EAGLE'S ISLAND

ALLAN BYRNE

Advanced Imagery

ISBN-13: 978-0615973173

ISBN-10: 0615973175

DEDICATION

To my mother, the librarian, who led by example.

CONTENTS

Contents iv

Chapter 1 3

Chapter 2 12

Chapter 3 26

Chapter 4 37

Chapter 5 48

Chapter 6 60

Chapter 7 69

Chapter 8 81

Chapter 9 90

Chapter 10 106

Chapter 11 122

Chapter 12 138

Chapter 13 158

Chapter 14 172

Chapter 15 190

Chapter 16 206

Chapter 17 218

Chapter 18 227

Chapter 19 238

Chapter 20 250

Chapter 21 262

Chapter 22 274

Chapter 23 287

Chapter 24 298

Chapter 25 311

Chapter 26 321

Chapter 27 337

Chapter 28 344

ACKNOWLEDGMENTS

This book would not have been possible without the help, and, especially, encouragement of friends and family. Despite the extended time in writing, they were always there to give ideas and proofread each new version.

CHAPTER 1

The man was, perhaps, in his early fifties, and his short, wiry beard was beginning to turn silver. His soft leather shoes dampened the sound of his step, and he padded across the stern of a small vessel. The frown on the chiseled face deepened as he looked out over the sea.

The object of the man's concern was readily apparent. Ahead of the ship a large cloud mass was building up quickly, and the sky was darkening. Open sea travel was not one of the typical duties of the ship, and he worried that a large storm might be more than it could handle. Besides, the rocky English shore menaced them off to port.

His reverie was interrupted as two boys arrived from the cabin. They both shared the sharp-cut facial features of the man, and it didn't take much to realize that they were his sons, and twins.

"Do you think it'll hit before nightfall, Father?" asked the more outspoken of the two.

"I don't know, Mark," he replied thoughtfully. "I would rather have it hit early, though. I don't want to fight the sea in the dark."

They continued to watch the quickly building storm and the scurrying sailors. The few sails of the ship were quickly being brought in before the storm hit. It was a necessary precaution to limit damage from the high winds.

Mark and his brother Robert were still watching the sailors when a shadow passed over the deck. The clouds had covered the sun, and the sky became dark quickly. The remnants of snow on shore had begun to melt earlier that morning, testifying to the approach of spring. Nevertheless, winter still lingered over the northeastern sea. It looked as though the warmth would be pushed off for another day or two.

Tempestuous little wind gusts blew sea spray across the deck, and the boys could hear the choppy waves slapping against the ship's hull. Up above, the last of the heavy canvas sails were beginning to tug at their ropes, making loud cracking sounds as they tensed and relaxed.

Shivering, the two boys returned to the cabin. Their

father stayed at the rail, the frown that creased his forehead deeper yet. His responsibilities didn't include the guidance of the ship, and he felt powerless watching the hurried preparations.

A few minutes later the waves began to swell to a dangerous size. As they grew, each successive wave knocked the small ship a little harder, and each wind gust pushed the mast further past its equilibrium. Green seawater sloshed over the decks and ran out through the gunwales.

Despite the efforts of the seamen, the ship was taking a beating. Her timbers groaned as they flexed in the heavy swells, little cracks opening and closing between the deck planks.

Captain Avery crossed the deck to have a word with his passenger, who was still leaning on the rail. They conversed for a few tense minutes, and then a burly mariner with a red cap was hailed and sent to fetch the boys. The captain and the merchant broke up and began to make preparations.

Over in the cabin, Mark and Robert were trying to keep themselves busy. Their attempted game of chess had ended after a particularly large wave had swept every piece onto the floor.

"I win!" said Mark, his legs sticking out from below the bed as he retrieved the pieces. "I got your king!"

The red-capped sailor poked his head in the door. "Your father would like you out on deck, boys," he growled. "We're preparing the leave the boat."

Robert looked up from the chess pieces. "Really?" he asked. But the man was gone, leaving the door swinging in the storm. The danger of their position began to set in.

Just as he was stepping to the door to close it, a smelly pile of cloth dropped over his head. He ducked and slipped it off his head.

"I think you'll want that, Robert! It's your oilskin coat. Amazing what you can find under the bed, huh?" Mark was grinning, not a bit fazed by the recent events. He grabbed his own coat and buttoned it up tight.

A few minutes later they stepped out of the cabin door. The ship was still groaning under the strain of the unbearable winds. Ropes hummed in the constantly changing wind, and waves crashed over the low deck. A coil of rope slithered by and a shattered handrail almost swept Robert off his feet.

At the edge of the deck, their father was motioning for them to come, and they stepped forward into the stormy evening. Water lapped around their feet with every step.

"Hold the rail!" their father shouted at them across the deck. Both boys obeyed, and began to inch closer to their father.

It was a short but perilous journey. When they finally arrived, they could see a small skiff bobbing in the waves next to the ship. It was already loaded with sailors, and only the three passengers and the captain remained to board.

Mark shielded his eyes with his hand, protecting them from the spray. Meanwhile, Robert was ushered by their father toward the boat.

Just as he was halfway down the small ladder, Robert heard a shout, and looked behind him. A large wave was coming in, swelling threateningly as it approached the crowded boat. He didn't hesitate, but let go of the ladder and dropped into the boat. In the next instant, the small craft was dashed against the side of the ship where he had just been.

Up above, Mark jumped back, letting go of the rail. In an instant, he was caught by the large wave as it crashed over the deck. He felt his feet pulled out from under him, heard someone scream, and watched as his father reached out to catch him. The hand fell piteously short. He felt the impact of the opposite rail, and then everything turned into foaming water.

In the boat, Robert struggled to raise himself to a sitting position as the saltwater splashed around him and stung his eyes. His fall had been broken by a burly sailor. The man now smiled at him and flexed his muscles, pretending to be none the worse for the wear.

Robert laughed and moved over on the bench to make way for Mark, who had been right behind him. When Mark didn't come, Robert leaned back and looked up the steep side of the ship. It now tilted at a dangerous angle away from the small boat. He could pick out the captain in the intermittent flashes of lightning, but his father and Mark were both gone. A sudden worry gnawed at him. He hoped they had just returned to the cabin.

The captain disappeared. A few minutes later, he reappeared and started down the ladder.

A moment later he dropped into the boat and took the seat next to Robert.

"Row back around the other side!" he bellowed to the oarsmen. Then to Robert, "Your father and brother were swept off the other side, I think. I didn't see them anywhere on board, Robert. I don't know if we can save them, but we're going to try."

The ship continued on, driven by the wind, and left the occupants of the skiff behind. The sailors rowed back and forth over the area, every one peering into the dark, misty shadows. Various pieces of ship's furniture and flotsam dotted the waves, but nothing remotely resembling a human being could be found.

For what felt like hours, the small boat crisscrossed the area. The loyal crew strained their eyes in the dim moonlit night. Then rain caused the visibility to decrease, and nobody could see past the next wave.

"Row for shore," Captain Avery finally commanded, placing his water-soaked arm across Robert's shoulder. Robert shrugged it off and turned around, putting his back to the captain and sailors. His eyes still scanned the restless waves.

Rowing to shore proved easier said than done. To Robert, it seemed like they were tossed up and down further than they went forward. The cold water sloshing around the bottom of the boat rose slowly, prompting the Captain to order every extra man to start bailing.

Robert got down on his knees and helped scoop the seawater out with his bare hands. Every other handful he threw out was dashed back in his face, the salty water temporarily blinding him. His knees were soaked in several inches of filthy brine as various forms of plant life swirled around them.

After what seemed like hours of bailing, he stopped to catch his breath. Resting his soaked forehead on the rough planks of the boat, he let his muscles relax.

 A second later, there was a large jolt as the boat was thrown against some solid object. His back slammed against the bench behind him and his neck snapped back. For a moment, his eyes saw nothing but sky. Then a large wave crashed over him. The boat, wedged in rocks, splintered and quickly filled with water. Every man aboard was caught in a confusion of breaking waves and shattered boat.

Robert's mouth and nostrils filled with water, and he choked as he felt his body thrown around by the waves. He couldn't see anything. The salty water was everywhere - in his mouth, in his nose, under his eyelids. Terror overwhelmed him and he tried to scream. The only result was a stream of bubbles.

He was dashed bodily against the large rocks, and his world was a mess of water, foam, and seaweed. The breakers spun him around, lifting him into the air and bringing him crashing back down again. He grabbed for the nearest rock and held on for dear life. After a few moments he was able to wedge himself in among the crags and shelter his face. The pounding waves broke over the rock behind him, giving him a brief reprieve.

Once he could see again, he shaded his eyes and peaked toward land. The shadowy shoreline was only a stone's throw away, but in between was an obstacle course of pounding surf and sharp rocks.

He began the treacherous journey quickly, but soon found that every ounce of his will was being put to the test. From one rock to the next. Rest. Another rock. His efforts were agonizingly slow, but he could see progress in between stops. His whole existence narrowed down to surviving the next step.

In the end, it was the perseverance of his character that took over, driving him forward when his body would have given up. His last step brought him onto a small beach, sheltered by a low ridge of rock. He collapsed into the sand.

CHAPTER 2

The wind whistled through the doors, blasting the remains of the deserted island castle. It whipped around the nooks and crannies as the snow fell onto the forbidding rocks below. Dimly, a lone figure could be seen making its way up through the ruins to a tower at its apex.

The boy crouched down and crawled slowly up the stairs. Gaping, jagged holes let the wind through, and he would shudder as he passed. Stacked debris cluttered his way, but he held on to the wall as he navigated the tricky ascent. After several short breaks and a near-fall, his journey was complete.

Mark looked out over the wide, open sea. Far below, he could see the jagged shore and the waves crashing against it. To the east, he spotted a small piece of timber lying on the rocks. It was his transportation, the only thing that had saved him through his hours of seaborne misery.

Considering it now, it seemed almost impossible that he had survived the long hours in the open sea, chilled to the bones, as he clung to the mast of the *King Alfred II*. Carried about by the waves and tossed from crest to crest, he had reached the island in a state of semi-consciousness.

Now, two hours later, he was peering down on the sea as it brought in the remaining pieces of his old ship. Sighing, he slowly let himself down with his back against the crenelations and watched the flotsam piling up on the shore. His clothes dripped water in a growing puddle around him.

After a short break, he made his way back down the tower. The storm had passed and the tempestuous winds had calmed down to a slight breeze. Snow was falling gently onto the ramparts of the castle, as if in defiance of the imminent onset of spring.

When he reached the bottom, he began to take stock of his situation. He was cold, hungry, tired. He studied the castle, trying to figure out where its storehouses and food supplies had been. Where could he find the best shelter? He knew he couldn't last long without some kind of nourishment and at least a small corner to dry off.

The small corner he found quickly enough. An old outbuilding had neatly deposited its lead roof in a heap at its center. Mark found that the tiles were even slightly warm where the sun filtered in through a second-story window. The old wall blocked the breeze as he wrung out his wet clothes and spread them in the patches of light. He huddled in the spare light, trying to retain what warmth he could as they dried.

When he put his clothes back on they were stiff and rough, but at least they were dry. After satisfying himself that he wouldn't die from the cold, he returned outside to the now sunny courtyard.

The cold air bit at his hands as he searched through the ruined castle rooms. The sun warmed him as he worked, and the walls around the courtyard blocked most of the wind, but everything he touched was still cold. He hoped he could find some food. A bag of stale bread, a barrel of salted fish, anything. Without food, he had no hope of making his way back to his father and brother. Assuming his father and brother were still alive.

When he had picked his way through the rubble to the outermost wall, he found the remains of what appeared to be the main gatehouse. It looked as though it had had been strongly fortified, back in its prime, but now the door had rotted through, and the rusted iron reinforcements sat alone in their sockets.

Entering the gatehouse, he began to look around. Several

doors had remained intact, sheltered somewhat by the lead-shingled roof. The first two doors proved to be useless leads, only opening to empty rooms. The last, a heavier door, only opened partway, and refused to budge. Scattered rubble and rock from the crumbling wall didn't let the door open any further.

Looking through the crack Mark could see a stairwell leading to the upper floor. This door was decidedly worth the effort of a little cleanup. Piece by piece he shifted the heavy limestone chunks and rotten wooden panels to the opposite side of the gateway.

As he pulled aside a fungus-covered piece of wood leaning against the wall, he felt his heart skip a beat. Where he should have seen the stone wall, he saw – nothing. A void. Empty. He looked closer. Running underneath the wall was a tiny passageway.

Completely forgetting the second floor of the gatehouse, Mark got on his stomach and entered the cold stone passageway. The sides were solid for the first ten feet. This part of the tunnel ran under the battlements, so its sides and roof had to hold the massive outer wall. After a small distance, the narrow passageway grew much larger. Mark pulled himself out of the small tunnel and stood. Directly in from of him was a paneled wood surface with a light layer of green moss.

Seeing a set of hinges on the left side, Mark pushed tentatively on the right. Nothing moved. He set his shoulder against the slightly slimy surface and gave it a shove. With a groan, the panel opened about the width of his finger. He gave another shove, then braced his feet against the far wall and pushed. The door slid open, screeching as the age-old hinges and swollen wood resisted the movement.

The hall beyond the door was nothing like the dirty tunnel he had just come from. Light wood covered the walls and solid oak beams spanned the passageway. The entire hall sloped downwards, with doors on either side.

As Mark stepped into the dim area, he couldn't shake the impression that it belonged in a different world than the rest of the castle. It was so... clean. Perfect. After a day of stumbling over chunks of debris, the smooth flooring was a relief. He walked to a random door and tested the handle. Locked. As were the second, third, and fourth doors he tried. He tried to force another one, but he knew before he started that he didn't stand a chance. Turning around, he decided to return to the surface and come back later, maybe with some tools.

As he went back to the small tunnel from the hall, he noted that the old door had been hidden behind a brightly colored banner. It depicted a silver eagle swooping down on some unseen target. At the bottom was a small coat of arms. The picture tugged at his memory, but he didn't know why. He paused a moment to feel the banner, marveling at how well-kept the cloth was, especially after seeing what the elements had done to tougher materials outside.

After crawling through the tunnel again, he exited the gatehouse toward the sea. The first thing he saw was the hull of the *King Alfred II*, which had settled just off the shore. For a moment, he wondered it if there were any survivors, but then he noticed that the ship was decidedly waterlogged and could not be seaworthy. Nevertheless, his spirits revived, and he began to run toward the ship. If there was food anywhere, it would be there.

Halfway down the steep slope, his foot caught on a piece of rotten wood, and he pitched into the wet snow and rubble. His hands shot out, scraping the icy gravel. Then, with a thump, his head hit the hard sand.

He lay there for a moment, the ice melting against his cheek. Then he picked himself up, brushed the gravel from his hands, and stepped forward. More slowly this time.

Wet and sore, Mark arrived at the ship. Pulling together what was left of his adventurous spirit, he clambered up the side of the ship and swung over onto the floorboards. Soaked and battered by the recent storm, they creaked loudly. A particularly weak board snapped under his weight, pitching him sideways into the open stairway. His quick grab for the rail revealed that it no longer existed, and Mark tripped down the stairs, arms flailing.

His face contacted the ground first, but the rest of his

body kept going, flipping him over into the room opposite the stairs. Gasping for breath, once again flat on the ground, he put his hand to his nose. It came back bloody.

A short section of his torn shirt sufficed to stop the flow. Pulling himself up into a sitting position, he took a look around.

Although small, this cabin was lavishly furnished compared to the crew's quarters and the berth where Mark had slept. On the left wall hung the remains of a shattered mirror. Next to it was a cabinet with the doors torn off and the shelves hanging askew. Straight ahead of Mark was a sea chest, battered and empty, the words "Captain Jonathon Avery" carved into the lid. On the wall to his right was the only unopened cabinet in the room.

Picking himself up slowly, Mark headed to this cabinet. When he tried to open it, he found that it was locked. No amount of force on his part could open the little doors. Mark decided that if the cabinet was being stubborn, he could be too. He turned and looked around for a weapon.

A broken table leg only made a dull "thump" against the well-built cabinet, and an unwieldy barrel served no better. But on the barrel Mark saw metal hoops. It was only the work of a moment to pound one off with the broken table leg.

Unfortunately, the round barrel hoop was not designed to open a cabinet either. Mark couldn't get the curved piece of iron to fit anywhere useful at first. But, with a little ingenuity and a lot more force, he managed to wedge it between the door and the lock hasp. A single twist of the hoop popped the door free.

Inside the cabinet were the personal possessions of the captain as well as some of his food: cheese, bread, and wine. Although somewhat wet, no food had ever looked better to Mark's eyes.

He snatched up the cheese and tore into it. After devouring all the food he could, he looked at the rest of the items in the cabinet. Sorting through the motley collection of carvings, buttons, and the odd chess piece, he found several pounds in coins. At first, he was tempted to grab the money. A second later he realized how little it would help him.

Searching deeper, he emptied the cabinet out onto the cabin floor. The motley collection of keepsakes didn't intrigue him in the least, so he turned his attention back to the cabinet itself. Deep in the corner, in a little indentation, was a tiny lever. Curious, Mark pulled it.

The action of the lever caused a spring to release. The side panel of the cabinet slowly swung out, revealing the most beautiful dagger Mark had ever seen. The sheath was made of supple blue leather and had a polished silver chape. The belt that accompanied it was also made of blue leather. Its buckle was silver, with gold inlay and the same design that was on the handle of the dagger and sheath.

Upon closer examination, the design appeared to be a coat of arms. Mark grimaced and wished he had studied his heraldry a little more back in South Shields, where he had grown up. Gules three castles triple towered argent... at least he knew how to say it right. It looked somewhat similar to the arms that he had just seen up in the castle. He knew the arms were familiar, but could he really be expected to remember heraldry after being washed up on an island? He went back to studying the dagger.

The hilt was made of iron, with a smooth flowing design inlaid in gold, like water flowing over rocks. The blade was sharp, and it shone like the sun, reflecting even the most insignificant sources of light. On the pommel was a fine blue gem set in silver.

Mark picked up the dagger wonderingly and hefted it. The blade felt alive in his hand, light and active. He placed it back into the sheath and buckled it to his waist. The dagger's weight gave him a sense of importance.

Satisfied, Mark left the cabin and entered the kitchens. Rifling through the cabinets, he found that very little of the ship's food had survived. Gathering up what food there was, he put it in a wet bag from the cabin and slung it over his shoulder. Moving on to the crew's cramped bunks, he found nothing of importance, except for some clothes to replace the worn pieces that hung about his shoulders. Attired in his new clothes, and feeling a little better, he optimistically opened the next door.

The creaking of the door was drowned out by the wild surf beating against the broken end of the *King Alfred II*. The rest of the ship, containing the armory and part of the storage, had been torn away.

Disappointed, but buoyed by his few finds, Mark made his way back off the ship, and climbed up the slope. This time, he took the trip carefully and didn't trip on any hidden objects. When he reached the gatehouse, he put the bag down in one of the rooms and proceeded to return to the tunnel.

He tried the first door on the left. Locked. Then he tried the one across from it. Surprisingly, it opened. Inside was a workshop with parts of ballistae and catapults in various corners of the room. He recognized the crock and beam from a catapult next to a workbench on which rested the firing mechanism for a ballista. Several chests in the corner held the tools used to make these siege weapons. The smell of wood filled the whole room, and wood chips covered the floor. To his right sat several finished siege weapons. All that was well and good, but it didn't help him any.

Mark left the room and moved on to the next one. It was locked. He skipped it and passed on to the large door a little further down the hall. It opened stiffly.

As soon as he stepped in, he felt the temperature drop. This room had apparently been a blacksmith's shop. There were racks for swords, pikes, and poleaxes, and a box for spearheads. Shelves on the opposite wall looked like they were meant to hold pieces of armor. Farming tools still leaned against the wall on the far side, partially obstructed from Mark's view by the large furnace and flue.

There were, however, no weapons of any kind left in the cold blacksmith shop. The flue rose to the ceiling, and seemed to be the source of the chilled winter air. Scattered on the floor around the large anvil were many metal shavings and chunks. The anvil's surface was deeply scarred by the blows of a hammer. Nothing useful caught his eye, so Mark turned around, glad to leave the chilly room. The warm air brushed past him as he returned to the main aisle.

Just then, he stopped to question himself. Why would the air in the passageway be warmer? Why wasn't it just as cold as the smithy? There was no reason for it to be as warm as it was. Unless…the island was inhabited. He banished the thought from his mind. There was probably a natural heating system, like hot springs, and it was incorporated into the tunnel system. The Romans did things like that, he knew.

The next room was locked, but the following room seemed to be sort of a meeting room. There was a long mahogany table in the center, with many chairs on either side, and a large, well-padded chair at the head of the table. The seat cushions were of dark scarlet velvet. They were soft to the touch, but very stiff. The intricate carvings on the backs of the chairs amazed Mark, and he stooped to examine them.

As soon as he did, he was immediately sorry. Once again that hauntingly familiar ensign looked at him. "Gules three castles triple towered argent." Robert would have known whose it was.

Suddenly, he had the feeling that he was being watched. He spun around, but there was nobody there. Mystified, he looked about the room. He was positive there had been a person in the room moments before, but there were no windows or doors except the one he had entered through. Was the old castle still occupied? It couldn't be! There was no way of survival on this barren stretch of rock. He wondered if he was starting to go mad. The sailors on the ship had told stories of marooned mutineers who quickly became insane.

Deciding to move past the issue, he left the room. The next few doors were locked, and Mark didn't try to force them. The last door was a stairway, leading to lower levels of the underground complex. Add a kitchen and barracks, which were probably behind the locked doors, and this place was self-sufficient. Every door was at least half a foot thick, made of solid oak with iron spikes. The walls seemed immensely strong and sure. At the end of the passageway was a winding staircase, constructed so that a defender from below had ample room to swing his sword, but an attacker's sword would hit the center column. In all ways, this underground system was designed to be a last ditch effort to survive.

At nightfall, returning from the third story down from the surface, he reflected on what he had seen. There had been an empty storage room, a couple of bedrooms, and a large training room on the second level, besides all of the doors that were locked.

The third level had been the smallest, with tiny compact doors that intensified the feeling of fortification. Everything was built to last. The doors looked even thicker than the doors on the first level, and had more iron reinforcements. There were peepholes and what might have been hearing channels too. Not that they went to anything exciting - just an endless hole or a view of the sea outside.

 Light came in through several holes that ran all the way to the surface, and the rooms had started to get dark as night fell. When he reached the top level, Mark decided to find a permanent place to sleep. He would need to establish somewhat of a base here. Retrieving his bag of food, he returned to the third floor down and felt his way to one of the bedrooms. He placed the bag on a small table, and then lay down on an old straw mattress. It seemed strange that he could just get shipwrecked, land on an island, and get into bed. But that was how it was, and he wasn't about to complain.

Lying in bed, he listened to the sound of the wind whispering through the light holes. Every once in a while, he heard things that didn't sound right, but he attributed it to the wind, and tried not to think too much about it. Eventually, he fell asleep.

CHAPTER 3

Robert felt himself come back to consciousness. He was lying on the cold ground, the sun warming only his face. His mouth was filled with sand, saltwater, and seaweed. Struggling, he tried to roll over on the wet sand and spit it out. His arms refused to hold him, and he collapsed back again, willing to lie there for a century if he could. The blackness was comfortable, and he slipped back into unconsciousness.

When he revived again, Robert was in a world of his own. It was all dark, although comfortably so, and he felt like he was floating. He could relax, rest, and forget about everything.

In the back of his head, he heard voices. They were soft, kind sounds, calling to him, and he felt like answering them, but that would mean leaving his comfortable blackness. He didn't want to wake and find himself on the beach again.

Eventually, though, he summoned enough strength to move his lips. No sound came out. His body felt like it was glued where it lay, and he tested each muscle in turn, growing more and more used to his consciousness again. Finally, he opened his eyes.

He was staring up at the underside of a thatched roof. Hung from the rafters were nets and ropes, and at the extremity of his vision he could see someone working. He moved his head to see what they were doing.

The man was a tall, skinny fellow, and his hands were moving deftly as they sewed up a large fishing net that was draped across his lap. His white hair and wrinkled skin showed him to be in the later years of life, but his quick movements and sharp look befitted a much younger man.

He looked up when Robert moved, and smiled. "How are you doing, lad? Perchance a cup of wine would do you well? Rolf thought I was crazy for thinking you would pull through." Robert smiled weakly and looked over to see another man sitting by the fire. Apparently the older man's son, Rolf was the mirror image of his father, except that he was in the prime of life.

"Well, I never really said he wouldn't…" he replied. The

old man grinned and glanced at him sharply.

"Oh you were worried, I could tell. You were a little wary of your mother's medicine," the old man shot back. At this a quiet old lady in the corner smiled slightly. She was even older than the man, but didn't look as though she'd weathered the years as well.

"Well, Mother's medicine is always good," the good-natured Rolf replied. "If it was only up to that, he'd be taking over our work pretty soon."

"I wouldn't bet anything on that," Robert squeaked out, his throat raw. The old man smirked in triumph.

"And he talks. Juliana has not lost her touch. What's your name, and where are you from, young lad?"

"Robert, from South Shields."

"And why, pray tell, did you go for a swim in a storm? Were you that thirsty?"

"I was not swimming. I was journeying with my father, and my brother. Have you seen them?"

Both men were taken aback. "Nobody sailed by this point," said Rolf. "We can see ship lights clear out to Moore's Island, and most come by on this side of it for shelter."

"Well, either you didn't see us, or I floated a good ways then."

"True… or you had covered the lamps. Maybe you were with smugglers. They often sail that way." Robert knew by Rolf's look that he thought they were smugglers themselves, not just with them.

"No! We wouldn't do that. My father is a merchant and he's often gone, but he took us with him this time, and--"

The old man broke in. "It doesn't matter. I suppose you are with us for now, till you can mend."

"You'll doubtless learn to mend nets faster than the fish can swim," said Rolf, "and after you're better, maybe we can help with finding your family."

"By the way, what friends do you have in the area?" asked the old man.

"I don't have any besides my family. Wait, I lived at the monastery."

"Which one? In South Shields?"

"Yes."

"There's your answer! You will be expected there, if anywhere."

"I… don't know. Father had rather I be with him, though I know matters have changed. I'll try to find him directly. After I get better, which I will soon."

The fishermen could see Robert was resolute, and they

went back to their work, the old woman admonishing him to get his rest.

The next morning Robert was feeling much better. He felt well enough, at least, to sit on the edge of his bed and sum up his wounds. There were numerous large scratches and scrapes, and the skin on the back of his left hand was shredded, leaving only a sticky mess. It was already hardening into scar tissue. His ribs were black and blue, and he suspected more than one of them was fractured or broken. Luckily enough, his limbs had survived any permanent damage, and he could move around, although slowly, as long as he could stand the pain from the bruises all over his body.

Rolf wasn't kidding when he had said Robert would learn to mend nets. Spring was just around the corner, and the fishermen were constantly occupied with fixing the tools of their trade. Robert quickly learned more than one aspect of the fishing trade, and received compliments from Rolf and Gerald alike.

It was several days before Juliana would let Robert venture out of the hut, but when he did, it was a relief. The early spring air was cold but refreshing, and he enjoyed it immensely.

He had decided to join Gerald and Rolf on a trip to inspect their boat, which they co-owned with their fishing partner. They had pulled it on shore for the winter at the end of the last season. It was sitting near their friend's house in the town of Ashington, several miles to the south.

The country they passed through was just coming out of winter, at the point where the beauty of snow had just left and that of spring had not yet arrived. The gray, misty flatlands were wet and muddy, and the cart path itself was in deplorable condition.

None of this mattered, however, to the three travelers as they walked briskly down the path. The spring air was fresh and sweet, and it was hard to feel down when the birds were singing in the trees.

Robert soon became amazed at the old man's knowledge of seaside birds. Gerald pointed each one out as they flitted from tree to tree. He was in the midst of showing Robert his favorite bird when Rolf unceremoniously edged them off the road. Seconds later, a group of horsemen galloped past, splashing mud on the three travelers.

"They must be in a hurry," commented Robert.

"Was that Roland, Rolf?" asked Gerald. "I didn't think to see any of Cogniard's men back so soon."

"Nor I, Father. But remember, he leads our lord's vanguard with his scouts."

"Cogniard will be here soon then."

"Or no. We can never tell."

"Ah, the way a single man can dictate our fortunes." The two men lapsed into silence as they continued down the muddy path.

Robert was somewhat mystified by this short exchange, but he forgot it soon enough when they approached the outskirts of Ashington.

They turned off the cart path just as the first few houses began to appear. A little ways into the bracken Robert noticed a small hut, and Rolf confirmed that it was their destination.

They were met at the door by Ulric, a blonde giant of a man who slapped Gerald on the back heartily.

"Well met, my friend, well met! Ready to get the old *Hibernia* in the water?" His voice boomed like thunder, and Robert saw Rolf wince as he clapped his shoulder in the vice of his large hand. "And who have we here? Gerald, I was under the impression winter fishing wasn't so good, but I might just want to try it now! What's your name, boy, Cod?"

"Robert, sir. You weren't too far from the truth on that fishing, though," Robert replied.

"We picked him up after that storm several nights past," Gerald explained. "'I was on a ship,' he says, but we never saw it."

"Ahhh, I see," the big man gave him an exaggerated wink,

and Robert groaned. He didn't want to revisit the smuggler thing again.

He saw Rolf wink at him as he asked "So, how have you been spending your time lately, Ulric?" In answer, Ulric held up his hands so they could see them.

"'Bout like you, I'll wager. Still, I didn't think my skills were so very lacking as I found them to be this spring." They all laughed. Ulric's fingers were so large that any needle would have a hard time missing them.

By this time they had reached the boat. It was on its side about one hundred feet from shore. It appeared to be a medium size boat, as far as Robert's experience with fishing went, and although it looked well kept up, it was very old.

"It hasn't been crushed!" Gerald exclaimed. "That maid at the Terrace Tavern must be feeding you something good for your sight, or you would have stumbled over it by now."

"A better fate it would be than being worked until it sunk," Ulric shot back. "I should do it a favor and step on it now, before you get your relentless hands on it!"

"Well, don't stand there, are you afraid of trying?"

Ulric immediately set about working for the welfare of the boat by climbing up the tilting deck and balancing himself on the upper rail. The boat groaned with his weight, and rocked slightly toward the three others on the beach. Only the small keel kept it from rolling out of its position. Robert laughed, amazed that the large man was still so agile.

"I think she prefers your smelly feet on the deck rather than the rail any day," said Rolf. "Let's get her in the water!"

Ulric jumped lightly, if that were possible for a man of his size, off the rail and onto a nearby rock. Then the group of men gathered around the fishing boat. With two on each side, they heaved the boat off the ground and walked into the water.

It was still only early spring, and the water was quite cold. Without hesitating, the men released the boat into the water as soon as it was deep enough, and pulled the bowline up onto the beach with them.

Robert looked back at the boat, noticing how it sat in the water. Even as he watched, the old vessel sank into the seawater, and disappeared under the surf.

"Hello! Guess it's time for a new boat, eh? Shall we buy that beauty that Finley has for sale?" Ulric's grin showed Robert that he was not too worried.

"I think she wanted to spend her days in the sea, where you couldn't ever find her, Ulric," replied Rolf.

"Don't be fooled, Robert," Gerald said, turning to the

boy. "Every boat will sink after being in storage for a season. The boat's timbers shrink without the water, and little gaps grow in between the boards. After the boat sits in the sea for a space, you can empty the water, and it will be seaworthy again."

The group retired to Ulric's house, where they changed clothes. Ulric found a set of fisherman's clothes for Robert, who hadn't had any extra to bring along. They were more than a little bit big. The shirt went down to his knees, and the pants had to be held up by a rope, but Robert was glad he had dry clothes after that cold dip in the water.

While they warmed up, Gerald told Ulric more about Robert's situation. Ulric seemed very interested, and suggested that Robert travel back to the monastery, where he could at least notify the monks, and then continue to search for his father.

Robert decided that this was probably the best idea, and determined that he should go to South Shields the next day and visit the monastery. He was hoping that the monks would have news of his father and brother, but he wasn't expecting much. He knew that he was the only one of the three who had made it onto the lifeboat, and even he had barely made it to shore.

The entire way home from Ulric's, he pondered what his life would be like now. Without his father or brother he would have to fend for himself. He had always had dreams of becoming a knight or soldier, but even though Brother Arnold had taught him many skills in that area, the monks generally frowned on it. Now that he thought about it, it seemed that Brother Arnold had done it as a favor to his father, who was gone so often.

He didn't even take part in the bright conversation of his fellow fishermen, and got ready to sleep as soon as they arrived back at the cottage.

"Going to take Ulric's advice, I see," commented Gerald. "You can make it back by evening tomorrow. If you do find your family, be so kind as to send word. If I don't hear about you within a couple days, I'm going to go look for you, hear?" Robert grinned and headed for the pile of fishing nets that he used for a bed.

"I'll just send another scruffy boy back here to do all your sewing for you," he replied.

CHAPTER 4

Mark woke late the next morning. Thin, weak beams of link shining dimly into his room didn't encourage him to get up any earlier, and the cold air made waking up harder than it should have been. He struggled out of bed and rubbed his eyes. He had no clue what time it was, but he was hungry, and it felt like every muscle in his body was sore.

His first thought of the day was food. He debated for a while about whether to eat some of his newly discovered stock, and decided that if he were going to get things done today he couldn't do them on an empty stomach. But he would be smart and eat the perishable food first.

He was still rubbing the sleep from his eyes as he broke the cheese into chunks and ate it. There was something about waking up in a half-lit room miles from any human beings that made him want to just roll over and wait for the monks to pull him out of bed. They would have done just that at the monastery. The next part, however, wasn't so comforting.

Heaving a sigh and standing up, he picked a few crumbs off his clothes and ate them, reminding himself that every particle was precious. Since he'd wasted some already, he would have to devote his morning, or at least what was left of it, to finding new sources of food.

As he stepped out of the crawl-space into the gatehouse, the warmth was already filling the air. The sun was high in the sky, and the birds were wheeling and dipping over the edge of the sea. He decided that if it was warm enough that evening he would sleep somewhere the light could reach. The bright light gave him energy, and would certainly make him get up on time.

Turning back into the castle courtyard, he saw the keep standing in the center, the tower rising out of the far corner like a sentry.

"Well, I guess I can always try looking there," he said to himself out loud. Then he chuckled. Talking to oneself was another sign of impending insanity.

He walked up to the doors of the keep and grabbed one of the iron rings. Bracing himself against a ledge in the stone, he gave himself a mental countdown, then heaved.

Instantly the door swung open. Mark yanked his foot out of the way as its bulk crashed into the stone wall. Losing his balance, he spun into an ungainly heap on the cobblestones. For the third time in two days, he found himself flat on the ground.

"Why me?" he grumbled as he picked himself up and shook off the dust. He'd chosen to pull hard because all the other doors were so stiff. Why did this one have to be so smooth? And it was outside too. Shaking his head, he pushed the thoughts out of his mind and walked through the door.

If it weren't for the handrail just inside, Mark would have been floored yet again. His head just couldn't tilt back far enough to see every inch of the magnificent arched ceiling. He felt a little dizzy, so he brought his gaze back down to the ground-level.

The entire interior was paneled with a light wood, polished until it shone. Intricate woodwork upheld a second-floor balcony, on which rested another balcony, this one at the third-floor level. A gracefully curving double set of stairs connected all three floors, and was covered in a dark red carpet.

But even the fine woodwork wasn't everything. The entire building shone with multi-colored light cast from the stained-glass windows that lined the second and third floors. The thick dust motes danced in the shaft of light as they drifted slowly downward.

Letting out his breath, Mark took a step further into the hall. Once he tore his eyes away from the awe-inspiring woodwork, he began to notice the everyday aspects of the building. The long tables that were laid out in the middle of the room were covered in a rotting yellow cloth that threatened to fall off the table it was so full of holes.

The floor was covered with layers of reeds, just like the floor of the monastery, and even the rail his hand was on was ready to fall apart. He noticed, too, how the polished woodwork ended at the third floor, and the beams that crisscrossed the ceiling above appeared to be darkened and cracked with age. It seemed that just the woodwork had made it through time unscathed.

Mark noticed how the upper tier of windows had been carefully arranged to allow for the amazing show of light. Even as he watched, the sun moved past the one perfect point and the brilliant light began to fade. He could imagine how the designer of this building had planned for the path of the sun and placed his windows to produce this effect just in time for the noon meal.

In the now-dimmer room, Mark began to explore. The first floor was simply an open hall, surrounded by little rooms on the sides and larger rooms at the ends. Each one of the little side rooms under the second-floor balcony sported a small fireplace and a rough bench.

At the far end of the hall he found the kitchens. They were dirty and cluttered, with various rough implements hung from pegs on the walls. It was obvious that nothing sanitary had come from this place in a very long time. Nevertheless, Mark opened each door, lifted each lid, and checked each fireplace for any sign of food. There was none.

A quick trip through the second and third floors revealed nothing more in the way of food. As he had seen earlier, the woodwork was spotless and the stairs were amazing, but the rooms that had housed the ruling lord were deserted, and a set of double doors revealed a library that was also empty.

What he did discover was a door that led out to the tower. When he had first climbed the tower, he had entered from a door at the ground level. This door opened just two floors below the top of the tower, and it was a short trip for Mark to arrive at the top again.

As he looked out over the island, he scrutinized it for its value to his survival. The first thing that drew his eye was a yawning cavern opposite the tower that opened into a small bay. It appeared to be large enough to hold a small ship, or even two ships, if they were small enough. The beach where he had landed was nothing but a clutter of rubble, but the far end of the island appeared to be more promising. A short, squat windmill stood in the middle of a large open area. Mark assumed that these must have been fields of grain, and the windmill would have served as the center of production. Deciding that this was well worth his time, he returned to the keep and made his way back down the curved stairs. In a way, having a castle all to himself was a bit of a perk, not counting all the food problems.

He struck out from the castle and across a few hills toward the windmill. On the way, he passed an old archery range, a small, empty outbuilding, and a two hundred foot cliff that bordered the bay he had seen from the tower.

It was only a few minutes' walk to the small mill. This time, Mark was more careful as he opened the door. It opened smoothly, however, and he entered the compact room. It was empty. A few shelves stood against one wall, and several impressions in the ground marked where more shelves had been.

Getting down on his hands and knees, Mark searched the floor in the dim light. Feeling around the empty shelves, he found what he was looking for. A few seeds had dropped from the shelves and remained over the years. Resting on top of the hard dirt-packed floor in the shade, they hadn't sprouted or rotted. With any luck, they would be ready to grow if he planted them. They certainly didn't represent any hope for food now, but in a year they would be ready. Assuming, of course, that he would still be on the island. He didn't want to think about that possibility, but he forced himself to gather up the few seeds that remained.

After checking the rest of the floor, he gathered them

together and placed them in his shirt pocket. He was just about to leave the building when a thought occurred to him. Turning around, he tilted his head back to examine the ceiling. Sure enough, a ladder was tied there. When he untied one end, the other swung down and settled in the dirt floor.

Slowly, testing each rung, Mark ascended the ladder into the machinery of the windmill. He was entirely unfamiliar with the cogs and levers that surrounded him, and the dim light didn't make it any better. But after tracing the mechanism from the main shaft all the way to the levers that activated the machinery, he was confident that he understood how it worked.

Stepping back, and making sure he was out of the way of all the machinery, he released the lever that held the system still. Only a slight creaking told him that he had done something right. Minutes rolled by, and he still didn't see any movement. Just as he was about to leave, he heard the wind pick up and the vanes above his head started to move. All around him the gears and shafts were spinning, and below him a grinding wheel slowly started to turn.

Encouraged by his success, Mark began to pull levers almost at random. He couldn't see what they were doing, but he could hear the difference in the machinery. Outside, the wind kept up a steady pace. Pretty soon Mark had some idea of what the other levers did.

"This one... makes it go faster if it's further this way, and this one... makes it go faster when it's over here. So if I put them both like this... it should go faster," he mumbled as he fiddled with the levers.

Sure enough, the machinery was really rolling now. Mark sat back and watched the grinding wheel with satisfaction. If he ever needed to make a tool, this was the spot.

Just then, a gust of wind shook the little mill. A loud "crack" echoed through the machinery, and Mark instinctively ducked. Pieces whizzed through the air. He could hear them bouncing off the walls and clattering to the floor below.

Then the grinding wheel rolled to stop. Mark relaxed. But when he looked back at the main shaft, it was still rolling. And fast.

While he watched, the shaft accelerated faster and faster. The building started to shake, and the straw in the roof filtered down past him to the floor below. Realizing that the main shaft must have broken, Mark scrambled back down the ladder and rushed outside. As soon as he was a safe distance away, he looked back and watched.

The vanes were spinning crazily in the sky, shaking the mill house and wobbling erratically. Without the restraining weight of the wheel, the vanes were spinning way too fast and tearing the whole building apart.

As Mark stood and watched, the entire roof of the mill

crumpled in a single second. Spinning vanes felt to the earth, cracking as they hit the ground, and sending pieces flying through the air. A moment later, all was silent.

Taking a deep breath, Mark felt his shirt pocket. Sure enough, the seeds were still there. His only consolation was that he had had the sense to collect the seeds before satisfying his curiosity.

He turned away the wreckage, now certain that a miller's life was not for him.

A short walk took him to the far shore, where he examined the various forms of vegetation that grew there. Nothing excited his curiosity until he noticed the small pools of water near the edge of the sea. The tide was just coming in, retrieving the little pockets of water that it had left there that morning. As the last large pool was being covered by the tide, Mark saw a large cod splash through and swim freely away.

Quickly, he ran over to the pool to see if there were any more, but that had been the last. He was sorry he had lost the fish, but he was quite glad he had seen it. Tomorrow he wouldn't be too late. He would find some way to capture those isolated fish and feed himself.

Although the fish had been able to get away, he noticed several patches of seaweed floating in ankle-deep water just a few feet further. Remembering the stories that Brother Arnold always told them about wandering soldiers, he grabbed the bunch of seaweed and spread it out on some rocks.

According to the Brother, there were several forms of seaweed that were actually edible, and a few that tasted fine. If things got bad enough, this could be another source of food. Not ideal, to be sure, but one more backup.

Once his mind was fixated on ocean food, it didn't stop. Oysters were another common food that originated in the sea, and he decided that those would be worth looking for. Leaving the seaweed on a few rocks high above the tide line, he strolled along the beach. He found a few crabs, some flotsam, and a piece or two of the *King Alfred II*, but from shore he couldn't see if there were any oysters to be found.

Remembering the temperature of the water, he decided against an exploratory plunge, and opted instead to head back to the castle. With chagrin, he remembered the now-defunct mill. If he hadn't been so careless, he might have been able to use that grinding wheel to make a float and a long hook to catch oysters. Of course, he still could, but now it would be much harder.

As he approached the castle, he noticed how cluttered the ground became. Deciding against a try at tool-making, he determined to clear a path from the beach to the gate. There were certainly a lot of things to be done, but clambering over the wreckage of old siege equipment and building materials was going to be in the way of everything he tried to do. Tomorrow was another day, he told himself as he rolled up his sleeves. Tomorrow, he would make a tool, find some oysters… maybe... light a fire.

CHAPTER 5

The birds were singing cheerfully as Robert strode briskly down the road to town. This morning he was bright and happy, and he had high hopes for his trip. The monks at South Shields were always friendly, and he was sure they would help him in any way they could. He was hoping he could be there by noon, so he could join the monks for their dinner.

Robert had started out as the sun rose that morning, and had been walking for several hours already. The path was smooth and the view of the sea was great, but he wasn't used to walking so much. Juliana had packed a small meal for him, and despite the early hour he already wanted to eat.

The morning air was crisp and cold, and he had done a

lot of planning on the way. He had decided that if nothing turned up at the monastery, he would stay with Gerald, Juliana, and Rolf. He was sure they would be glad to have him. He wasn't sure how much he wanted to fish for the rest of his life, but he knew he was lucky to have met them. There were always other opportunities, but he was in no hurry.

Pretty soon that line of thought got a little depressing and he hoped he wouldn't have to put any of it into action. By far the best case scenario would be if the monks had news of his father and brother. He didn't want to spend any more time assuming that they had drowned.

By the time he reached the outskirts of the inhabited area that included towns of Newcastle and Tynemouth, as well as North and South Shields, the road started getting a little busier. The small shops randomly scattered along the road were collecting a few customers, and the artisans inside were hard at work. Apprentices hurried to fill their masters' tasks, and carts rumbled past.

Eyeing the carts made Robert start to realize how tired he was becoming. Thinking that he could save some time and effort, he started looking for one that had room. Sure enough, several minutes later he looked over his shoulder to see a cart stacked high with barrels. It was being pulled by a yoke of oxen, and driven by a portly man who was happily singing.

Waving the man down, Robert asked him if he could

catch a ride to the Black Friar's monastery.

"But of course, of course. Hop on up and keep me company. From where do you hail?" The man's tone was friendly, and soon Robert was in a lively conversation about South Shields and the surrounding area.

"The best cakes are from Margaret's Bakery, son. Trust me. I used to work with her in the castle, and not a meal in my life matched those I had there." The man shook his fat finger to emphasize his words.

"To be honest, I am not an expert in the cake area," Robert replied, "but I certainly had a good selection of food at the monastery. Why don't you still work at the castle? Or shouldn't I ask?"

"You mean to say you've lived here your whole life, and you don't know the history? Well, a few years back, the Earl who ruled this area was banished by our lord the king. A good earl, he was. The new Earl is always gone. Still looking for the first earl. At that time I was the head cook in the castle. We had a good time! Until our new lord came in and claimed his cooks were better." The large man looked slightly disgruntled, but his face brightened. "Now I have my own little winery, and in truth it's almost as good as being head of the kitchens."

"How is it, in the castle? I had never a chance to be anywhere near it."

"Well, it's a friendly castle. Well, at least it was. Now

some of the servants and retainers are imported from the next county, and they take a negative view of us in general. It was called the Eagle's Nest, but now that the bird has flown the coop, they just call it Tynemouth Castle." The ex-cook laughed at his own joke, and Robert joined in.

"If you look there, now, just above the wall - that large roof… that's the lord's kitchen, and that was my home for many years. Oh yes, and I can still taste Margaret's cooking. By the way, her shop is down that road there." He pointed down a wide lane paved with red brick that led to one of the more prosperous areas in town.

When they arrived near a main intersection they stopped and the friendly driver sent him on his way. "The monastery is just down there. I'm off to deliver provisions to a ship, so I'll bid you farewell. I wish you luck finding your father!"

"Thanks for your help!" Robert replied, and hopped off of the cart. He waved to the man, then strode off down Low Friar Street. It was a familiar road to him because he had grown up in the monastery. Many times he had played with his brother in the streets and alleys around it. They hadn't been the best of kids, as far as the abbot was concerned. There were other boys, he said, that behaved much better and didn't spend their time playing war games either.

The comment wasn't far off the mark. Both boys had

enjoyed their knightly fantasies immensely, and Robert had many memories of the lanes he was passing through now. Of course, he told himself, it had only been a few weeks ago that he left this place. However, one old memory in particular stood out.

It had been a quiet Friday studying in the monastery, and after their church-approved white-meat supper, Mark and Robert had decided to let some energy loose. They had a game that they played, in which one boy would start on the far side of the monastery and the other would wait on the monastery grounds. The first boy had to get past the second, but that was only part of the challenge. He also had to ring the supper bell that hung at the front gate to notify the other that he had gotten through. This turned out to be no easy feat, as the monks soon caught on to the tomfoolery and severe punishments were threatened.

But this Friday night was one of the first times they had played this game and the monks were still humoring them. Robert had been watching Mark closely the past few rounds, and he thought he had seen a pattern emerge in the other boy's actions. If he followed the pattern, Mark would sneak up Dispensary Lane, to the east of the monastery, then cut through the jumble of buildings to come at the bell from behind. This time, Robert vowed, he wouldn't make it.

As soon as the game started, he crept up a small crevice between two buildings that led to Dispensary Lane, and poked his head out to make sure Mark wasn't coming yet.

The left was clear, but when he looked to the right, he saw a familiar cloak disappear around the corner. He was shocked. There was no way Mark could have come that far without really sprinting. He ran down the road as quietly as his soft leather shoes would allow, and once again saw the cloak just ahead. He rounded the corner and leaped.

Halfway through the air, he knew something was wrong. The man was way too big to be Mark, and he was wearing a hat that Robert definitely did not recognize.

The instant he hit the man, he was on the road, rolling along the rough cobblestone. His ear hadn't missed the swish of a blade coming out of its sheath, and when he looked up a bright sword was inches from his nose.

The laugh was soft and friendly, and when Robert had refocused his eyes on the man, he laughed too. It was his father, wearing the same cloak he had given his two boys, but looking just a little more tense than he usually did.

"I guess I should have been paying more attention, huh?" his father said as he sheathed his sword and gave Robert a hand up. From an alley down the street Mark shouted in surprise and the three headed to the abbey together.

Robert remembered this story particularly because it showed exactly what his father was like. He would always come quietly, unannounced, and leave the same way. He was quiet, kind, and yet somehow there was a side to him that was as keen as edge of his sword.

The memories left Robert as he approached the main gate of the monastery. The large oaken doors were shut and barred, but his hand automatically reached for the bell on the right side.

A hand closed over his. "Might not be a good idea right now, Robert. Let's go down a few doors."

Something was wrong. Robert's heart started to pound just a little bit faster. The figure beside him was in a robe and cowl, and his hand on Robert's shoulder was more than politely guiding him away from the gate. Robert tried to snatch a look at his face, but the man's gray cowl prevented him.

They continued down the road, and then stepped into a midsized home on the right side of the street. Inside there was a small foyer, and Robert's companion asked him to sit in one of the two armchairs. When Robert sat, the other man sat in the opposing chair, and Robert finally saw his face.

"Brother Arnold!"

"Yes, it's me. You don't know how lucky you are, young man. That monastery was thoroughly searched yesterday. They did not find the object of their search, but evicted every scribe, monk, and abbot residing there. Most traveled over to Tynemouth Priory, but I've stayed here."

"What were they looking for?"

"It was empty, and they would not have been very kind to any visitors showing up on their doorstep, especially one of the order, or one of the occupants." Robert noticed how he had neatly sidestepped his question, but said nothing. The monk continued.

"I didn't realize you were going to be coming back, Robert. Where's Mark?" Then Robert told him the story, as he had told it twice already. He noticed that each time he told it, the reality set in a little stronger. When he told about losing his father and Mark, Brother Arnold became noticeably disturbed, and broke in to ask Robert where he had been staying.

"I hadn't gotten there yet," Robert replied, with a wry smile. But to Brother Arnold, it didn't seem so much of a laughing matter. Robert continued his story, and told Arnold how he had been staying with Gerald and Rolf, the fishermen.

"What are your plans now, Robert? If you want to stay in South Shields, I'm against it. There is nothing for you here anymore." Robert told him what he had been planning, and Arnold seemed to agree.

"Where can I find this cottage?" he asked. "I've an interest in your well being, my lad." Robert told him how to find Gerald's cottage, and the monk wrote it down on a scrap of parchment.

"Well, I have an opportunity for you, but the time is not yet right, I dare say. Maybe I'm wrong, but I will keep in touch with you."

Robert left the monk's house shortly after noon, and began to make his way out of the now-bustling city. On a whim, he decided to walk by the docks to see if any ships had come in. Maybe they could give him news of his father or brother.

The castle was directly in front of him as he walked down Front Street and he could see busy people crowding the gate and heading to the wharf. He turned onto Pier Road, and saw that they were either loading or unloading some ship at the mouth of the river.

He figured that must have been the ship that the friendly cart driver had been talking about. It looked like a nice ship, well made and ready to weather the ocean's storms, unlike the one he had ridden on. He also noticed that there were quite a few soldiers standing around. He guessed that meant it was a ship being sent or received by the castle itself, not one of Tynemouth's typical cargo ships.

He stopped a burly laborer who was carrying an impossibly heavy sack of grain, and asked him if the ship had just come in.

"That 'un? She's getting ready t' sail, son. Some day you'll learn t' just stay outta the way, and not ask questions, y'know. Mebbe it'd be wiser." Confused, Robert watched the man walk off. He hadn't seemed unfriendly, but...

"'Scuse me, you the nosy one? I think you'll be coming wit' me, boy." A hand dropped on his shoulder, and Robert twisted away. It was an impulsive movement, but when he glanced back and saw the look on the man's face, he knew the impulse was a good one.

Escaping wasn't quite that easy, however. The man was attired in the castle's livery, and was armed with a pike, which he quickly dropped in Robert's path.

Once again, instinct took over, and Robert snatched the pike's haft, and giving it a shove into the man's gut. The guard grunted and wheezed, then grabbed his stomach. He appeared to be in such pain and surprise that Robert was halfway inclined to apologize for his hasty action. But then the man's arm snaked out at him and tried to snatch the edge of his shirt. Robert quickly dodged. Then he took off running.

Behind him, he heard the man shouting, raising the alarm. Dodging quickly into a small alley, he moved two streets over, then tried to walk calmly. He could feel his heart thumping in his chest and his face turning red, but as far as he knew, the guard hadn't gotten a good look at him, and he would have no idea who he was. Neither would anyone else who was trying to help. Running would just make them positive they had their quarry.

His guess was accurate. Several minutes later, a handful of pikemen marched down the road at a quick trot. They didn't even glance at Robert. Smiling quietly, he watched them disappear into the distance among all the busy city occupants.

The way back to the fishermen's cottage was largely uneventful. He managed to get a ride with another fisherman returning from the market, and discussed the fishing business for the major part of his ride. Nearing Hartford Bridge, they saw a troop of horsemen approaching. To Robert, they looked like the same men who had passed them on the way to Ulric's. Now, given time to look at them, he was impressed. They were clean, trim and efficient looking men, all riding well-groomed and athletic horses. The leader, a skinny, graying man in his fifties, nodded to Robert's companion as he went by, prompting a proud look from the man.

"That's my friend Roland. He's the leader of our earl's scouts. He and I never missed a joust back when we were still kids in Consett. He's always on missions from the earl. Helping him catch the latest lawbreaker, probably."

They rode on until the fisherman stopped at his cottage, a little south of Ashington. From there Robert continued on foot. The sun was setting to his left, and the reds and yellows were painting the sky in a beautiful mural.

It was just dark when Robert stepped into the fishermen's cottage, thankful to have these friends. Without them, he would be on his own, with nowhere to go.

CHAPTER 6

Mark woke the following morning, wondrously comfortable for once. He'd built a fire the night before to cook his supper, and the extra warmth it provided was an immense improvement over his first night.

He revived the fire by blowing on the coals and adding some fresh wood. His breakfast consisted of several strings of seaweed cooked over the fire. It was the same thing he had had for his supper the night before. He decided that if he didn't find something else to eat he would have to invent other ways of preparing his seaweed. The small bag of food from the ship was still by his bed, but he didn't want to break into his reserves.

After finishing breakfast, he got thinking about how long he would be on the island. He hadn't even given a thought to trying to leave. His only concerns had been food and water. Now he decided that the only chance he had of getting off the island was to attract a ship. After all, he could never hope to leave on his own unless he built a boat. Following this reasoning, he allotted his morning time to gathering wood for a bonfire.

The first step was finding a good location. After cleaning up his fire-making and seaweed-cooking mess, he left the small room and climbed the steps up the tall tower overlooking the bay. It would do for a place to build a fire, he thought.

The next step, bringing wood up to the tower, was not as easy. He broke off several trees' worth of branches from the small orchard in the castle's inner court, then carried them up to the top of the tower one scratchy armload at a time. The thin whip-like branches caught on every corner and snapped back at him, and the top branches were always scratching his face.

After ferrying a suitable amount of fuel up to the proposed fire location, he returned to the room he had slept in the previous night. Thankfully, the fire was still lit. He used a chunk of wood to ferry the flames up to the tower.

The thin branches were still green, and didn't light very well. His varied attempts proved unsuccessful, until he found some dry wood and lit that first. Once that was started, the fire spread slowly to the green branches. They didn't catch fire easily, but once lit they produced thick clouds of smoke.

Satisfied, he sat back against the crenellations that lined the tower and watched the black clouds boiling into the still air. After a few minutes a tall column of smoke had arisen that could be seen from miles around.

Mark was exhausted after all the climbing, and his skin was cut and scratched from the branches. Little red welts were forming on his arms, and his fingers sported tiny cuts all over. The heat from the fire didn't help either. Mark had to retreat down the stairs to a lower window to watch the sea after the fire became too hot to bear.

It wasn't long before his short rest turned into a light sleep. The fresh ocean breeze mixed with heat wafting down from the fire and wrapped around him like a blanket. His head nodded once, twice, and finally rested on his chest.

Some time later the snapping fire roused him, and he lazily looked out over the ocean, which stretched endlessly into the distance. He was about to close his eyes again when he saw something edging into his vision from the side of the window.

He craned his neck to get a better look. It was a ship! Every scrap of its canvas fluttered in the light breeze. It was heading straight for the island.

Adrenaline coursed through Mark's veins. All drowsiness

gone in an instant, he tore down the stairs. His stings and scratches were forgotten. He covered the courtyard at a dead sprint and clambered over the piles of ruined war vehicles as fast as he dared. When he slowed to a stop at the edge of the water, the ship almost appeared farther away. Still, he was certain it was coming.

Glancing back at the fire, Mark immediately noticed a change. The tall black column of smoke was no longer pouring out of the top of the tower, and any remnant of it was quickly dispersing into a rising west wind.

He paid no further attention to it, however, because the ship was now furling its sails and casting anchor in the water a short distance from the island. He watched eagerly as a boat was lowered from the tall sides of the ship. It took only a few moments to load, and was soon heading for shore.

The heavily loaded boat sank low in the water as it headed toward shore. Nevertheless, it cut through the water at an incredible pace. Even the quickly moving boat was too slow for Mark. He had an urge to jump into the water and swim out to it. Remembering his last encounter with the freezing water, however, he held himself in check.

Now the boat was getting closer. Mark could see the sun glinting off of swords and pikes. Immediately an uneasy feeling rose in his stomach. There was no reason for them to fear a single person on an island. He backed up a ways onto the shore. The men seemed to be holding a conference as the boat swept closer and closer. Mark could hear short sections of their conversation, and he didn't like it.

"...to the left...he doesn't get away...could hide anywhere on that island...we have to...otherwise..." As Mark became increasingly alarmed, the boat beached on the island.

The men clambered out onto the rubble-strewn beach. They quickly split, and groups of men sprinted to either side of him, effectively cutting off retreat to anywhere except directly back.

Mark turned and ran. Instantly, he realized his disadvantage: he had to navigate the tricky clutter of ruin extending from the castle walls. The men on his left easily kept up with him, using the path he had so laboriously cleared just the day before. Mark didn't have that option as he scrambled, panting and scared, up the slight incline toward the castle.

In the midst of glancing back at his pursuers he felt his foot slip into a hole. His ankle twisted savagely, and his body hit the ground so hard it knocked the breath out of him.

His pursuers were there in seconds. Lying on his back with his leg twisted under him, Mark could only watch as the leader stomped to a halt in front of him, leering.

He was a tall, muscular man with an air of authority about him. His clothes were well-kept and the hilt of his sword was polished, shining in the sun. The leather belt was tightened against a mail shirt that had no remnant of rust or dirt on it. Bulging arms were enclosed by bronze vambraces, and his fingers were strong and calloused, yet lean enough to handle a weapon with skill.

His hand was just reaching for his sword when he uttered a short grunt. His body jolted as if somebody had just kicked him full in the chest. A second later he slammed into the ground. A crossbow bolt stuck straight up out of his chain-mailed bulk. He lay there, unmoving, as men gathered from every side, confused.

Seeing one last chance, Mark tried frantically to gain his feet again. His ankle felt like it was on fire. Hoping it was just out of joint, he tried to force it back into place. The pain was incredible, but it was nothing compared to the shock when the joint popped back into place. Shaking, he heaved himself to his feet.

The men saw his actions and stepped toward him. Instantly, a hail of arrows cut the air. Flinching, Mark instinctively covered his head with his hands and curled up into a ball on the ground. Arrows whistled around him. He could hear them landing in the ground with a soft "thud" or puncturing weapons and armor with a sharp "crack."

In seconds the hail had stopped. All Mark could hear was

groaning. Tentatively, he uncurled himself and took a look. Many of the men were still unhurt, but they no longer concerned themselves with him. They began to drag the wounded back to the boat as quickly as they could.

Like magic, swordsmen began to appear out of the rubble, closer to the boat than they were. Mark could see them materializing from behind a small knoll, forming up into a company. It was an eerie scene: the swordsmen in their blue dress with highly polished chain mail walking slowly toward the boat.

When they had reached it, the company executed a smart about-face and fanned out in front of it. Every man's sword was pulled from its sheath at the same instant. The fleeing men were stopped dead in their tracks.

Mark's mysterious attackers were spread out, but they formed into a motley group and dashed at the front of the semi-circle, trying to get to the boat. To Mark, it almost seemed like they were melting into the line of blue. As fast as they approached, they were cut down. Within minutes there was a pile of bodies and a group of quavering men with hands in the air.

The surrendering men were quickly and efficiently gathered up, and the mysterious rescuers silently led them away. The little group of prisoners had a shocked, disbelieving look on their faces as they were prodded up the path to the castle.

Mark looked toward the ship as the men began to walk away. There seemed to be confusion. For a moment, it looked as though another boat was going to be sent. It was halfway down the side before it was quickly pulled up. Without a hint of hesitation the ship piled on sail and began to pick up speed.

As the sounds of the men receded, Mark sensed someone's presence next to him. He looked over and saw a young man in his mid-twenties standing next to him. He was dressed in the same clothes as the other swordsmen, the shining mail coat under a brilliant blue surcoat emblazoned with a silver eagle. His mailed hand rested lightly on the hilt of his sword as he gazed out to sea.

Following his gaze, Mark saw that he wasn't looking at the fleeing ship, but at another, smaller ship that was racing toward it. The small ship was clearly trying to overtake the larger ship, and it looked as though she were going to board.

As the gap between the ships narrowed, arrows began to fly from both sides. The ships began to take on the likeness of pincushions. Little splashes in the water and twitches in the sails gave evidence of the ferocious stream of projectiles.

When they closed, there was a flurry of action. Grapples flew through the air. Men jumped over the gap. Then the ships hit.

Mark could see the men on both boats stumble as the ships collided. Shock waves pulsed through every spar. The men of the larger ship were clearly outnumbered due to the loss of the landing party, and as the ships drifted off into the distance the end was not in doubt.

The young man next to Mark turned abruptly and said,

"Come. I imagine you'll want something to eat besides seaweed right about now." With a wry grin he gave Mark a hand as they walked up the slope to the castle.

CHAPTER 7

It was still dark when Robert followed Rolf out into the cold early morning air. The high oilskin collar chafed against his chin; the entire coat felt stiff and uncomfortable. It was a typical seaman's clothing: high pants, coat, and large hat made from sailcloth with a thin layer of tar. The "rough weather clothes" weren't always necessary, Rolf said, but Robert was glad to have another layer of protection at this time in the morning, especially with a chilly breeze coming from the northwest.

He followed the two fishermen down the road to Ashington, ducking his head into his collar to keep warm. They were walking along at a brisk pace, eager to be out fishing again, but Robert wondered how many people were crazy enough to get up this early in the morning and spend hours on the freezing ocean.

At least one more person was that crazy, apparently. Ulric met them on his doorstep with several mugs of warm apple cider. The drink really hit the spot after their long and dreary walk.

They didn't stop long, however. Fifteen minutes later they were stepping onto the deck of the *Hibernia*. Ulric had named the boat after Ireland, known as Hibernia to the Romans. One of his ancestors had led a Roman cohort to Ireland, and his campaigning stories had filtered down through the years. Ulric readily admitted he had never been there, but he still named the boat after the legendary land.

Gerald, Rolf, and Ulric had pulled the boat back out of the sea and stocked it with the necessary supplies while Robert had been "gallivanting with the monks," as Ulric put it. The fishing boat was now ready to sail, and Robert would be joining the three experienced fishermen on their first trip of the season.

Despite Robert's hopes, the wind didn't decrease as they cast off from the little dock, but began to blow colder and stronger as they pulled away from shore. Gerald soon had Rolf and Robert busy baiting and tying hooks. It turned out to be another reason Robert was convinced fishing was for the insane. Rolf laughed at his clumsy attempts to attach the bait to the large hooks. After Robert had speared himself multiple times, the young fisherman gave him a few pointers that made the process much easier.

They were attempting to catch fish by towing a main line equipped with drop lines, or small, baited extensions off either side. Periodically they would haul the entire line into the boat to retrieve the fish and replace the bait.

Their success turned out to be only mediocre, but the work still kept Robert busy. They ran two lines; one would be baited while the other was out. They rotated the lines to make the most of their time. The pace of the work was not all that fast, but Robert was not used to it, and he envied Rolf's habitual precision. Rolf could carry on a running argument with Gerald and Ulric while baiting twice as many hooks as Robert.

In the back of the ship, Gerald and Ulric were kept busy gutting the fish. They would pass buckets of waste up to the boys, who then baited the lines with the chunks. Robert could see them working quickly with short, deft movements of their sharp knives. They could gut a large fish in only a few quick actions.

It wasn't long before a small pile of fish was beginning to form in the back of the boat. It didn't take much longer than that for Robert to start aching from the cramped quarters and fighting his clumsy fingers, which were getting stiff with the cold.

"The cold won't last long, happily," Rolf said. "It's only bad early, and then only for a few weeks." He was right, and Robert was relieved. The nighttime air lost its chill, and he even got used to baiting the hooks after a bit of practice.

And then Robert witnessed one of the best benefits of a fisherman's life: the sunrise. A thin layer of mist was rising from the sea, and the tendrils that rose were caught by rays of the sun as it edged over the horizon. In a few moments, the entire area was bathed in soft golden light, and Robert could see that they were not alone. Several shadowy sails were outlined in the quickly dissipating mist, and they made the scene even more beautiful.

Robert had always been more conscious of the "finer things in life" as he called them. His brother Mark had more interest in fact and realism, but Robert thought that even he would be impressed by the living picture in front of him now.

The men had stopped working for a moment, and were gazing at the sunrise. In time, though, the picture was erased, and work began to be an all too imminent thought in Robert's mind.

"Hey, there's Glen," Rolf announced. "He still hasn't fixed that sail of his." To Robert he said, "Glen and his boys usually fish where we do, and last year they lost their mast to a larger ship's spar. They fixed the mast, but it looks like their sail still needs a little help."

"Ahoy there, Glen! Ahoy the Bumbling Bumble Bee!"

Rolf's shouts were answered by an equally humorous voice;

"Why don't you old men just move to Hibernia, 'stead of talking about it so much!" The words were spoken by a boy of about thirteen, who sat in wet oilskins in the stern of the boat. He was baiting hooks just as Robert and Rolf were. His father looked up and waved to Ulric and Gerald, then returned to gutting the pile of fish that lay before him.

Robert soon became used to the brisk pace. The fresh sea air made his job much more pleasant, and he started to enjoy the work. He was also kept entertained by the friendly banter between fishing ships, as the various crews began to wake up from the hard work that had kept them occupied the last few hours.

The work continued for a while, until, as the sun began to reach its peak, Gerald straightened and called for the lines to be hauled in. Rolf and Robert unhooked the fish that were on it and coiled the line neatly into its container. As they did so, they removed the hooks to keep the lines from becoming tangled.

There were still a few more fish left to be gutted, so Rolf and Robert lent a hand. Although considerably slower than Gerald and Ulric, the two boys helped reduce the pile of fish until it was nearly gone. Soon Gerald ordered them to set sail for shore, which was now only a large gray mass on the horizon.

Robert had no idea how to sail the vessel, but Rolf taught him. He told him which ropes to pull, when, and how far. The sail began to flutter in the slight breeze as the ropes slid through his hands, and he felt the boat begin to catch the wind. In a matter of moments, they were headed for shore.

They docked at the small pier by Ulric's house and began to unload the fish into a large basin near the shore. Meanwhile, Ulric ran to the house and procured a farmer's cart, into which the fishermen loaded as much fish as they could.

Gerald and Ulric were known as the "fresh fish" sellers in Ashington. As soon as they came in from fishing, they would load up the cart and head for town to sell their goods. Gerald reasoned that this was much simpler and easier than preserving the fish and trying to ship them off to the big towns to sell.

It wasn't long before they were approaching Ashington with their smelly cargo. A pot-bellied, balding man with an officious air met them at the gate.

"And what do you have, Gerald?" At the response, he began to scribble some numbers on his pad. Robert leaned over and watched him write. It was all he could do to keep from laughing as the man straightened and announced:

"The tax will be four fish, with, ahem, one for the town

improvements going on." He accompanied them to the city hall, where they left the "tax," and continued to the market.

"Did you see his scribble, Rolf?" Robert asked.

"You can read? What did he write?" Rolf replied.

"He wrote nothing but the number of fish, and the rest made no sense, to make you think he was figuring the tax!"

"I suspected as much," grumbled Ulric. "That old tosspot has been 'taxing' different amounts every time we come in."

"But, the, ahem, town improvements," Gerald imitated. The group burst out laughing.

"Look there!" cried Rolf. "He only wanted one for breakfast!" Sure enough, the tax collector was walking quickly away from the town hall with a large cod in his hand.

"You may as well let it lie," said Robert. "At the current tax rate he undercharged you by two fish anyway. Lot of good that 'figuring' did for him." They all laughed again as they entered the center of the town, where the market was bustling with life.

"Fresh fish! Fresh fish! Just caught this morning!" Housewives, innkeepers, and merchants flocked to the call for the first fish of the season. In only minutes the large cart was empty, and the fishermen returned to refill. They made several more trips, and on the last one, Robert noticed the scout whom they had seen earlier. Rolf noticed as well.

"Look, Father, Roland is accepting recruits." The graying man was standing behind a small table, where several young men were gathered.

"Hmmph. Good luck with that," Gerald said. "None of those boys are cut out for it, and he knows it."

Just then, a young man walked up, grabbed a quill, and began to sign his name to one of the papers. Even from a distance, the men could hear Roland's sharp voice.

"Not so fast, Mr. Denton. You have to meet my requirements first."

"Really. Too bad for you, then." Cogniard's officer was about to reply, but his gaze went past the young man and rested on another person walking up to join them. He heaved a sigh and replied, "Very well, sign there."

"Is there a problem here?" An older man, fashionably dressed and appearing quite self-interested, joined the group.

"Roland is giving me trouble, Father," the young man said, even as he signed the paper.

"Not at all, Mr. Mayor. As you can see, Harry is signing as we speak."

"Very well, then. No more trouble, eh? And that will be Mr. Denton from now on, eh?" Harry smirked as he finished his signature with a flourish.

"Well, Mr. Denton, it seems you have filled our vacancy. Shall we be going? Roy, lend him your horse."

A disgruntled-looking young man from Roland's group of scouts dismounted and handed the reins to the boy, who smiled and went to mount. With his father watching, he placed his foot in the stirrup and gave a small jump, landing on the small leather saddle.

Like lightning, the horse's back arched. His head went down as he let out a snort and tried to launch the young rider into the air. Through sheer luck, Harry managed to grab a hunk of mane, and he hung on for dear life. Bucking and snorting, the spirited horse took off down the road in fits and starts. His hapless rider was jerked in every direction.

As the wild pair neared the group of fishermen, Robert slipped off the cart, and ran out into the horse's way. He waved his arms wildly, stopping the horse dead in its tracks, although not calming it down any. When the dangling reins came in his direction, he snatched them up, holding the horse where it stood.

"Get off while you can!" he shouted. The boy began to slide toward him, but he suddenly stopped and grabbed Robert's shoulder, hard.

Wincing, Robert yelled at him to hurry up.

"My foot's stuck!" the frightened boy yelled. Just then, the horse half bucked, moving away from Robert. The boy's hand on his shoulder pulled him along, and he almost lost his balance.

Knowing that the only way to save the boy was to get his foot out of the stirrup, he placed his own foot in the near stirrup, backwards, and reached across the horse to get at the other side, where the boy's foot was thrashing wildly, and hopelessly entangled. The horse, now burdened with two people, kept jumping around as a struggle ensued on his back.

Robert, one foot in the left stirrup and one hand on the horse's mane, was trying to cut the stirrup leather. Meanwhile, the boy was trying to free himself, but only succeeded in giving Robert a bloody nose and bruised shoulder.

Then for a moment Harry was still, and in that time Robert managed to slice the tough leather leading to the stirrup. Immediately, Harry began to fall toward the ground. Robert grabbed him around the waist with his right arm and heaved him bodily off the horse, dumping him in an unharmed heap in the road.

There was no lack of volunteers to help Harry, but Robert had to worry about the horse. It had calmed down considerably but was obviously still spooked. Thankfully,

Robert had always taken an interest in horses, and was no mean hand when it came to controlling them. He calmed the beast down, then mounted it himself and rode it back to its owner, who was leaning against a doorpost down the road.

The young man's face was still somewhat dissatisfied in its appearance, as Robert had noticed before, but he was obviously enjoying the scene that was playing out before him. The spoiled Harry was being assisted in any way possible, while his father could be heard saying, "Maybe it isn't quite the time for you to join the scouts, son."

The horse's owner, whom Roland had called Roy, looked up, surprised, at Robert when he rode up.

"Amazing," he said. "I've never seen anyone ride old Carmen except me." Robert laughed, catching on to what had just happened.

"A surefire way to get rid of recruits, huh?" he said. Roy nodded and managed a grin. "We've had our share of overconfident buffoons who think they can ride. Carmen never fails to remind them that they can't."

Robert laughed and handed over the well-used reins. "Enjoy," he said, turning to leave. Just then, a gloved hand fell on his shoulder.

"What's your name, young man?" Robert turned around and found himself looking at Roland, the head scout for the Earl of Newcastle.

"Robert Sheffield, sir."

"Where did you learn how to ride? That was no piece of fool's work you just did."

"I lived at a monastery for a while, and they considered it an art worth learning."

"You lived at a monastery… where do you live now?"

"I'm staying with them," he said, pointing toward Gerald and the others.

"I see, and… Gerald! I haven't seen him in ages! I'll have to see what he's been up to lately. But to return to my earlier train of thought, you don't really sound all that decided about your life. Do you have any plans for the near future?"

"Actually, you are right. I lost track of my family, and it seems I won't see them again soon, if ever."

"Hmmm… I'm sorry about your family. Would a position as a scout help you with your plans for the future?"

CHAPTER 8

Mark sat back from his empty plate, a gluttonously heavy feeling weighing down his stomach. There was no remnant of the repast left to speak of, and he was finally full.

The young man-at-arms returned, and, while trying to hide a smile at the empty plate, told Mark to follow him. They left the dining hall, which had been one of the large locked underground rooms, and walked past several doors. Then they stopped at the last door before the spiral stairs. The man-at-arms knocked, and there was a flurry of movement before the door was opened and a tall, lanky youth peered out.

"Yes?" he said, looking back and forth between the two of them.

"The sergeant would like you to entertain this young man until he returns," said Mark's guide.

Mark was quick to notice the special emphasis on the word *entertain*, and saw the knowing glance that passed between the man-at-arms and the boy.

"Hi. My name's Jan. Let me introduce you to the rest of the people here," said the boy. The man-at-arms left and Jan led Mark into a small dormitory that was overflowing with boys.

"Thomas Allen, the sergeant, told us to stay in here while he took care of the chaps outside," said Jan. "I'll start by introducing you to my friends."

He led Mark to the back corner of the packed room to a group of boys about his age. They were sprawled over several small beds and conversing with each other. All conversation stopped when Mark and Jan came up.

"Hey all, this is the would-be survivor master," Jan said. Mark blushed at this comment, but Jan went on. "Mark, these vagabonds are generally considered to be my friends, although I would never admit it publicly. The short scheming analyst is Ijn. He generally keeps his mouth shut, a trait not commonly found amongst us except when the upperclassmen are present." He waved his hand toward a group of surly unshaven young men lounging by the room's only fireplace, who were watching the introduction.

"The big guy over here is Richard, who we generally call Rich, even though he's far from it. Mr. Studious over there is referred to as Louis." When Jan said his name, the average-sized boy in the corner looked up from his book. He looked appraisingly at Mark, then returned to his reading.

"Over here is Pieter, my most beloved, or not, cousin, who unfortunately looks just like me. Which is not such a good thing at times, seeing as though he's a bit of a mischief maker." The last boy did look like Jan, and grinned at Mark.

"Now that you know who we are, could we have the honor of knowing your name?" Jan asked. Mark told him, and then Jan took him on a quick tour of the people in the room, spitting off names so fast that Mark could never have remembered them all. One person he did remember was one of the "upperclassmen." His name was Lukas, and he seemed to have nothing in common with the other upperclassmen. He was quieter, more polite, and seemed to take an actual interest in Mark. His classmates looked like they wanted to ridicule him, but some form of respect kept them from voicing their opinions.

After meeting the masses of boys, Mark returned to the friendly group in the corner and was soon bombarded with a barrage of questions.

"How did you get here?" from Pieter.

"Did you actually think the island was deserted?" asked Ijn.

"Were you really hungry?" the large guy, Richard, asked.

The questions were endless, but Mark had no problem answering them all. His normally outgoing nature responded quickly to all the questions, especially since he hadn't talked to anybody in days.

After the boys spent some time asking questions, Mark started to ask some of his own questions about them. He learned several things about each one. Ijn had come from Japan with his father, who was now the third in command of the island fortress. Ijn's father, a Samurai from Japan, had left because of a growing dislike of the shogun he had served. He and Ijn had traveled across Europe and met up with one of the fort's resupply ships in a port in the Netherlands. Being completely free from any restraint, he accepted the chance to start over again on the island after having heard all about it from the ship's captain. He had started as a low ranking officer but had moved quickly up, impressing others with his tactical know-how. Ijn had followed in his father's footsteps, and was recognized, at least among his friends, as a tactical genius.

The other boys' stories quickly followed. Richard had always lived with his father, who had been just one more wandering knight, glad to accept a job. Pieter and Jan had been living on the street in Amsterdam when Pieter had snuck aboard a resupply ship, bringing a reluctant Jan with him. They had been discovered before the ship even left the port but were allowed to stay.

Louis was the son of one of the officers. His father had been with the Earl, the ruler of the castle, throughout the conflict with his scheming neighbor who had taken lands and title from him. Louis spent his time studying or reading. He entertained dreams of becoming an officer like his father, who was now an aide to Ijn's Samurai father, Aronii.

After what seemed like only a few minutes of talking, there was a knock at the door. A servant had arrived to inform the boys that they were free to go.

Mark got up quickly, and followed his new-found friends through the door. They walked down the halls and up the spiral stairs into the tower. A heavy wooden door led to the main building, where the stained glass windows had been arranged with such precision.

Once inside, they skirted the unused dining hall and entered a small hallway off to the side that led to a spiral staircase. The stone slabs were cold on Mark's feet as he descended the rough stairs, and he became increasingly aware of the cool, damp smell that was wafting up from below. After reaching the bottom of the stairs, they followed a long corridor that slowly curved to the left.

Just as his brain figured it out, they entered an astronomical cavern, the same one he had seen from the tower. They had entered the cavern at the middle, and, due to the wide mouth, Mark could see where he had stood in the tower. Looking the other way, he saw a large open space, filled mostly with water, and a wooden walkway around it. The back of the cavern sloped sharply down, leading to a small waterway that disappeared underground.

While Mark had been looking at the cavern, all the boys had been focusing on what was happening at the mouth of the cave. A small ship was entering, and quite a few people were standing by to support the operation. The compact, solidly-built ship eased slowly into the cavern. It was pulled by a group of husky sailors, their bare feet straining against the wooden planking of the dock.

When the boat slowed to a halt, a gang plank was set down and a detachment of soldiers disappeared below the decks. Several minutes later they reappeared with a scraggly bunch of dejected-looking soldiers, apparently the occupants of the captured ship. These were led away, and the ship was slowly pulled back out of the cavern.

Mark was ready to head back, but the other boys were waiting, expectant, as though something important was supposed to happen. Just as Mark was ready to think they had never seen a ship unloaded before, the cavern grew dark, and the captured ship loomed in the entrance. The mainmast had been removed, but the mizzenmast didn't fit, and several chunks of dirt and rock fell into the water as it came to rest just outside the cavern.

The aggressor's ship was well-built. It was constructed of thick timbers, with several heavy weapons mounted on its decks. The strength of the hull was readily apparent, and deep scars in the wood showed that this ship had weathered many storms and most likely many battles as well. The style of construction dated the ship only a few years old, but it looked as though it could have been twenty.

As the ship stopped, a distinguished looking nobleman appeared from behind Mark and his friends. The crowds seemed to part before him as he made his way to the ship. He was accompanied by an entourage of several officers, and Mark could easily pick out Ijn's father by his Oriental features.

"The nobleman there - that one - is Lord Cornuel," whispered Jan. When Mark threw him a questioning glance, he explained.

"Lord Cornuel is the second-in-command of the fortress. He's the commander now, because the Earl of Newcastle is late in returning."

The tall, commanding man strode onto the deck of the ship and looked around. His piercing eyes missed nothing, and they scanned the ship quickly and thoroughly.

As he turned to enter the cabin, his eyes fell on Mark, and rested there a split second longer than what would have seemed normal. Then he entered the large cabin of the ship. Aronii, Ijn's father, also picked up on this oddity, and his gaze focused on Mark as well. Then he gave a curt nod in the direction of his son's friends and disappeared into the ship.

Mark was left with a strange feeling. The looks that he had received up until now had been curious but not all that interested. Now, Lord Cornuel, the commander of the island, had seemed to study him intensely for a split second, and Aronii had seemed to see whatever the commander had seen. He felt like he was left out of a joke, except that this joke seemed pretty serious.

After several minutes, the commander and his retinue filed back off the ship, and the curious island dwellers began their own inspections of the recently captured prize. The boys flooded onto the deck of the ship with everyone else. Mark could feel the rough-hewn deck under his bare feet, and smell the salt water that had recently been used to scrub the decks clean.

Ijn moved quickly and surely, looking at everything, and examining the damage that had been done, although it was slight. Mark soon began to appreciate Ijn's way of thinking as the boy explained the strong points of the design, as well as apparent defects. The boys continued to inspect the ship, and by the time they had finished, the vast majority of the people had left. Only a few stragglers still scrutinized the vessel.

Mark and Ijn stepped off the ship, engaged in conversation about the design. They were quickly accosted by one of the men Mark had seen in Lord Cornuel's retinue.

"If you don't mind, sir, the sergeant would like to have an interview with you."

The words were framed as a suggestion, but Mark knew them to be a command. He bid farewell to Ijn, and followed the man up the stairs.

CHAPTER 9

There had only been a slight mist when Robert had gotten up that morning. Now, as he stepped out of the fishermen's cottage, he noted that the rain was picking up. Gerald and Rolf stepped out behind him, and he felt the old man's hand on his shoulder.

"Well, it was good having you around, even if you did have a questionable background, Robert." The comment still offended Robert, but he laughed it off and shook the man's proffered hand. Rolf gave him a punch in the shoulder.

"If you need more pricked fingers or fish guts, you know where to come!"

After assuring his friends that he would look them up

soon, Robert took his leave and started off down the road. It hadn't been too hard of a decision, joining the scouts. Roland had told him to be in town by noon if he wanted the position, so he was able to discuss the proposition with Gerald - after Roland had bought his old friend a drink, of course.

He and Mark had always dreamed of being war heroes of some type, although their plans had differed somewhat in their emphasis. While Mark had favored large battles and raw courage winning the day, Robert had placed his emphasis on skill and thought. Which was why the scouts appealed to him. They relied on speed, stealth, and skill to affect the outcome of not only a battle, but a whole campaign.

His love of horses had also influenced his decision. So had Roland. Gerald had unconditionally recommended Roland as "the most honorable, courageous man you will ever serve under." Robert had only one drawback. When he joined the scouts, he could no longer search for his father or brother. However, Gerald's unfailing realism had convinced him that chances of surviving a shipwreck were low enough. Add the cold water and there was really no hope.

The rain had not abated by the time Robert reached the stable where the scouts were preparing to ride. Roland welcomed him in and led him to the back of the stable, where a scout was leading a young sorrel horse out into the aisle.

"Never mind, Fulke, the lad's here. I think he can handle this. Robert, meet Fulke Cheverell, one of our archers, and our best runner. Fulke, this is Robert, the newest scout."

"Pleased to meet you," the young man said. He handed the reins over to Robert, and pointed to the pile of harness-leather on the floor. "There should be a serviceable bridle in there, and as far as saddles go, we're not carrying any extra, so…"

"You can find one next door at the cordwainer's," Roland broke in. "Tell the clerk to bill it to the scouts. After you get saddled up, wait with the rest. We're almost ready to head out."

Robert spent a few minutes in the cordwainer's shop, making sure the saddle he picked was the perfect balance of weight and strength. From what Gerald had said, the scouts were constantly on the move, almost always on horseback. They were one of the best light-horse units in the country, and Robert didn't want to be left behind for any reason - especially not because of a broken saddle which he had picked out!

His choice made, he quickly saddled the dark red horse and led him to the front of the stable, where most of the troop were waiting. Seeing them mounted, he did the same. Except that he didn't make it quite all the way up.

As he placed his weight in the stirrup, the entire saddle

slid around, almost dumping him back on the ground.
Robert's instinctive reaction landed him on his feet, but
his face turned a darker shade of red as he realized his
mistake. Several chuckles and a short laugh didn't help his
composure any, but what really irked him was the fact
that Roland had just appeared out of the stable, and
though his face didn't change a hair, his eyes laughed
merrily.

Quickly, Robert righted the saddle and re-tightened it,
this time giving the horse a good poke in the ribs. The
first time he had saddled, he had failed to make sure the
horse had let out his breath, resulting in the loose girdle
when the sorrel had exhaled later. It was a beginner's
mistake, and he knew it. What was worse, the men
around him knew it, and by his estimation they wouldn't
let him forget it very soon.

Roland's look of approval at his quick reaction was lost
on him as he swung up for the second time on his mount,
giving the horse a good pat when he mounted
successfully.

Within a few minutes, the stragglers were saddled and
waiting to be off. Roland disappeared into the stable one
last time, returning with a blanket roll which he tossed to
Robert. Then he swung up on his own horse, and took a
headcount.

Satisfied that all the scouts were present, he motioned
them forward, and the group headed west through the

center of Ashington.

It wasn't long before Robert learned to appreciate the discipline of the scouts. They rode at an efficient, mile-eating pace along the westerly road, stopping only for short breaks to water the horses. The group was around fifty men in all, split loosely among the main body, vanguard, rearguard, and two flanking groups.

As they pushed their way westward, Robert got to know his horse a little better. The same could not be said for his human companions. Conversations were not unusual, but as a rule the scouts rode silently, their eyes scanning every inch of the way ahead.

In the rare occasion that someone did crack a joke or comment on a passing site, it was never directed toward Robert, who felt somewhat left out. To be sure, the scouts were never impolite to him, but he didn't yet fit into their way of doing things, and as far as they were concerned, he didn't exist.

It was already dark when they caught up with their own vanguard. The group had prepared a sheltered campsite, and the men were bringing in wood for the fires when the main body came up. Gratefully, Robert slipped off his horse and led him to the small stream that ran nearby. As the horse drank, he removed the saddle and bridle, setting them on the ground nearby.

"You can keep those near you when you sleep. Just don't

lose track of them. It's not uncommon for small-time country thieves to try and make a quick profit by reselling a good piece of harness." The voice belonged to Fulke, the scout who had brought his horse out at the stable.

"Thanks," Robert replied. "By the way, do you know the name of my horse? Or was he just bought in Ashington?"

"That's Amaury you're riding. He belonged to Simon before... good horse, that one." Robert was going to ask what happened to Simon, but he got the feeling that any probing would not be appreciated.

After Amaury had finished drinking, Robert followed the lead of the other scouts and hobbled him near the troop's horses. Then he dragged his tack over to one of the fires, where he began to spread out his blanket.

"Hey you there, we need some more wood stockpiled for the fire!" One of the scouts that had been traveling with the main party motioned toward the central pile of light brush. Wearily, Robert left his blanket half-unraveled and joined several young men procuring wood from a nearby stand of trees.

He began to break off light, whippy green branches of the trees, but one of the men stopped him and pointed toward a smaller plant.

"We want wood that's dry and dense, as well as easy to gather. Green wood is none of those things, and you'd be here all night if you tried to light that stuff." With a number of the scouts helping, it was only a few minutes before the men had deemed the pile large enough.

Intending to finish unrolling his blanket, Robert returned to his place by the fire and found that it was missing. He looked suspiciously at the other scouts, who had not left their spots since he was called to get wood, but he could not discover anything from their stony faces. As far as he could see, none of the scouts at his fire had more than one blanket roll. Keeping a sharp lookout, he went for a stroll around the now-settling camp.

He could feel many eyes following him as he tried to nonchalantly discover the culprit. It was useless. Every man returned his gaze unflinchingly, and some even seemed to be laughing. Determining that the longer he looked, the more foolish he would appear, he decided that two could play at this game.

Robert returned to his place after checking on Amaury, and sat cross-legged before the small fire. The evening meal was being served, and Robert was thankful that the thief had left him with his bowl and cup, for he could not have eaten the soup very well with only his hands.

It turned out to be very good soup. When he asked, Robert learned that it had been made with some small game caught by the outlying scouts while they rode. As they ate, he tried to scrutinize the men without making it obvious. Nobody was talking, except two men discussing the ailments of one of the horses. It seemed that everyone was tired, but Robert guessed that they were always this quiet.

With no talk, supper was finished quickly, and the men almost immediately got ready to sleep, setting out sentries and checking the horses one last time.

Without a bedroll, Robert had no idea what he was supposed to do, but he decided to play along, and when the men lay down he did too, just not with a blanket or pillow. Cushioning his head on his arm, he closed his eyes and tried to sleep. Unfortunately, it wasn't as easy as he thought. The hard ground quickly made his hip and shoulder sore.

The pain was enough to jog his memory. He and Mark had always listened to stories from Brother Arnold with great interest. This was especially true when the stories were about his friend's campaigning in the army. The particular story he remembered now was about this very situation – sleeping on the ground. Apparently, if you scratched out a little hollow for your hips, and did the same for your shoulders, the position would be much more comfortable.

He immediately tried this out. With a small stick nearby, he scratched out two little hollows and lay down. Unsatisfied, he got back up and adjusted them.

"Sleeping in a hole won't help you any," one of the young men nearby quipped.

"We might think it's a pit toilet by mistake," another offered.

At that point, an older man walked up and boxed their ears. "Don't you know a good trick when you see it? This is a classic. If you're ever out in the woods by yourself without a blanket, I'll bet my bridle you'd wish you were as smart as he was."

By this time Robert had adjusted the slight depressions in the ground, and lay back down to test them. It was perfect. He had just enough time to wearily grin at the old veteran before he drifted off into a sleep of exhaustion.

The next morning he awoke to the bustle of a camp ready to move out. Each man took care of his own breakfast, grabbing some dry food from the bags they carried. At this point Robert sorely missed his own bedroll, which he assumed had contained some of the same food.

He wasn't wrong. A grinning young hulk of a boy, probably the largest in the group although only around Robert's age, sat on a stump eating out of two bags. He was making it obvious that at least one wasn't his. Robert was hungry. He was not, however, going to let this imp tease him.

Taking a seat next to the over-indulging young man, he asked him how much he weighed.

"Oh, uh, I don't know. What, you think I should only have one breakfast? I'm twice as big as you!" This was said in a loud, mocking tone that could have been taken as either a sarcastic joke or an attempt at an insult.

"My point exactly." A few older men standing nearby tried to cover their grins. Robert continued "Do you need my horse as well?" The boy's face turned red, but he caved in and laughed with the rest of the group.

"All right, here's your breakfast!" The men were still laughing when the clear note of a hunting horn called them to mount.

Eating his breakfast on the road, Mark found that bright skies had replaced the dreary rain of the previous day, and sunnier dispositions came with. He rode along next to Fulke and Ted, the boy who had stolen his breakfast. Ted was a happy individual, although he was given to practical jokes, as Robert had found out.

Conversation kept up a lively pace all the way until they stopped at midday after riding through several small towns and villages. They took a lunch break in the town of Consett, where Roland announced that they would most likely meet up with Cogniard before the evening meal.

This news was received with great surprise by most of the men, and Ted told Robert that they had expected Cogniard to be moving west. If he had been, it would have taken much longer to catch him. Now, if they were to meet him before supper, he must have either stopped or turned around.

Fulke confirmed this news as he returned from an armourer's shop down the road, where he had met several of the officers. They had soon bored of the pitifully small collection of weapons and were discussing the recent developments. Fulke learned that Roland had sent several scouts ahead to alert Cogniard to some recent developments. The entire army would soon turn around and head back to the eastern shore if Cogniard liked what Roland had to say.

All the scouts knew, of course, that they were pursuing an enemy of Cogniard, and this news meant that they might see battle soon. Cogniard was a man quick to action, and his recent movements betrayed the fact that something was up.

They rode hard that afternoon, knowing that they would have a good rest that evening, and there was no time for talking. Robert and Fulke had been sent into the vanguard, and they were the first to spot Cogniard's camp as they came over a rise and looked down into the valley.

It was an expansive array of tents and wagons, with cooking fires and stockpiles arranged helter-skelter around a central tent. They could have learned something from the Romans, Robert thought as he recalled the lessons at the monastery.

"How many men are here?" asked Robert as they let the

horses pick their way down the steep slope.

"Cogniard's own forces number about a thousand, and he's hired another five hundred or so from around Newcastle to accompany him. It's one of the biggest armies around, especially in this area."

"So why is it way out here in the middle of nowhere? He must have had some reason to come this far away from home."

"Well, the guy we're after isn't a fool. Apparently, he tricked Cogniard into thinking he had assembled an army in Lancaster, and that's where Cogniard was headed. Obviously, Cogniard isn't too happy. Roland believes this usurper is in his own backyard, on an island."

"Where did you hear that from? I would have thought Roland would keep that to himself."

"Well, you'll learn soon enough that secrets aren't kept very well in groups this small. I was in the party that was with Roland, and I'm not deaf, at least not most of the time."

By this time they were riding through the outskirts of the camp, past soldiers polishing swords, cooks preparing supper, and pages running between tents. The camp alternated between small, makeshift tents just about ready to fall over and large, grandiose tents festooned with all the colors and pageantry of the knight.

Of course, the largest tent was in the middle, and Robert didn't need to be told that it was Cogniard's. Officers and knights in several stages of undress could be seen discussing the latest events with furrowed brow, or hastily instructing their pages to carry messages to their men.

The entire vanguard rode up to the tent, and the leader dismounted, disappearing inside the ribboned tent flap. He soon reappeared with a short, stocky man who emanated toughness.

Cogniard's actions were quick and curt. His bulging muscles twitched at every move, and the scars on his face and arms belied the bright, pretty decorations on his tent. This was not a man to mess with. His hawk-like eyes scanned the hill where Roland and his troop were just starting to descend into the camp.

"He's pretty sure, is he?" asked the new Earl of Newcastle.

"Without a doubt, Lord. However, you'll have to talk to him for specifics." The Earl grunted and turned to go into the tent. His adjutant quickly stepped out of his way, and turned to the leader of the vanguard.

"We've got some room for you over by the Blyth men. Make yourself comfortable." He also turned back into the tent, then turned back to say "Make sure Roland reports here immediately."

Fulke was dispatched to relay this request. The rest of the

vanguard put their horses in the makeshift corral and walked over to the section of camp where the Blyth men were passing the time. Their tents were easily recognizable by the red-white-and-blue adaption of the Tynemouth coat of arms, with ships representing the port of Blyth.

Nearby was a small empty space of ground that the scouts immediately set about making habitable. It wasn't long before the rest of the scouts, minus Roland, rode in, and soon the area was packed with the fifty scouts and their horses.

Supper was a delicious, noisy ordeal, with the men completely at home in the festive atmosphere of the camp. There were no worries about security or food preparation; all was taken care of by the larger army.

After supper, Fulke, Ted, and Robert took a walk through the large camp, each one pointing out familiar family crests and coats of arms. Robert was surprised by the large number of women and children in the camp, but Ted told him that this was fairly common. They were camp followers, and were composed of the family of the soldiers as well as any enterprising individual who thought he could make a shilling or two off the army.

The small group stopped at one of these shops, run by an old, shriveled man who sat on a bench as he sewed together a saddle. Behind him, a girl about the boys' age sat polishing several pieces of tack.

As the boys browsed the used harness equipment, the girl looked up and gave a sniff of disgust.

"Oh, it's you." Her comment was obviously aimed at Ted, who colored and grunted to his companions, "How 'bout we move on, then." Ted and Fulke's embarrassed looks, combined with the sheer disgust on the girl's face and the sound of the old man saying "Now, then, Kate, we can't have..." made Robert grin as they beat a hasty retreat.

"So... anybody going to explain?"

"Well," said Fulke, "maybe Ted should do that."

"Not so fast!" retorted the indignant Ted. "You started it!"

"Well, it's like this..." started Fulke. "Ted-"

"Maybe I should tell this story!" Ted interjected. "If I let you, I'll get all the blame!"

They had stopped just a few feet from the tent, and the girl called Kate poked her head out.

"It began with a girl and a pile of snow, and ended with two very embarrassed boys."

Quickly the boys began walking again, and Fulke explained. "She thinks she saved a poor girl from a good face-washing, and she also thinks she dumped us in the selfsame pile of snow."

"Did she?" asked Robert with a wide grin.

"That's debatable."

"Unproveable!"

The sound of laughter behind them proved that Kate had good hearing as well.

After returning to camp, they sat at one of the cooking fires with several of the senior scouts, who had just been talking with Roland.

"So he says we're headed home, at least," an older man said.

"Not to rest though! If what he heard was correct, we've got our quarry caught in a trap!" This was from a younger man, brandishing a short sword he had been busy polishing.

"We don't know that yet," cautioned a grizzled warrior across the fire. "We're going by a wisp of smoke, literally."

"And the ship's sails," broke in the first speaker. "One ship leaves, and you see two sails on the horizon. Then the first ship never comes back. You can guarantee there's been foul play!"

CHAPTER 10

Mark sat in the comfortable armchair and watched the sergeant closely. As he shuffled papers and organized his great expanse of a desk, the heavy oak door behind him opened. Lord Cornuel entered, followed closely by Aronii. The sergeant nodded to several empty chairs behind his desk, and the new arrivals sat. Mark was surprised at how the sergeant seemed to give no special respect to the commanders. From his experience, the sergeant's rank put him a long way below Cornuel.

"As I understand it, your name is Mark. Am I correct?" His short, quick words matched his exterior: quick, and to the point.

"Yes, sir," Mark answered.

"Good. My name is Thomas Allen, and this is Lord Cornuel, and Aronii, both commanders here. We would like to know how you got here and what you noticed about the fortress before Cogniard's men came." He saw Mark's questioning look and said,

"Suffice it to say Cogniard is our nemesis at this point."

Then Mark began to tell his story. He told how he had left from home in South Shields on a voyage with his father. After several stops, they had turned back toward home, and had been shipwrecked near the island. He had hung onto a piece of wreckage, and landed on shore, exhausted. After reviving enough, he had explored the island…

"That's good. We know what happened from there." Thomas Allen interjected. "I'd like to ask you several more questions before this interview is over." He proceeded to ask a multitude of questions about Mark's father, brother, and his home in South Shields. Mark told him how his father was gone a lot, and how he had stayed at a monastery in South Shields. He had lived a normal life there, and had been taught by the monks who inhabited the monastery. When asked about what his father did, Mark replied that he was a merchant, and had traveled to many lands, which was why he was gone so often.

"One last question," said Thomas Allen. When he pulled out the dagger that Mark had found earlier, Mark almost fell out of his chair. He hadn't even realized that he had lost it.

"Where did you find this?" asked Allen.

"I was searching through the remains of the ship, and it was in the captain's cabin," said Mark. "It was in a secret compartment in the closet."

Mark wasn't sure, but he thought he saw a flicker run through Aronii's face. A split second later, he coughed. Mark put what he thought was two and two together and forgot about the look on Aronii's face.

"You should take better care of your weapons, young man," the sergeant said. "That's all. I'll have someone take you to the boys."

He rang a bell, and a moment later a servant appeared. Mark noticed that the instant the bell was rung, the dagger had disappeared under the table. The servant motioned Mark to follow him.

By the time Mark reached the boys' rooms, or, more accurately, barracks, it had grown dark, and several boys were already in bed. He was pointed to a bed next to Ijn. The two boys briefly discussed Mark's meeting with Allen, and then they rolled into bed.

As Mark adjusted his covers, one of the upperclassmen walked by. He strode down the aisle to Louis' bed, and kicked the unfortunate sleeper. Groggily, Louis looked around.

"Hey, you! Get up! You've got work to do." The voice echoed through the barracks, and Mark saw several boys look up in silence.

Louis obediently got out of bed. Mark could see that he had been asleep for some while. The upperclassman proceeded to berate him on what his faults and misdoings were, and then commanded him to polish his boots and armor.

"What's gotten into him?" Mark asked Ijn.

"Get used to it," Ijn replied. "The upperclassmen think they can lord it over the younger guys, and they take it a lot farther than I would like."

"Why don't you do something about it?' whispered Mark, as the irate upperclassman glared in their direction.

"It's been going on for a while," replied Ijn, "and there's not a whole lot to be done about it."

Mark watched in indignation as Louis groggily dressed again, but the other boys just turned over and went to sleep. Frowning, Mark followed their example.

He was awakened early in the morning with a repeat of the scene that had happened just hours before. Another upperclassman was yelling at some poor soul to get going. From what Mark could gather, several of the boys were supposed to get things ready for the upperclassman, and, due to the preceding day's events, had overslept and forgotten to get up and do their tasks. Burning with indignation, he turned over and started to ponder what was to be done.

Minutes later, he heard a gong being hit repeatedly. The inhabitants of the barracks stumbled out of bed and began to prepare for the new day. Mark followed their example and was soon caught up in the mass of boys heading to the underground hall for breakfast.

They sat at a long table near the back of the large room. He pulled up a chair next to Ijn, and nobody seemed to object, so he assumed that it could be his spot as long as he stayed.

As long as he stayed… When that thought came up, it triggered other thoughts. Until now, he had been caught up in the hubbub of life at the fortress, but now he realized that at some point he had to return home and find his father and brother, if they were alive. He was about to ask Ijn about it, but the boy put a finger to his lips, and just then a priest stood up. Everybody bowed their heads, and the priest began the meal.

After breakfast had started, Mark asked Ijn when he could return home. Ijn gave him a queer look, and then started laughing.

"Look, Mark, you had better give up all hope of going where you call 'home,' because this is your home now."

At Mark's distressed look, he continued.

"This island is a fortress, and we aren't here playing games. The reason that you thought this island was uninhabited is because we are hunted men. You weren't supposed to see anything. There is somebody out there who is after several important people here, and anybody who dares to stand up for them is in danger of losing his head on the mainland.

"Lord Cornuel will never let you leave. You know too much. At any given time, you could be apprehended and forced to give out information regarding the location of the island, and especially the way into the underground part. Cogniard doesn't know we're here, but he knows we've gathered a large force, and we aren't going to give up very easily."

Mark pondered this information. There was a good chance that his father and brother were still alive. He had seen Robert get in the boat. He didn't know if his father had made it, but he'd been right by the rail. If his father had fallen in and floated with the tide, as Mark had, he would have drifted to the island. Therefore, he must have been in the boat. He was probably with Robert right now.

That momentary rush of optimism made up his mind and let him stop worrying. He knew the commanders of the fortress well enough now to know that they wouldn't let him go in this kind of a situation, and he didn't want to be a danger to the rest of the people on this island anyway. Besides, he would wait for this to boil over, and then go to find his father and brother.

"How did you manage to stay hidden all that time, anyway? I was pretty sure this island was deserted."

"Like I said, you were supposed to think that. When you drifted in, we tripled the watch and locked everything down. You had Lord Cornuel, Aronii, and Allen all in a boil about what to do. We'd always had some plan for enemies coming, but not for a marooned sailor. It seemed too coincidental, and in the end they must have decided you were a threat. Maybe a spy, sent by Cogniard. Regardless of who you were, we were being careful.

"Allen was in charge of removing all evidence of our existence outside of this underground section. He cleared out the mill and the keep in record time, but we weren't counting on you discovering that tunnel. We didn't even know about it. Thankfully, we've got a pretty good scout system here, and you were being watched at all times. We were all herded into our rooms while you were crawling through the tunnel, and believe me, it was quite a feat."

Mark was astonished. "So there were people all around me the entire time? No wonder I felt like I was being watched!"

Ijn laughed. "That one time in the Earl's meeting room was Allen's fault. He was heading the effort to watch you, and that was the last time he tried it himself. Just imagine

Sergeant Allen tiptoeing around the halls!" Everyone in the immediate vicinity joined in the laughter. Mark laughed along, amazed he'd been so carefully watched.

The breakfast was brought in by servants who bustled about and made a lot of fuss, but Mark noticed that the food was prepared well, and there was plenty to eat.

"Where does all the food come from?" he asked Ijn.

"Resupply ships go out every month," Ijn replied "We're still waiting on the last ship. The Earl was on it. He normally doesn't go on supply ships, but there was a lot of secrecy about this one. And I noticed that the scheduled return date allowed much more time than usual. Not that anyone else thought that was significant. Anyway, we have enough food for several months without the ship returning, so there's no need to worry about lack of food for a while."

Mark didn't spend a lot more time thinking about the food - he just ate it. Despite the large meal the night before, he devoured the delicious food placed before him. There were eggs and bacon, along with several types of bread and several choices of beverages. He enjoyed himself immensely, trying everything, and Ijn laughed when he saw the rate at which Mark consumed his food.

"If you keep eating like that," he said, "you won't be feeling very comfortable after training."

"Considering how good this tastes after almost starving, I

don't think I'll mind," Mark replied. He did consider the advice, though, and decided that he had better follow it.

After everybody had finished and the priest had closed the meal, Mark followed Ijn toward the training ground. This was one of the features that Mark had earlier noted between the remains of the castle and the farms that were on the other side of the island. As they walked, he noticed that the air was rapidly growing warmer, and the dirt path was already turning from mud to dust.

Several groups of boys were standing around and talking when they got to the training ground, and others filed in quickly. Mark could see Thomas Allen standing in the corner of the partially walled area, watching the young men as they entered. Satisfied that everyone was present, he walked to the front. The boys automatically grabbed swords from a rack and moved to certain positions on the field, marked by pells, or thick posts. Mark was motioned to an empty spot near several upperclassmen.

"Okay, everybody, listen up. Today you need to go through your basic drills first, while I show Mark what to do. If you get done before I do, start over, or practice your own variations." Thomas Allen's voice was loud and commanding, and Mark saw every boy obey quickly. The swinging and hacking ensued as Thomas Allen snatched a sword from the rack, tested it, and came over to Mark.

"This class is on sword fighting, and you're a little behind, because it started a while ago. We drill first, and then we work up to one-on-one. What you need to do is practice certain moves on the pell."

He swung the sword so fast it whistled through the air, and chunks of wood came flying off the post faster than Mark's eyes could move. Allen stopped as quickly as he had started. Then he explained each swing carefully, as if the post were a human opponent, and showed Mark how to get the maximum effect out of every swing. The series was familiar to Mark, with a couple variations; when he tried it, Allen gave a few quick corrections and walked back up to the front.

Mark swung away at the post, going through the exercise as quickly as he could. Several people had already finished, and by the time he had completed the task everybody had moved on to different exercises.

When Allen saw that Mark was done, he called the boys to attention and explained their next drill. Each person took put their sword in its sheath. Allen then had them pair up with the person next to them. They were to fight with the padded swords and extra safety equipment.

Mark was paired with an upperclassman who looked as though he could have eaten three times as much as Mark. While Mark fastened the buckles on the extra pads, the upperclassman merely threw the pads on loosely. He stood looking nonchalantly on as Mark struggled. After fumbling through the unfamiliar leather straps, Mark straightened and picked up the sword. He never expected what hit him.

The burly young man rushed at him with a vengeance. His sword hissed back and forth through the air, hitting Mark several times before he could even think. When he recovered, he spun around, out of the way, and assumed a defensive position. The upperclassman was on him instantly, but this time Mark was ready. He stepped to the side and spun. Then he swung his sheathed sword in an almost complete circle, catching his opponent as he came headlong past the spot where Mark had just stood. The sword slammed into the upperclassman's stomach.

To his credit, his the young man moved his large bulk quickly, and was back at Mark in seconds. Mark parried his thrusts and watched for an opening. As the battle ensued, more and more people stopped their own matches to watch. Mark's innovative but desperate swordplay was being tested against the pure power and well-trained skill of the upperclassman. Sweat began to drip down both of the combatant's faces. On top of that, Mark was beginning to tire. He had practiced swordplay, but only as a hobby, not something that he intended to save his life with.

The next swing from the giant was a low cut, aimed at Mark's legs. It was a dirty move, because there was less padding on his legs than anywhere else. Thinking quickly, Mark saw his chance. He jumped into the air to avoid the swing, and then brought his sword into play. Its tip seemed to sizzle in an arc that ended behind the hilt of his opponent's quickly-moving sword. There was a loud clang. Mark almost dropped his sword because of the vibration. But, because he had hit the other sword from behind, the lightning swing knocked it straight out of the upperclassman's grasp. It tumbled through the air, coming to rest in the scraggly brush just outside the training ground.

Mark stepped back, breathing hard and unsure what to do. He couldn't continue the fight if his opponent didn't have a sword, but it looked as though the embarrassed and enraged young man was ready to fight with his bare hands. He didn't have to make a decision though. Allen stepped in. He returned the sword to its owner and without a word led the class through a series of fast-paced maneuvers.

After the session was over, Mark was three times as tired as anyone else. He was obviously a little out of shape, and his so-called "practice" didn't help any either. He trudged back along the dusty path to the castle, falling in step with Ijn and his friends. He was glad he had someone to hang around with. Without them, he didn't know what he would do.

The rest of the day was spent in various learning sessions, on topics mostly familiar to Mark. Several were new, including tactics and several hands-on activities about making almost anything. He soon got to enjoy moving from topic to topic with his friends, and met a few new people. The teachers, who were really castle workers with extra time, welcomed him to their classes, too busy with the rowdy boys to do much more.

The thing that Mark liked most about this way of learning was the fact that there was no after-hours studying. Students were expected to learn in class, and there were no assignments. This was fine with Mark, especially because he enjoyed his freedom in the afternoon. He and Ijn explored the castle together, getting in the way of the cooks, butchers, bakers, scribes, and all sorts of tradesmen. The pair traveled all over the island, visiting every place they could.

Mark's favorite was the blacksmith's shop, the same one he had visited earlier. The blacksmith, James Drydon, was a huge man, with fiery red hair and thick eyebrows. He enjoyed having Mark and Ijn around his shop, and explained to them everything he was doing. After leaving the smithy, they wandered around for a while and then went to the underground hall for supper.

During the meal, Lord Cornuel stood up to speak. "As you all know, we have recently had an encounter with Cogniard. I have decided, in lieu of the Earl's presence, that we will double our efforts on our building projects. To do this, everyone here will help in some way. Each person will be assigned a job. Some will have more than others depending on the amount of free time they have, or their current position."

He looked around, and Mark had the feeling he was

waiting for sounds of disapproval. None came, so he continued.

"We have nearly completed the interior of the castle, and we will hopefully start on the exterior soon. Your job assignments will be posted on the doors to the hall after we breakfast tomorrow. Any questions should be addressed to Sergeant Allen." He sat down again.

Mark watched the reaction of the people. Many nodded, but there seemed to be two opinions running through the group. Many of the tradesmen and men-at-arms were in agreement, looking as immovable as the gray walls of the castle. Standing with them, although not necessarily looking so tough, were the high-ranking members of the Earl's household in their fine clothes. A striking difference was seen on the other side of the room, where crowds of serfs and laborers sat. True, Mark could see a good number of men-at-arms there as well, but they were the lowlier sort, given to drinking and brawling. All these folks were scowling, and Mark felt that, given time, they could easily start to cause trouble over this new schedule.

After supper, the hall emptied and Mark found himself heading outside the walls with his friends.

"What are we doing now?" he asked.

"The upperclassmen practice their archery after supper, and we collect the arrows for them," Pieter said.

"And... why? I wanted to see what Drydon was up to in

his shop," Mark replied indignantly.

"Tell that to those grumbling ogres," said Louis.

"Have any of the officers actually told you that you have to do what they say?" Mark asked Ijn.

"No, not explicitly. But they've never tried to stop it. It's been that way ever since we started here," he replied.

"Well, I'm not going to do it. It's shameful the way they carry on when they aren't catered to all the time. They can get their own arrows for all I care. Come on. Let's go find out what Drydon's doing."

Pieter and Jan, along with Ijn, were inclined to do what Mark said, but Louis and Richard balked. After some convincing, however, they decided to risk it. The entire group turned around and walked back toward the castle.

As they approached the gate, one of the upperclassmen came out with his bow.

"Hey," he said, "get to the archery range. You're going to be late."

"Maybe tomorrow," Mark, the unspoken leader, replied nonchalantly.

"What?" The young man stopped in his tracks. "Who do you think you are anyway? Get down to the range."

"I know one thing," Mark replied, "and that's that I am

not your slave, or anybody else's."

Mark faced the older boy, both standing on the dusty path outside of the time-worn castle gate. The drab stones behind the upperclassman made his face stand out as it turned several shades of red. Mark tried to be nonchalant. He was not successful.

"If you don't turn around, I'm going to tan your little hide right here and right now." The upperclassman was hovering right in front of him, but Mark stood his ground. He could see smeared potato on his opponent's chin.

On an impulse, he straightened his shoulders, lifted his chin, and spat into the face of the obnoxious young man. The effect was instantaneous.

The older boy's fist came hurtling into Mark's stomach. He reeled backwards, crashing into Louis and Jan. The others tackled the upperclassman. As they pulled him off of Mark, two more came out of the gate and immediately joined the fray.

Mark took a shaky breath and followed Louis and Jan back into the battle. Given the numbers, the fight would have gone badly for the older boys if Thomas Allen hadn't stepped out of the gatehouse.

CHAPTER 11

Robert was up at dawn the next morning with the rest of the large military encampment. Cogniard had decided to head to the coast, convinced by Roland's evidence.

With such a large army, it would take most of the morning before they could even think about leaving. Robert was assigned to help pack up the portable smithy, and he worked alongside the short, pot-bellied smith who sweated like a pig and moved even slower.

"If'n somebody would make up their mind, I wouldn't hafta cart all my stuff down into this valley and then all the way back up and out again," the smith said. Robert wisely kept silent and let the man complain to himself, an occupation the smith obviously wasn't unfamiliar with.

"Ever since he got this bright idea in his 'ead to go conquesting, I've been riding up hills and back down, over the roughest terrain, driving the roughest wagon. All to find some enemy o' his that is apparently so dangerous he's more important than the time of hundreds of men."

Robert began to ignore the man, thinking instead about his brother. Mark had always shown an interest in smithing and had learned a bit about it at the monastery. They had even made a few small items together, although their tutor was the only one impressed with the novice workmanship. Mark had always wanted to do more, but Robert had grown bored quickly, more interested in the games they played on the monastery grounds.

"Heads up!" A barrel came rumbling his way, filled with pieces of scrap iron and worn-out implements. He managed to stop it without getting crushed, then lined it up with the ramp they had placed at the back of the wagon.

"Be right there!" called the smith. He lumbered over a second later. Together, they heaved the heavy barrel up the incline, slipping on the slightly wet grass. With a "thump" it rested in the back of the heavy-duty wagon, and the smith grabbed his hammer.

"Thass it," he said through the nails he was holding between his lips. One by one, he pounded them into the back of the wagon. The man may have been slow, but he sure knew how to hit a nail. Robert figured that if he swung only half as hard, the nails would still have been buried forever in the back of the wagon.

"Maybe that would be it if we had horses," commented Robert.

"That could be true. Stupid critters! Why don'tcha fetch them for me, son."

Robert headed toward the edge of the camp where the horses were under guard while they grazed. Those that remained, anyway. Most of them had been claimed already, and Robert had no problems picking out the large black Shires that the smith had described to him.

"Excuse me sir, those are the smith's horses. You looking to take them?" Robert turned around to see one of the guards eyeing him with a suspicious glance.

"The smith wanted me to pick them up. We just got done loading his wagon."

"Is that so?" The guard was bored, apparently, and Robert spent the next five minutes convincing him that he really was going to bring the horses to the smith. In the end, the puffing, pot-bellied smith himself came storming into the corral.

After that, it took only a few minutes to get the matter cleared up, and Robert was free to return to the scouts. When he got back, they were all mounted and ready to go. Grabbing his bedroll, he ran back to the corral, shooed away the same guard, and led Amaury back. When he returned, the scouts had moved out. Robert rushed to saddle his horse and quickly headed off in pursuit.

Threading his way through the lines of supply wagons, he slowly moved to the front of the line. Almost there, at the foot of the trail that led out of the valley, he was stopped by a snarl in the caravan. It was caused by two wagons, both trying to merge onto the same narrow trail. With the wagons so close together, the horses became nervous. Just as Robert rode up one of the horses half-reared, spooked by the other cart.

The already overloaded wagon twisted sideways, and the contents shifted to the back axle. It broke with "crack!"

Now the only usable trail out of the valley was blocked by the broken wagon. The situation was further worsened by the fact that the two drivers obviously knew each other and were not on friendly terms. They immediately fell to arguing.

Seeing the predicament, Robert pushed Amaury forward and used the advantage of being on a horse to get control of the situation.

"Excuse me, sirs, but if you could stop arguing, we could get the rest of this company out of the valley." The wagon drivers glanced at him, and returned to arguing about whose fault the accident was. Meanwhile, the horses were tangling themselves in their harnesses, and the carters behind the accident were getting impatient.

Robert leaned down and put his gloved hand heavily on the closest man's shoulder. "Enough is enough," he growled, and gave the man a shove toward his horses. "Cut those horses loose and let's get moving!" The man cast him a surprised glance, and hurried to obey. The other driver looked at Robert; then, deciding he was worthy of a little respect, asked him what he should do about his broken cart.

"Pull it off to the side for now. You can stop the carpenters on their way through and try to get it fixed then." The man agreed and set to work freeing his own horses.

While the horses were being loosed, Robert rode a few carts back and rounded up several volunteers. They pushed the broken cart to the side, clearing the way for traffic.

Seconds later, the next two carts almost repeated the same accident, both vying for the small opening. Seeing that there was no easy solution to this, Robert moved his horse over and motioned the smaller cart through first.

It was a bit awkward for Robert to be telling everyone what to do, when he had just joined the scouts, but his elevation above the crowd got everyone's attention, and soon traffic was flowing smoothly through the choke point.

With the end of the line in sight, Robert saw a cluster of horsemen ride up with Cogniard at the head. The Earl's glance told Robert he wasn't pleased with the stalled cart, but he bypassed Robert and talked to the drivers. The voices of the group floated over, and Robert could hear the story being repeated in more and more glamorous terms as the drivers tried to blame each other for the accident. He soon began to ignore them and returned his attention to his self-imposed job of making sure every cart got through without accident.

After the last straggler came through, he turned around to see Cogniard watching him.

"Who are you with?" he asked. "Your unit will be wondering where you are."

"I was just hired by Roland, your Lordship," he replied. "I should be able to make it to him quickly and explain."

"Ah, I see. The new scout. Roland did mention you, and now I see why he was impressed. Good work on this little accident here. The cart drivers might not be friends, but they both agreed that you solved their little problem pretty quickly, and saved the army several hours at least. Or, actually, several days by the time we got to the end of the story." His eyes twinkled merrily, and he motioned several of his accompanying riders forward. "You've obviously proved yourself well enough. Now I need you to bring these men to Roland. They know their mission, and you can tell Roland that you are to be among the group that accompanies them to the shore."

Robert reddened at the compliment, and glanced at the men. They were both in their thirties and riding well-built, spirited horses.

"Yes, your lordship," he replied. He wheeled his horse away and the men followed him up the trail toward the retreating caravan. The Earl gathered his riders and came up behind.

He reached Roland fifteen minutes after passing the rearmost carts and threading his way up the line. The gray-haired commander was riding easily along at the head of the column, conversing with his advisors, and not at all surprised to see Robert ride up with the two men.

"From the Earl?" he asked. When they all nodded, he pointed at the wagon behind them. "Grab some extra food and head out right away. You'll need all the time you can get. Robert, why don't you accompany them where they're going. They'll explain what's up. You can grab a friend or two to ride with you, if you'd like." Robert nodded, not bothering to tell him that the Earl had already suggested that he escort the men.

After retrieving the extra supplies, Robert and the two men set out at a quick pace, hoping to quickly overtake the vanguard, where Robert assumed Ted and Fulke were. The small group soon found the guard. Robert learned that Fulke had been dispatched to join the scouts on the left flank, and only Ted was riding with the vanguard. Ted willingly joined Robert and the two scouts, though, and the leader of the vanguard suggested that they take Roy as well, to make their company a group of five. Even though they were traveling close to home, highway robbers were everywhere and they didn't want to take any chances.

It was mid-afternoon before they got well under way, and Robert estimated that they would reach the coast late the next night. He would have preferred to be in the castle earlier, but when he mentioned this to the men who rode with him, they disagreed.

"Not for what we need to do, son," said the first man, small with a dark complexion. He looked Spanish to Robert. "We've got to be under cover once we reach the coast, so nighttime is perfect."

"So what's happening when we get there? Are you trying to…"

"Spy? Yes, that's our job. You'll be helping us acquire a boat of decent size, and we'll be trying for that island that's supposed to be out there. Fred here is an expert sailor, and we'll do what it takes to get on the island without anyone knowing. Even if that means risking the open sea in a fishing boat."

Robert was beginning to dislike this assignment. It didn't sound like these men meant to buy or borrow a boat, and besides, he didn't have a good feeling about spies anyway. To him, this kind of spying was underhanded and crude. If you couldn't beat your enemy fairly, you shouldn't beat him at all, as far as he was concerned.

Considering the long journey ahead, he decided, somewhat riskily, to voice his opinions to these practitioners of the craft. He was surprised at what they said.

"You aren't the only one who thinks that," replied Fred, a burly, red-faced man with large hands. "We don't think about it as underhanded at all, just an extension of normal warfare. Any king, prince, or noble has spies. Also, any person, anywhere, hears about things without seeing these things themselves. That's primitive spying, too."

"But this goes beyond chance hearing," argued Ted, who seemed to fall in on Robert's side. "Jumping in someone else's house and hiding under the bed is a whole separate matter."

"Well, when a man really needs to get things done, and isn't stopping to bandage his opponent's wounds, spying is a necessary thing. Life isn't fair, and war is even less fair. War is all about who can get the best advantage and exploit it, whether it be well-trained men, high ground, or spying."

Robert began to see the spies' position, although he didn't necessarily agree with it. But Ted pushed on, grilling the two spies about what was honorable and what wasn't. Roy chose to ignore them altogether, riding slightly ahead and watching the road.

It was a beautiful spring day, and with the argument continuing in the background, Robert watched the scenery go by, noting the fresh buds on the trees, the bright blue skies, and the creatures of the forest coming to life after the short winter. Every once in a while Roy's horse Carmen would skitter away from a squirrel scampering across the path, or a hawk taking flight.

Up the hills and into the valleys the party continued, traveling at an easy, mile-eating canter. The horses were fresh and well used to the running, having served in the scouts their entire lives, or, in the spies' case, picked from the best of the army.

With the on-going argument and the fast-passing scenery, Robert was surprised when the sun dipped behind a hill and they found themselves traveling in increasing darkness.

Without warning, Roy, up in the front, pulled his horse to a side-trail and motioned the others to follow. Somewhat peeved at this erosion of his assumed leadership, Robert was inclined to be ornery. However, he decided that prudence was the better side of leadership and followed his fellow scout into the small path where he led them.

Slowing their horses to a walk, they traveled for several minutes on the winding, briar-ridden trail in the fast-darkening forest. Then Roy stopped and pointed to the left, indicating several men, only mere shadows in the night, crouched in the bushes next to the road they had just been traveling on.

One of the men looked like he was holding a wire taut, but Robert couldn't see any wire. He didn't have a chance to look longer, because as the group started to ride away, one of the men turned and saw them. Roy hadn't seen the man turn, but he was instantly on his feet in the stirrups when the man's shout echoed through the woods.

Robert snatched a glance back and saw every member of his party urging their mounts forward, and the would-be brigand picking up a longbow from the bushes.

His own horse moving at a gallop now, Robert had to look forward. In front of him, he saw Roy glance back. From the expression on his face, Robert knew he had seen the threat.

In a single fluid motion, the scout wheeled his horse out of the way of the rest of the party. Snatching an arrow from his quiver, he notched it on the string of his bow. When the horse was broadside to his target, he released the shaft and kicked his horse back into a gallop.

The entire motion was so quick and smooth that Robert hardly had time to grab his own bow to help. The horse had never stopped moving; he merely switched from gallop to spin, and back to gallop again. As far as the success of the maneuver, Robert had no idea if the arrow hit; but he knew that no arrow had come their way, and no other sounds came from the direction of the formerly hidden men.

Back on the main road, well down from the sight of the incident, the group slowed to a trot. A small town was just ahead, a few lights winking in the darkness.

"Where did you learn that, Roy?" asked Robert. "I didn't even think about getting my bow out, just hanging on tight and wishing Amaury would go faster!"

"It wasn't too bad, was it?" Robert saw Roy truly smile for the first time. "I've done a lot of training with the scouts since I was young, and that's one I've never really tried before in real life. I hit him, though. Right in the shoulder, if I saw correctly."

"That's some good shooting!" Ted's thoughts were echoed by both spies as they all reigned in their horses in front of a small inn.

Named "The Hunter's Lodge," the small inn was a far cry from what Newcastle offered, being more on par with the scout's tents in the main army camp. In the main room, a large fire roared and several patrons were busy discussing the latest gossip.

Nobody paid any attention to the Earl's men as they

walked in and found an empty table. Tired from that day's ride, they all ordered large meals. After eating, Robert arranged for sleeping space for that night.

It was early the next morning when they set off again, first eating a hearty breakfast, then getting their horses from the stable and setting off at the same pace as the previous day.

The sky had just become fully light, but Robert could tell that today wasn't going to be as nice of a ride. The clouds on the horizon were low, and tinged with red, indicating a storm that day, or at least a bit of bad weather.

The weather showed itself just as they were stopping for a midday meal. Large drops of rain came splashing down, and thunder rumbled ominously in the distance. At Robert's suggestion, the group mounted again and rode off, eating their lunch in the saddle. If they were to make it to the coast by nightfall, they needed to be on the road constantly, and a storm certainly wouldn't help any.

As they continued along, the roads began to get wet and muddy. The large hooves of their horses spattered every member of the group with the red clay.

The mud didn't only make them dirty; it slowed them down as well. More and more effort was required of the horses as they rode through the thickening slop. Several times they took detours to avoid a large puddle in the road or a growing mud pit.

Even with the obstacles, the horses kept up a decent pace, and that evening after dark Robert led the group into the suburbs of Tynemouth, the location of Cogniard's second castle. Here Donald took over, as their journey had come to an end, and they would now do whatever it took to launch the spies in a boat headed at least in the general direction of the island.

Donald led them around the main city, outside its walls and far enough away that any watchmen wouldn't see them. When Robert asked him why they needed to hide in their own home county, the spy replied that if Cogniard was sending spies to his enemy, there was no reason why his enemy couldn't send spies to him. Chances were, he said, that if they stopped in at the castle, news would spread quickly that they were there, and their quarry would be awaiting them.

It didn't take them long to reach the shore, and Donald led them along it until they came to a small fishing smack, sitting in the shallows, with several inches of water in it.

"It's a pity they couldn't have brought the boat out a day earlier. That would have been great to use, huh, Fred?" Donald wanted to get to sea quickly.

"Without a doubt... but I see another boat down further that would do better. And... it doesn't have half the sea in it." They moved down to check the boat out, and it quickly had the approval of all. Besides, of course, Robert and Ted, who both had second thoughts about helping spies steal a fisherman's boat.

"It probably came from Cogniard anyway, boy," said Fred, noting Ted's disapproval. "They can always say it was stolen and have the castle pay for it, seeing as though it's supposed to be under their protection anyway, right?"

Donald cut off all further argument by putting them all to work. With their shoulders and backs against the boat, it slid easily into the water and righted itself in the shallows. Roy, Ted, and Robert watched as Donald and Fred loaded the boat with the small number of provisions they had and prepared to push off.

"How are you going to navigate to an island you've never seen, in a boat you've never used, in the middle of the night?" asked Robert.

"I won't," replied Donald. "Fred will."

Fred explained a little better. "When Roland left here several days ago, he ordered that a beacon fire be lit in two places along the shore tonight. One in the priory castle on the hill and one on the beach below. We can line ourselves up with those beacons to point us in the direction Roland believes the castle to be, based on what he saw."

Robert looked down the shore line. Sure enough, there was a beacon fire lit close to the water. There was also one in the castle tower, which rose high above the cliff under which they now crouched in the pouring rain.

"I've never done this before, but I think it should work," said Fred. "Provided Donald doesn't fall asleep on the way."

The head spy grunted and pointed at the boat. "Also provided that Fred doesn't spend all of tonight teaching his spies-in-training how to be late for an appointment. Let's go."

Fred chuckled and waded out to the fishing smack. With both men in, the boat settled in the water, and then began to float out toward the open sea.

"Thanks for the escort! Enjoy your night!" came across from Fred, and the boat slipped into the darkness.

CHAPTER 12

"So. What do you have to say for yourself?" The stern look bored into the boys sitting across from the sergeant. They were in Allen's office.

"We're sorry." said Mark, "I mean, sorry that I had to fight. But I would do it again in the same situation."

"Why?" The look on Allen's face was anything but understanding.

"We aren't here to do anything for other people. For them, I mean. Everyone here is a person on their own, and we can take care of ourselves. Just because the older boys happen to be stronger doesn't mean they can be lazier."

"Maybe you haven't noticed, but Lord Cornuel has servants."

"He has a rightful authority. He needs them to do his job more effectively. The upperclassmen are no different than us. They are still going through training, and they have the same responsibilities as we do right now. They don't require any help."

"Well, at least you're not both a troublemaker and treasonous," Allen grumped. Then he continued.

"All right, Mark. I don't want to catch you fighting again. The best way to resolve issues is negotiation. Fighting separates people, and we can't afford that right now. That goes for you as well." He nodded curtly to the other boys. "Whatever you do, do it the right way. At the moment, the right way is negotiation. I don't want to see you in here again. You are dismissed."

The boys left his room, and headed up the stairs to the main courtyard. They felt the semi-chilled air breeze past them as they strolled out through the heavy doors and down the stone steps. In the large, open area they relaxed, sitting with their backs against the sun-warmed stone wall, discussing the recent events.

"That's what happens, Mark. You can't just decide it's time to stop doing something, and expect everyone to bow before you," said Jan, nursing a bloody nose. "That's not saying I didn't enjoy the fight, but there are a lot more than three upperclassmen."

"There are a lot more than six of us too, you know," Ijn replied. Mark was surprised. He wouldn't have expected anyone to stand up for his bull-headedness. Ijn continued. "If we start something, we have to finish it. There's only one acceptable way out of our situation."

"I didn't know we were in a situation." said Louis. "Life goes on, you know."

"Not after I spat in Harold's face," said Mark. "That, combined with the fact that we didn't back down, is going to cause an all-out war. Ijn's right. This could be a lot bigger than we think it is. I bet his 'one acceptable way out' is to get everyone we know on our side, to help us."

"Exactly," said Ijn. "We have to get all of our friends and show everyone that we are serious. After we get everyone together, we talk with the older guys, if only to satisfy Allen. They won't listen anyway."

"And if they don't listen," said Mark, "we have full right to pursue our best interests militarily." Ijn nodded. But the others had their doubts.

"You really think we can force the upperclassmen to do something?"

"They have fewer people than we do."

"They're also quite a bit larger."

"And we can be smarter," Ijn and Mark both replied.

"Tactics win wars," said Louis, coming in on Mark's and Ijn's side.

"Whoa! When did this turn into a war? I thought we just wanted to skip archery practice."

"We can't do it halfway. That's how you lose," explained Ijn.

"What are we waiting for?" asked Jan. "Archery practice is almost over, and we're about to have some mad hornets on our tails for what we did."

"Where can we find more help?" asked Mark, rising. "We need to get some people together."

"Most are at archery," Richard replied, "but the rest normally relax out on the armory terrace."

The boys trooped back down the stairs and into the underground area and followed the hall past the blacksmith's shop to the next door. It opened into a warehouse full of weapons and armor. Mark breathed in the fresh air, and deduced that this room must have an opening outside. It did, and as they walked past the rows of weapons, they could see the cloudless sky.

The weather had warmed considerably, and many boys their age were relaxing on a terrace that was walled in by rock but open to the sky. The slight breeze wafted in and out of the open area. Mark asked Jan where they were in relation to the rest of the castle.

"Right this way, please," Jan replied, and he walked to the edge of the terrace and started climbing a steep set of stairs carved into the rock. They curved slightly, and came to a flat, round area, enclosed by more of the same tough granite. A path through solid rock led either way, but Jan went forward and stepped up onto a ledge that allowed his head to reach just above the gray stone. Mark followed and saw that they were on the rock cliff across from the cavern where the ships were stored. He looked behind him and the tower loomed straight up.

"Amazing," he said. "What do you use this for?"

"Generally it's just used for observation, but the two small fortifications to either side of us have the capability to be fitted with siege weapons, which we can use against ships that come too close to the cave."

They returned to the terrace, and found that Ijn was already discussing their proposition with the other boys their age. The general attitude was positive, for doing jobs during their free time was never popular. Although the same doubts came up again, Mark and Ijn were able to gather a solid following.

"As the general opinion seems to be for rebellion, we will proceed by appointing delegates to speak to the upperclassmen," said Ijn. A questioning murmur ran through the listeners. They had been expecting a fight right away.

Ijn explained that it was a technicality, and that they would do it to satisfy the sergeant. Then he described what had just occurred before archery practice, and hoots went up when they heard that Mark had spit in Harold's face.

"After that," Ijn said, "We'll probably get in a fight just talking to the upperclassmen. You'll have your fight yet, believe me."

Mark watched Ijn weave his magic among the members of the group. He quickly noted that Ijn was a master with words, and it looked as though the boys were ready to swim across the channel at his next word. Mark didn't have that eloquence, and he decided that if the group was in need of convincing, Ijn was the man for the job. Or Robert, who had the same skill, even though Mark didn't plan on seeing him anytime soon.

It turned out, however, that they didn't need a delegation; the older boys came to them. Five upperclassmen and Harold walked into the armory, straight for Mark.

"You Mark?" asked the leader, growling.

"Actually, yes. We were about to go and talk to you about this, uh, chore issue. We don't think you need help with anything. Well, maybe with thinking…"

"Funny," said the giant, as the younger boys tried to keep

from laughing. A large, meaty fist shot out. Mark jumped to the side.

"Listen, we seriously want to talk first. Think about how many people are in here, ready to help us. It would make sense if you stopped threatening me."

"We don't need to talk. Just do as we say and you'll survive the next few days." The giant gave up trying to fight, and walked through the group of boys to the door and out. Harold seemed ready to continue the discussion alone, but he knew it would be dangerous. Dozens of eyes followed him and his friends out, and then snapped back to Mark.

"Okay," said Mark. "We obviously need to have a plan of action. We can be fairly certain that they'll turn violent if we offend them. Therefore we need to stick together." He thought for a moment. "This isn't a problem in the morning, while we learn, but the later afternoon is when we need to do it. It's my opinion that we should split into groups and always be near each other. If you choose not to join a group, do so at your own peril."

There was a murmur of agreement to his statement, although a large number of the group looked unsure. Ijn continued.

"We also need leaders for each group, and leaders for our entire group. We need a system that can react quickly so that we can be able to outnumber the upperclassmen whenever possible."

They discussed the organization of the groups, and how many there should be. In the end, Ijn and Thomas, another well-known boy, divided the boys into groups with their friends. Then Thomas brought up a question.

"How do we keep the groups together if we are all getting assignments for work in our free time?" Nobody had considered it. If all the boys were separated, as they would most likely be, there would be no defense against the older boys. Thomas answered his own question.

"We have to talk to Allen. He can put us to work together. All we have to do is group ourselves according to what work we like, and tell him. If we ask politely, he can hardly deny it."

"Yes, he can deny it, but if he doesn't see any reason to, he won't," said Ijn. "He makes his decisions fairly, and he won't tell us 'no' if we put the groups together well and work hard."

"Let's take care of that now," said Mark. "Thomas and I will go talk to Allen. Ijn, can you see if you can get us together in some more appropriate groups for this?"

There was general agreement, and the two boys threaded their way through the masses on the way out. Thomas walked ahead, and Mark followed.

"How do you think this will all turn out?" asked Thomas.

"We can only let it turn out one way," Mark replied. "We can't accept it any other way."

"Stubborn as a mule! You're just like Ijn, you know that?"

"I don't know if I'd go so far as to compliment myself to that degree."

"Well, don't, then. We can't lose to those thick-skulled giants with all the help we've got."

They had arrived at Allen's door, and Thomas knocked on the rough wood. There was a pause, then a voice called them in. Thomas pushed the door open, the heavy wood creaking on the strong metal hinges.

Allen was sitting behind his desk. The expression on his face was just short of a glare.

"What do you need?"

"Well, we--" Thomas and Mark both started at once, then Thomas let Mark speak.

"We took your advice, sir. We selected people to go talk to the upperclassmen about the problem, but we never got there. They came to us and threatened us first. But we talked to them anyway, and they wouldn't listen. They didn't dare harm us, because we were in the armory, but you know as well as I do that they will try their best to get at us separately."

Allen raised his eyebrows. "And you blame them for that?

What will it take to show you that spitting at people isn't healthy? Maybe I should let you learn your lesson!"

Mark blushed, then pushed on.

"We decided to split into groups for protection. We thought this would work out fine, until we remembered the new work schedules. We know that this could separate us, and mean problems for us. We thought we could split ourselves into groups according to our interests, and help as a group in each interest, if you agree." Mark stopped talking. He watched the sergeant.

"Bring me your list of groups and I'll check them over. If they're good, and they'd better be, I'll help with this. If it works out, you can keep the groups. But time will tell. I need the groups before tonight, and I'll put the schedules out tomorrow."

The boys took this as a dismissal and left the small office. When they were out of earshot, Mark said, "I'm glad he didn't chew me out right there. If I were him, I wouldn't even bother with people like us, especially with the castle's situation right now."

"And yet," said Thomas, "it's the little things that make the difference, especially in morale, and he has enough experience to know."

"I can tell. But I hope I don't have to talk to him too often."

They arrived back at the armory and found that Ijn had divided the boys into groups. Mark's group was composed of boys who wanted to work in the blacksmith shop and the armory, producing weapons and parts. Ijn led a group willing to work with horses.

Mark hadn't even known there were horses on the island, but he was told they were kept on the other side, in a lower area that was fenced in and camouflaged. There weren't many, but they needed stables and pastures, and that was the work Ijn was volunteering for.

Thomas led one group, and Gregory, the son of the priest, led the other. They were assisting in the block work and carpentry in the castle. Ijn had chosen his groups well, because these four categories were exactly what Allen would be looking for to help repair the castle.

The two building groups, those led by Thomas and Greg, were larger, with about twenty-five boys each, while Ijn had twenty, leaving Mark with ten boys. He had fewer than the others, but they were all strong and ready to fight, so he didn't worry about safety.

"Obviously, if the entire class of older guys attacked one group we would have problems. We need to keep track of each other and support each other. Besides having messengers running back and forth, I don't have any ideas. Does anyone here have a suggestion?"

"If we were close together," said Thomas, "we could use

whistles, but that won't help across the length of the island."

"Most of us will be fairly close together, right?" asked Mark. "We'll be in the armory and the smithy, and Thomas and Greg will be on the castle grounds. Where will you be working, Ijn?"

"They haven't picked a site for the stables and corrals yet, but my guess is that it will be directly outside the castle walls," he replied. "Most of the upperclassmen will be inside, with the building projects, I would imagine. That should help us out"

"For now we can just use whistles," said Greg, "and we can figure out what works best later."

"If that's settled for now," said Thomas, "we need a meeting place."

"The armory should do, right?" asked Ijn.

"Sure. It's large, and open to the outside for fresh air. Besides, we're always here anyway."

"Sounds fine. Anything else?" asked Ijn. There was a general shaking of heads, so the boys got up and separated into their groups of friends.

"So, captains, what's the news?" queried Jan. "Are we raiding the upperclassmen's belongings tonight?"

"No, not unless they do it to us. We have to act as a

passive coalition," Ijn said.

"Okay, okay, we get the point. You're smart," said Pieter, "but for the weaker minds among us, nobody in particular, what does 'acting as a passive coalition' really include?"

"We have to remain defensive," said Mark. "Besides refusing to work for them, of course. We can't just provoke them into attacking us."

"Exactly," said Ijn. "We have to keep Allen on our side."

The large group of boys talked together for a while, then started to drift off to the barracks. Mark and his friends were some of the last to go, walking out of the deserted armory as the sun began to set. Jan made a quick run to Allen's office to drop off the lists, then he too was soon in the barracks, getting ready for bed.

After a deep and restful sleep, Mark was awakened by upperclassmen berating someone in the room next door. As he began to come to out of the deep fog of sleep, he saw shapes moving tensely past his bed. Ijn was already up. Mark threw off the covers and rolled out of bed. Jan and Pieter were waking up on the far side of the room as he hurriedly dressed.

Mark and Ijn rushed out the door of their room with several other boys behind them. Entering the next room, they saw a row of boys confronting several upperclassmen. The upperclassmen were holding two boys that had refused to work. Greg was talking, his voice deceptively casual, hiding the tense feeling they all had.

"Let them go. You don't stand a chance. If you want to fight, we'd be more than happy." Mark and Ijn walked up and stood next to him. Bleary-eyed boys filled the room, and several upperclassmen woke up to find themselves in the middle of a standoff. The three stubborn older boys refused to back down. Mark found the situation increasingly dangerous, and his suspicions were confirmed when one of the upperclassmen reached under his bed and pulled out a knife. The blade reflected the wavering yellow light of the bedside candles as it moved.

"Everybody back off. These two have work to do." He flourished the long dagger threateningly. Mark stepped forward.

"Put down the dagger." His eyes hardened and locked on the upperclassman. He moved forward again. The older boy assumed a defensive position, his knife held ready. Mark walked forward until he was right in front of the offending boy. They glared at each other.

The room was tense, silent. Mark knew that if he backed down, everything would be lost. In one fluid motion, he grabbed the knife arm of the boy and pulled it past him. As the boy came forward his head went down. Mark's knee went up. The knife clattered out of the boy's hand, and Greg grabbed it in a flash. The room burst into pandemonium.

The two boys being held attacked their captors and were assisted by a crowd of others. Upperclassmen watching from their beds were pinned down by still more boys and then, just as fast as it started, the fighting stopped.

Thomas Allen stood in the doorway. All eyes watched him as he took in the frozen chaos. His eyes were mere slits as he pointed a finger at Greg.

"Whose knife?" Greg pointed mutely at the upperclassman sprawled on the floor where he had fallen.

"He pulled--" Mark was cut off by Allen's look.

"There will be no fighting with weapons. Clean yourselves up and come to breakfast. I shouldn't have to be your nursemaid." He turned on his heel and walked down the hall, where a gong was being sounded to wake the rest of the castle. The boys were motionless for a second, and then they slowly untangled themselves from each other and returned to their respective rooms to change their clothes for the new day.

Mark had scraped his arm, so he headed to the infirmary after getting directions from Ijn. It wasn't bad, but he didn't want to have it bleeding during his classes or work.

The infirmary was housed in the lowest level of the three-level complex. It contained a few beds and a small area for dressing wounds. The attendant, Charles O'Neill, had apparently gone to breakfast so Mark helped himself to some soap and bandages. At first the soap stung as he cleaned his arm in the pail of water, but after he rinsed it off the scrape looked and felt better. He wrapped a few lengths of the bandage around his arm for good measure and then headed off for breakfast, a little late.

When he entered the dining hall, the mood was tense. The work lists wouldn't be posted until after they ate, so everyone was in suspense. Mark was concerned that after this morning Allen might redo the schedule and not be so kind to them. He was silent as they ate, ignoring those who were energetic enough to talk in the early morning hours.

After breakfast was finally finished, the majority of the castle gathered around the lists posted on the door to the hall. The priest was reading them out loud, but nobody could hear him in the chaos.

The boys couldn't get to the lists at first, but after the crowd had cleared out, they stepped forward. Mark saw that he was assigned to work in the blacksmith shop. Allen hadn't changed it! He checked the other boys in his group. They were all there.

"My group checks. How about yours?" he asked Ijn.

"Mine's good. I think the other two are as well."

"They are," said Thomas, appearing beside them. "I checked both of ours. We have to report to Lockhart, and Greg reports to Lamartine, the mason."

"Phew!"

"No kidding. Allen didn't seem too happy, especially about the knife."

"Well, I'm not too happy about the knife either," said Mark. "For one, my arm is starting to feel like it's on fire. And really, once we get into weapons, this turns deadly."

"Just imagine a fight in the armory," said Thomas. "The swords and halberds would be out in moments."

"That had to be what Allen was thinking. I wonder what he plans to do about it."

"I doubt he'll do anything. He said 'no weapons' in front of everybody, and he's used to being obeyed."

"I'm sure we will obey him - if anyone doesn't, they're not part of us, no questions asked. But the upperclassmen - I say, we're going to be late to swords. Let's get out of here quick!"

The four boys sprinted out of the castle. They weaved in and out of the busy castle traffic, arriving at the fencing yard just as Allen called the class to order. He ignored their flushed faces and heavy breathing as he led the class through a new variation of the drill.

After they had practiced the new drill several times, Allen told them that they were getting new positions. They quickly moved to different pells as Allen read off the names. Mark noticed a conspicuous split between the upperclassmen and the lower levels. Allen wasn't taking any chances.

Once again they practiced with each other. Mark was glad Allen hadn't put him with another upperclassman. His partner was with a younger boy who wasn't advanced as he was. Mark enjoyed helping through the moves, showing how to hold the sword for a certain strike and teaching him how to catch someone off guard.

Mark also noticed a bad habit his practice opponent had, which he had seen a few times. People he saw on the island tended to rely on their sword too much, always using it, and never seeming to realize that they were crippling themselves by only thinking inside the box. Mark showed the boy, Alfred, how to fake with his sword, and how to follow through with a kick or hit with his shield. He also showed how many people held their shields loosely, only expecting impact from the front. You could grab their shield with both hands, and kick them in the stomach, as long as you moved quickly. The move could wreak havoc on an opponent, mostly due to the factor of surprise.

Mark was showing Alfred several other tricks when he noticed Allen watching him. When he caught his eye, Allen barked, "Since you find it important enough to tell Alfred, why don't you tell us all."

Reddening slightly, Mark hesitated, but then began again. The older boys pretended to ignore him, but the sergeant's glare straightened them out. Mark's repertoire of moves wasn't large, but the class continued even though the gong sounded from the castle to bring them to the study rooms.

Since Allen had just ignored the sound, Mark had moved on. Instructors wandered down from the castle, intent on bringing their students to class, but ended up stopping to watch the demonstration.

When Mark's bag of tricks ran out, he straightened up and said, "That's all, sir." The sergeant nodded and the class was dismissed. Several of the instructors watching the performance went immediately to Allen and expressed their disapproval of his actions. Allen responded with a well thought-out "Harrumph."

While they were being herded back to the castle by irritated pedagogues, Ijn asked Mark, "Where did you learn all that?"

"I learned self-defense from the monks in South Shields. They assumed you weren't carrying a sword, but they taught it anyway. The way they taught, though, concentrated more on non-weapon tactics, which they implemented nicely with swordplay."

"I'll say. You had Allen in fits with jealousy."

"I wouldn't say that, but at first I thought he was punishing me. I guess he really meant it."

"He tends to be that way. He doesn't care if he intended to punish you – even though he probably did. He has the guts to reconsider, as long as you prove what you were doing was worth the infraction."

They had arrived back at the castle and they took their seats as the instructor harried the tardy boys. Many glances were thrown Mark's way and when classes were over he was approached by several people in the armory. He was kept busy by explanations of "his" tactics until a hush fell over the room. An upperclassman had entered the armory.

Mark looked up and breathed a sigh of relief. It was only Lukas, the one decent older guy. As he took a seat near Mark, the silence held. He looked around, and then said, apologetically, "I'd only intended to listen." Mark grinned and continued to answer a question that Thomas had asked him.

When the short break ended Mark watched Lukas leave. There was a funny look on the upperclassman's face. Mark wondered what it was all about. He felt as though Lukas were different than the others, especially since the boys regarded him with such deference.

CHAPTER 13

It wasn't long after they left Tynemouth the next morning that Robert and his friends met the vanguard of Cogniard's main force. The small group of outriders had bypassed Newcastle to arrive at the shore quickly. Roland was in the lead, having replaced the leader from the day before, and he was eagerly awaiting news of their efforts.

"We put the spies to sea right under the cliffs of the priory castle, Commander. It was with an appropriated boat, and they seemed fairly confident of their success, given the quality of the boat and the time of departure." Robert put a distinctive lilt on the word "appropriated," conveying his dislike for the task of stealing a boat. He might be won over to the value of spying, but he would never believe it was right to steal a boat out of a fisherman's back yard.

"Thank you, Robert. Why don't you fall in behind us. I've got another mission for you to take care of as well."

Robert saluted and wheeled his horse around to join his friends in the back of the column. It was another bright day, the preceding storm having left during the night and only the slight trace of mud on the roads betrayed the fact that there had been a storm recently. The forests seemed to have benefited from the outburst of rain, and the little green buds were already larger and brighter than several days ago.

With the jingling of harnesses and the slap of leather, Robert and his friends rode along in relative silence, their thoughts wandering to the events of the previous day, wondering how the spies were getting along, wondering if they had even made it to the island.

"What really are the chances of a fishing boat surviving out on the sea?" asked Ted after a space, frowning.

"Not too great, to tell by my experience," replied Robert. "I was shipwrecked fairly close to that spot, and as far as I know I'm the only one that survived."

"You could almost be a minstrel! Say that again with a little more vigor and I'll actually believe you."

"I said I was shipwrecked off that coast, and nobody else made it except me."

"So you're serious? How did you manage to survive?"

Once Robert got started, he was a decent storyteller. He could weave in all the elements of a great tale. The story of his shipwrecking stretched to twice its original length, and by the time he got done, it was so obviously fabricated that Ted replied, "So, after being knighted for saving the mysterious noble under attack by the sea dragon, what got you here in a humble scout's position?"

They both laughed and Robert was about to shoot back a cutting reply when a voice interrupted from behind them.

"In most stories, no matter how ridiculous, there is a grain of truth. What really happened, Robert?" It was Roland, riding close behind the boys and smiling as though he knew they didn't expect him there. Neither boy had seen him drop off to the side of the column and then come up behind them. He had intended only to relay his latest mission to Robert; but, having been caught up in the tale, he stayed to the end.

Robert, nothing loathe to repeat the story, did so again in a little less joking manner. By the time he was done, he was in a much more somber mood. He realized that this story wasn't about the glamour of the experiences he had been through, but about losing his father and brother and most likely never seeing anyone from his past life ever again.

Roland sympathized with him, recognizing that Robert

was now completely on his own and fending for himself. However, he had come to send Robert on a mission, or so he said, and he began to explain.

"It's a fairly straightforward assignment, this one. You'll ride back to Tynemouth with the vanguard, then you and I need to arrange for the troops of the main contingent to be housed and fed while the rest of the van return to Cogniard."

"So if you're going to be there, why do you need me?" Robert asked, interested in this proposition.

"Why don't come up to the front and ride with me for a bit and I'll go into a little more detail." With that, he pulled his courser out of the column and led Robert up to the front. Ted and Roy stayed in the back.

"When I started this scouting organization, it wasn't anything more than little Roland riding around on his lord's extra horses to find the latest news. At the time, Cogniard was little more than a poor, although noble, landowner. He was despised by his neighbors north across the river Tyne and directly to his east.

"My missions for Cogniard went from small-time errands to real and effective scouting. I would ride into the next counties and pick up the news, gossip, and even a few documents that later turned up as 'lost.' It was with these services that Cogniard managed to beat his neighbors in the little game of politics that ensued, and he became

Lord of Newcastle through what you might call, well, maneuvering. Essentially, by hook or by crook.

"By this time, though, the scouting force had grown from one man into a small, tightly knit community of expert horsemen, led by the best in the army. Cogniard never denied me the right to pick anyone I deemed capable for a scout's position, even right out of his own bodyguard. The scouts are the guiding eye of his army, and he can't do much without them.

"So I guess I mean to say that I'm always keeping a good eye out for men, even when they are still young, to join, lead, and command my scouts. When I saw you in Ashington I thought you might be a potential leader, and since then I've kept an eye on you.

"I want to train you, as I have many others, to become a leader in the scouts. Not now, probably not even soon, but I want you to get used to the idea that someday you might lead a section of the scouts. For example, Roy will soon be leading a small group."

Robert was amazed that he was listening to this. He had always liked Roland, but never expected to be talking to him of promotion within days of joining his scouts.

"So, how would that work? Do you want me to follow you around?"

"Not completely. I'm going to give you assignments that I think will be worthwhile for you to do, and try to give you as broad a range of experiences as possible. But as far as this one goes, I'd like to introduce you to the castellan there, and the other people of importance that you might come in contact with. I would have stopped back at Newcastle to introduce you there as well, but, as you can see, we're in a little bit of a hurry to get to Tynemouth so Cogniard can move forward with his plans. Which, by the way, are a continuation of that story I was telling you earlier. The man we're after was the Lord of Newcastle before Cogniard ousted him, and he doesn't have such good feelings toward Cogniard. What he does have is a lot of money and men, and this won't be the stroll in the park that most of our men think it will."

When the vanguard arrived at the gates of the Tynemouth Castle, Roland stopped the group and addressed himself to a short man riding behind him.

"I've got business to attend to, Geoff, so you'll need to take charge and report back to the main body. Don't forget to tell Cogniard about the potential hideout we saw on the way, and remind him that we'll need to pay the mercenaries when he arrives. Robert, you're coming with me."

The two scouts, leader and novice, presented themselves at the Tynemouth Castle barbican for admittance. The relatively new gates swung open on oiled hinges and a stocky little man in parade-clean armor strolled out. Or, as Mark would have said had he been there, he rolled out.

"Greetings, one and all. Or two, I should say! Happy to have you here at the Tynemouth Priory. Should I admit you brothers to the cloisters? Or would you prefer the chapel first? Good to have you back, Roland!" The happy little man was beaming as he jokingly bowed to the two scouts. "And who have we here? A new recruit, to be sure. How do you do? And pleased to meet you!"

The man shook Robert's hand and laughed as he welcomed the two within the castle's outer set of walls. The large priory rose straight out of the ground like a chunk of ice dropped there in a windstorm. It competed with the keep for the largest building in Tynemouth, and housed one of the most beautiful sanctuaries in the area.

"You'll want to know, then, young man, why we have such a splendid religious institution here. It dates back to..." He went off into the story of the Tynemouth Priory, also telling of the men who were buried there, including several kings.

"...which, of course, is why we have such a nice priory, and the castle is here to guard it!"

"What he means, Robert," Roland broke in dryly. "is that the natural features of the area and the proximity to Scotland, as well as the River Tyne, make this a critical spot to defend for anyone interested in dominating a large section of the English continent."

"You always were a little biased toward the military half

of Tynemouth. Must get dusty following that horse around, though. Anyone up for a refreshing, ah, cup of water?"

"Once again, our friend Benedict is withheld from saying his true meaning by the hood and cassock that he should be wearing. What he means is that we should join him in his home for a drink of wine. You see, Benedict is, although you can't tell, the abbot here, as well as the castellan." Benedict's face followed along with Roland's words in its expression.

"Well, about the hood and cassock. See, the monks and priests all think I should wear that, while all the stewards and officers are dead set on me wearing armor. So I just wear what I want."

By this time they had reached the keep, and the friendly Abbot and castellan led them up a few flights of stairs to a decent-sized room that contained a desk, a few chairs, and a small table. As well as a wine rack.

"Never did get the priests to agree with the wine rack, nor the stewards with the stained glass windows, but we have them both." He deftly played his fingers across the protruding necks of the wine bottles, and pulled out a dark red wine.

"Light on the alcohol, heavy on the taste. Of course, they all are."

Once they were seated, the conversation leveled out into

a more serious discussion of the issues at hand. Robert found that Benedict was not as fickle as he seemed, and that he held his opinions as strong as the next man, if not a lot stronger. He was shrewd in his reasoning, and it seemed as though he had a handle on every topic from halberds to rosaries.

He was of course an Anglican abbot and a skilled soldier at the same time, and knew what he liked in both areas. Robert understood why castle and priory were loath to let the other have him, and why he was needed in both.

After extensive discussion, from which Robert learned quite a bit, Roland suggested a tour of the castle and priory ground so that Robert could familiarize himself with them. Without further ado, they left the keep and began at the stables.

A short, curly-haired man was supervising the repair of a stall as they strolled trough.

"Hello, Martin! Ademar giving you trouble again?" the abbot asked, stepping by the sweating laborers into the stall.

"Took out the hinge in the night. Seems he can't keep quiet for more than a day." The man's eyes flickered between the abbot and Robert, a suspicious look in his eye.

"Well, we can't spare him. Not now, anyway. I take it you're keeping him in the foaling stall?"

"It's the only one big enough right now. He doesn't like it much, but it'll have to do."

After inspecting the repair work, the abbot's group moved on. It wasn't too soon for Robert. The stablemaster's eyes had been a bit too sharp, and he had felt briefly uncomfortable under his stare.

The whirlwind tour went through the armory, kitchens, workshops, and other miscellaneous outbuildings of the cliff-top castle. When it was over Robert was worn out, and he and Roland headed back to the keep where they would be staying that night. Benedict had been intercepted by a page requesting his presence in the castle for a ceremony. Despite the page's insistence that he should have been there an hour earlier, Benedict was unfrazzled and had left with a wave and a smile.

On the way to the keep, Robert and Roland were intercepted by their own messenger from Cogniard. He relayed the news that the army would be staying in Newcastle that evening and they could expect them in Tynemouth a little after noon the next day.

After dealing with the messenger, Roland led Robert to their rooms in the keep. They were directly adjacent to the room of the castellan, and Robert was amazed at the prompt and polite service of the attendants who brought them blankets and clothes.

It wasn't long before all were called to the great hall for a late meal. Roland and Robert found themselves ushered to the head table, where they sat next to Benedict, who served as the host and priest at the same time.

The five-course meal was a lengthy affair, with food appearing out of nowhere at Robert's elbow and drinks being refilled as fast as they were emptied. He hardly had time to notice Roland's amused smile at his surprise, although he did note that while the head table received amazing service, those sitting "below the salt," or in the lower tables, did not receive the same.

After the delicious meal that was so long it was almost physically exhausting, Roland and Robert retired to Benedict's office where they once again discussed affairs of great importance. This time, however, the talking was specific and to the point, centering on the spies that Robert had dropped off earlier.

"Well, we did receive their signal the next morning." Benedict's eyes twinkled.

"And..." Roland replied, leaning forward in his chair. "Come on, I can't believe that it actually worked!"

"Oh, it worked like a charm, my friend! Early this morning we saw the pigeon return to its nest, and it had with it the message that they had arrived and had safely hidden the boat. It also gave a few more specifics, at least as specific as you can be, of where the island is exactly."

Roland turned to explain to Robert. "The spies carried

with them some pigeons. Message pigeons, the man called them, that Cogniard and Benedict here were certain would fly any distance to return to their nest. In any case, we sent them with our spies, and it appears that it was true!" Returning his attention to Benedict, he asked, "When do you expect another message?"

"We should get another tonight. In fact, I wouldn't be surprised if the pigeon was on its way now."

"Well, where does it roost? Let's go wait for it!" Robert's reply was immediately seconded by Roland, and the three quickly left the room. Benedict led them into the priory, up several flights of stairs, and into the rafters of the large building.

Just before entering the cramped area, Benedict grabbed a torch from a sconce on the wall and motioned the others to do the same.

"We usually don't go up here, and leave it dark for the pigeons, but we'll need light now."

When he ducked through the small door, Robert was amazed at the complexity of the system of rafters. Beams crisscrossed each other from the strawed floor to the lofty peak in the center. Dust motes swirled about the lanterns. As he walked he could hear a soft cooing coming from the darkness beyond his torch.

When they found the pigeons, they also found the pigeon man. He was lying on his back, snoring softly. At least, until the light of the torches hit his eyes.

"Welcome, milord. I'm awaiting the second message." His eyes darted nervously from one visitor to the other, but Benedict put him at rest.

"I think I'd fall asleep up here too, in the dark with gentle cooing all around me. Sounds so nice, I might just move up here. After all, I'm the abbot, right?" They all smiled, and each took a seat on the rough wooden floor. It was covered with dust stirred around by pigeon feet and textured with pigeon droppings.

Without further ado, Benedict leaned his round head against a pillar and went to sleep. Roland chuckled and began to discuss more tactics with Robert, who tried to listen but felt more like lying on his back and staring at the stars through the open hatch.

Sometime later, there was a flutter of wings, and a pigeon landed on the lip of the hatch. After a few inquisitive coos, it continued into the building and found its own perch.

The pigeon man was quick to retrieve the message from its leg. Roland woke Benedict, who really wasn't asleep after all. With baited breath, they waited for the abbot to read the message.

"Island small. Many people, rebuilding large fortress. Recommend siege equipment. Contact with target. Success. High hopes. Arrive as soon as possible. Progress continues."

The men looked at each other in silence until Robert just had to ask.

"What exactly does 'contact with target' mean?"

"Well, we sent them with quite a few missions, in hopes that they could finish at least a few," replied Roland. "By far the one with the most potential but the least chance of success was contacting an official who formerly knew Cogniard, and could be friendly to us. It looks like they have succeeded."

CHAPTER 14

The group boys watched closely as James Drydon maneuvered a strip of metal on the anvil. It was glowing red hot. Drydon's hammer slammed down, and the fiery piece of metal sparked with the impact.

A few "taps" later and the horseshoe was quenched in the bucket of water next to the anvil.

"And that is how it's done, chaps," Drydon said, his deep voice heavily tinged with a Welsh accent. "You'll be doing this for the next few days, I suppose. As soon as you can get me two hundred of these we can move on."

The group of boys looked dubiously at the finished product.

"Can you do that again?" asked Sven. "I'm not sure I can quite duplicate that..."

"Better, you try it," said Drydon. "Here you go. I'll walk you through it." He backed away from the anvil and motioned to Sven.

"All right. Start with the metal here, right?" Sven grabbed the tongs and positioned a strip of metal in the fire. "How long until I can take it out?"

"Wait till it's beyond red hot." Drydon beat John O'Dell to the bellows and started pumping them to provide air for the fire. It flared up quickly as the brawny blacksmith pumped away.

When the strip of metal was hot enough, Sven brought it over to the anvil. Grabbing the hammer Drydon handed him, he started pounding away at the edge of the metal. A slight curve slowly appeared. Before he'd gotten too far, however, the metal had cooled off and the color had changed back to a dark gray.

This time, John grabbed the handle to the bellows first and started pumping as Sven immersed the metal into the fire again. He soon found that the job wasn't as easy as it looked, even though Drydon could do it without breaking a sweat. In a few minutes he was breathing hard. By the time the horseshoe was hot again, he was red in the face and panting.

"Guess you won't be jumping for that job again, huh?"

Drydon laughed.

Sven started to work on the horseshoe again. After several trips back to the fire he succeeded in producing what Drydon called a "borderline" horseshoe.

"If you can make it that good, we're alright. Anything less and you'll have to keep working or start over." The burly smith eyed the group for a minute, then started pointing locations of tools. Somehow he'd scrounged up anvils for all of them, but there weren't quite enough hammers, and even fewer tongs.

"Guess you'll have to share," the smith said. "Once you get in a rhythm it shouldn't be too bad."

The first hour of work produced so many bad horseshoes that Mark started wondering if it was worth it. He himself hadn't made a single passable horseshoe. Most of the time he'd been standing by another boy's anvil, waiting for a tool.

It wasn't too hard for him to punch the holes at the end of the process, but he found that every time he punched a hole he had to put down the hammer and move the shoe. Then when he went back to grab the hammer it would be gone.

"I can't believe how frustrating this is!" he said to John.

"You aren't joking, either," John replied. "I can bend these things pretty well once I get the tools. But every time I turn around, somebody grabs whatever I was just using."

"You'll just have to keep holding the tools. Then nobody will think to grab them," Mark joked.

"At the same time as moving the shoe, and holding the punch? How many arms do you think I have?" John reached over and snatched a hammer from the next anvil and mockingly tried.

"Here." Mark grabbed the tongs from him and positioned a freshly heated iron strip on the horn of the anvil. "Fire away."

John started pounding at the metal. As he did so, Mark moved it slowly around, allowing John's hammering to shape the iron.

"Perfect!" John said as he wiped his forehead. "Heat that thing up again and I'll be able to finish this one off."

As he stood waiting, Pierre, another one of the students, walked up. "While you're standing there could you bend this one too? I noticed it didn't take you very long."

"Even better!" John was getting excited. "You and Mark just rotate, and I'll just keep shaping."

Pretty soon the group of three was out-pacing all the other groups combined, at least when it came to bending. After the bending was done, John struggled with getting the nail holes punched correctly. Sven stopped his work to watch. Frowning, he turned to look at the other boys, who each slaved away at their own piece, most still making mistakes.

"Hey, Charlie!" he shouted across the room. When his friend looked up, he waved him over. Grabbing one of John's bent horseshoes with a pair of tongs, he threw it on his anvil and handed Charles the hammer and punch. "I'll hold, you punch."

The two went at it with a will. In a few minutes they finished off the pile of bent shoes that John had created.

Mark noticed the new self-made group, and stopped for a moment. He headed over to Drydon and got his attention.

"See how we're working here?" he asked. "We've got to be making five times as many shoes as everyone else."

"Good work," said Drydon, not stopping what he was doing. "Keep it up and we'll promote you. Double your pay, in fact."

"From zero, huh? That's not what I meant, though. If five of us can work together and make shoes faster than everyone else, we should take the other five and get them doing the same."

"Hmm." Drydon stopped and examined the group. "Alright, we'll try it." He stopped the other boys and lined them up similar to the first group. Within a few minutes they had decided who was the best at bending and punching, and their line started to produce horseshoes as well.

Both groups were producing quickly, and each had noticed how fast the other group was. The competition started at the end of the line, where the hole-punchers would race to put the next shoe into the pile. Of course, they had to have prompt service from the benders, who were quickly informed when they were being sluggish. By supper time, the pile of newly-made shoes was growing rapidly.

"Time to clean up!" Drydon called. There were only a few minutes until the evening meal, and the boys were a mess.

During the meal, the conversation centered on their work. Even the other groups were interested in how the mundane job had turned into a competition.

"I bet I can lay more bricks than you!" Thomas challenged his friend.

"Not if we're doing the same job, you can't." the boy replied. Mark smiled as he saw spirits flaring up all over the table.

"You really started something, you know," he said to John. John smiled too.

"It's not really about the competition, though. Not the

part I started. I think we went faster because we were each doing what we liked," he said.

"You think I like holding horseshoes on an anvil?" Mark scoffed. "No, it was definitely the competition that made us faster."

"Then why were we going faster even before the other group got started, huh?" John shot back.

"You think you two could agree that it was a combination and shut up?" said Rich, who was sitting between them.

"No, I think Mark has a point," said a grinning Jan, poking his way into the conversion.

"Of course I do," said Mark. "You see, when..." Rich groaned and plugged his ears. Jan butted in again as John was replying.

"No, that's just wrong, because umph mrrph-"

Pieter was covering his mouth.

"If you'd stop intentionally egging people on, some of us might be able to eat in peace. Now if you don't keep your mouth shut I'm going to shut it for you."

The grin on Jan's face showed that he'd been caught red-handed.

"Well, even you know how funny John looks when he's mad..." The whole table burst into laughter and the argument died away as the boys continued to eat.

That evening after the meal, Mark returned to the smithy. Drydon was still clearing away the mess from that afternoon.

"So how did we do today, Drydon?" Mark asked, grabbing a few tools to put away.

"Not too bad... at the end. At the beginning you were, well, awful. See that pile of horseshoes over there? Every single one has to be melted down again. Wrong size holes, flattened too much, you name it." He put the last tool in its place and walked over to the pile. "You busy?" he asked.

"Nope," said Mark.

"Good. A little help will make this go a lot faster." The two of them worked together, talking back and forth over the roar of the fire.

"What do you like making the best?" asked Mark.

"Whatever's hardest," the smith said with a grin. "Swords. You can't compromise on sword quality. No second-rate smith is going to come close to a true swordsmith."

"What's the hardest part about making a sword?"

"Well, the process for any sword is pretty tough, but for me, the hardest thing I've ever done – or, actually, not

179

done – is create the sword that the Earl wants me to make."

"How is it any different than the ones in the armory, or those over there, for that matter?" asked Mark, motioning to a rack of finished swords behind the smith.

"I'm not sure," said Drydon with a wry grin. "I do know it's different, but I'm not sure how. That's the problem. I've tried a number of different materials and processes, but I can't get it."

"Is it better, though?" asked Mark. "Why would you want to make that particular sword when you could just make these?"

"It's... well, have you seen the Earl's sword? Oh, of course not, you just got here. Well, it's strong and flexible and all that. Sharp too. But the real different is that it inspires people. See, the house of the Earl was always known for their knowledge. They've come up with unique solutions for a number of their problems over the ages, and this sword is just, well, is a symbol of that, I guess. Nobody else can make it."

"So how come you don't just ask the Earl?"

"Well, you nailed it. That's the problem. He doesn't know. The process got lost somewhere, and he's desperate for another sword. All of Cornuel's subjects are pretty loyal to their leader, and want Cornuel to be equal with the Earl. The Earl has always said Cornuel was just as important as himself, but that claim is starting to wear thin. Just imagine the Earl's face when Cornuel's men started asking the Earl to give Cornuel a sword just like his. If he can't deliver – if I can't deliver – we'll start having trouble with more than just the few hired men we've got. And Cornuel's men aren't weaklings."

"Nothing like a little stress," Mark grinned as he helped Drydon pour the last batch of molten horseshoes into a set of molds. Then he straightened.

"What do you usually try?" he asked with a suddenly serious expression on his face.

"What do you mean, what do I usually try?"

"What is the process for these swords?"

Drydon shrugged his shoulders and rattled off a list of metal contents and quenching times that almost made Mark dizzy.

"A little slower, please?" he asked, grinning.

This time Mark broke in when Drydon listed the metals he used, suggesting a little more of one of the metals. Drydon looked at him suspiciously.

"Since when were you a swordsmith?" he asked. "I usually do, in fact, use that much when I try to make the Earl's blade. But no, it doesn't work out."

"Hmm. Keep going then." Drydon gave him a funny look and kept going. This time Mark stopped him when he got to talking about quenching.

"Excuse a second question, but have you ever tried a shorter quenching time with colder water?"

"No... I didn't have any colder water and certainly didn't seem that important to me." The smith's forehead was creased. "Now tell me where you're getting this from. I watched you today, and I know you haven't had more than a day's practice with a hammer. Where would you be getting these ideas from?"

"Well... did you know I used to live at a monastery?" Drydon nodded. Mark continued. "When I was there, my brother Robert and I did a lot of learning, Robert more than me. He did a lot of reading, too. There was one time, after we learned about smithing from one of the Brothers, that we got all excited about making our own swords. So he dove into Brother Arnold's books and I started looking for metal around the monastery grounds. I found a few old rakes and stole a skillet from the kitchen. Robert had been busy too, and found a well-worn entry in one of the older books that described how to make a sword.

"Since we really weren't supposed to be reading Brother Arnold's books, we both memorized the process and snuck out to the little monastery forge in the middle of the night. Needless to say, we didn't get very far. Brother

Arnold was a better sentry than we thought, and he stopped us just before we melted the skillet."

Drydon's eye's twinkled with laughter. "I bet you boys probably got a good beating for that."

"Nope. Brother Arnold never beat us. But the other monks would have. Especially the cook. It was his favorite skillet," Mark replied. "So. Do you think we can try it?"

"Well... not tonight. There's not much time left. But maybe tomorrow. Speaking of which, you'd better head off to your room. It's starting to get late."

Mark put one more mold away, then said goodbye to Drydon and stepped out into the hallway. It was getting dark and the only sounds he heard came from the direction of the stairs. But as he started to walk to the dormitories, he heard quiet footsteps behind him.

Tensing instinctively, he looked over his shoulder. A hand snaked out and wrapped around him, covering his mouth. He twisted his body viciously and kicked back with his feet, but the hold was too good. He did, however, get a good look at his assailant's face. It was Harold.

"Ummph grmph merrgh," he managed to get out.

"Shut up. You're going to get what's coming to you, you puny lout," Harold hissed in his ear. The older boy forced him to the ground and raised his hand for a blow.

Wriggling, Mark tried to squirm away, but Harold only paused and made his grip more sure. The cold stone floor bit into the back of Mark's head. Without preamble, Harold raised his hand to strike Mark.

Just then, Mark heard Drydon walking to the door of the smithy. So did Harold. The upperclassman crouched down and leaned toward the wall, trying to hide in the shadow. Mark hoped Drydon looked in their direction before he went down the stairs to his room.

Just as the door opened, Mark began to squirm and tried to shout. Harold twisted his neck painfully, but Mark only squirmed more.

It worked. The slight sounds were enough to attract Drydon's attention.

"Harold!" he shouted in surprise and anger. "What do you think you're doing?" The burly giant was there in just two steps, lifting Harold off of Mark with one hand.

A few blubbering words came from Harold. Mark winced as Drydon smashed the helpless boy against the wall and let him drop.

"Get to your room. You know better than this." The two boys walked down to the dormitories as Drydon stood in front of the smithy. Shaking his head, the smith walked toward the stairs as the two disappeared into their own rooms.

The next day after classes there was more competition in the smithy. Mark's group, although the first to discover the efficient process, turned out to be a hair slower.

After three hours, Drydon called a halt and the work ceased for several minutes while the boys relaxed on the smithy's benches. Mark wiped his brow with his hand. When he looked at it, soot covered his entire palm. John laughed at him. "Go look at yourself in the quenching trough, Mark."

Mark heeded his classmate's suggestion. When he saw his face he laughed. His forehead was black with soot, and the dripping sweat made ashy streaks down his face. He wiped them off with his shirt and returned to his seat.

"How are we doing?" he called across to Drydon.

"Not bad, Not bad. We might get done tonight."

"We won't get done if we don't get back to work," said John. "Let's go."

The boys returned to their tasks, some weary and reluctant, a few still intent on their goal. The process began again. As the shoes began to collect at the end of the lines, they were stacked on pegs placed in wooden racks against the stone wall. The larger sizes started at the left hand side of the wall, and as the racks were filled the iron wall began to grow. As the hours passed, the line of horseshoes continued to spread across. Four hours later, when Drydon called a halt, it was touching the far wall that adjoined the armory.

"This may be a stupid question," Mark said, "but why so many horseshoes? We don't have that many horses, and the few we have can't use that many very quickly."

"Actually, it serves somewhat of a dual purpose," said Drydon. "The Earl always wanted extra, you see, because he's always wanted to return to the mainland after Cogniard. He knew I'd be overwhelmed if we did that, because he'd need a lot of smithing done, so he always told me 'just make a lot now, and if we don't use them we could always sell them.' "

Mark nodded, deep in thought. "What was he like?" he asked. "The Earl, I mean."

"What *is* he like, you mean," said John. "He isn't in the past, you know."

"That's just it. He isn't the past, but he's everything else. He's our present and future, and if he goes, we all go."

"Basically," said John, "he's the visual essence of a dream, especially for those whom he personally recruited."

"Yeah, those hired riff-raff aren't much to speak of, are they?" commented Drydon.

"To answer your question though, Mark, he's the best ruler many of his followers have ever had. Most of us here would follow him anywhere he went, even to the edge of the world if he decided to go down that way. He's fair, but perfectly just. Iron hard when he needs to be, but he has his softer side as well. You won't catch him yelling at his servants or criticizing the food. He's what we all aim to be."

The boys slowly cleaned up and drifted off to supper. Mark was impressed by the description he'd been given of the Earl, and he wondered if he would ever get a chance to meet him.

After supper he made a beeline for the smithy, walking in just after Drydon had stoked the fire.

"So. You ready to make a sword?" Drydon asked.

"Sure thing. I can't wait to get started," Mark replied.

It had been a long day as it was, and now the torches flickered low in their sconces as the work began in earnest. Waves of heat rolled from the forge as Mark worked the bellows. Drydon rummaged through his stock, looking for the best pieces. With these, he began to work.

Heating, pounding, quenching. The cycle never seemed to end. Varieties of metal too obscure for the average shop combined with the most common iron in long, thin layers formed the core of the new blade.

After hours of hard work, the sword began to take shape. As it neared its final shape, excess metal was scraped off and the blade was tempered. When the metalwork was finally done, the edges were still dull and the surface unfinished, but it reflected the firelight unlike any other sword.

"Sure looks like it worked to me," commented Mark.

"Yes, it looks rightly like that other one," replied Drydon. "The Earl will be pleased, and that's an understatement. Now how did you say we had to do that cooling bit again?"

Mark explained one more time the technique that he and Robert had memorized. They put it into action, and then Drydon called it a night.

The large man reverently wrapped the unfinished blade in an oiled cloth and placed it on the shelf. The two were about to leave the smithy when Mark turned and went back to retrieve the cloak he had left lying on a bench. Just then, they heard voices. Both Mark and Drydon froze. Mark couldn't tell where the voices were coming from, but Drydon motioned toward the armory, next door.

"What news?" It was an unmistakably French voice. Mark had never heard it before, but by the deep frown on Drydon's face, he could tell the smith had.

"We've got all the information we need. If you can get us out, and slow down Cornuel, we'll have it done," replied a low, gruff voice.

"Don't forget to mention that the Earl isn't here. Cogniard would have our heads if he spent all this work for just a fort."

"Don't worry. We've got it all down. That's why we need to get out, fast."

The voices drifted away into the hall, then came toward the smithy. Drydon was standing frozen in the doorway when he realized they would be able to see him. He stepped back and slowly closed the heavy door. Mark breathed a sigh of relief as the door slid shut on well-oiled hinges. He started to walk back toward Drydon. Then the latch on the door fell into place.

It was the loudest click Mark had ever heard in his life. It seemed to reverberate through the shop, echoing off the solid stone walls. Mark thought it would never stop.

The footsteps outside the door stopped, as did the whispered conversation. Mark saw the door move, but it was latched shut, and didn't open. After a period of silence the footsteps receded down the hall, quieter now than before.

Drydon took a deep breath, and then turned to face Mark.

"I don't trust it. Something is going to happen."

CHAPTER 15

The next morning Robert woke refreshed and happy. He was, after all, an honored guest in an important castle. Roland was already up and impatient to start the day. He was reviewing charts and maps on a table near the door, and motioned Robert to have a look.

"See, according to the spies' first report, the island looks like it should be about here." He pointed to a spot not far from the shore. "And this..." he said, pulling a hand-drawn sketch from the stack, "is about what it looks like, from what I can decipher."

It looked like a backwards capital "B" to Robert, with a tiny castle drawn in one of the bumps. "Which way is north?" he asked.

"Up. Up is always north, on any map you draw. If you can't tell which way is up, look at the text.

"In this case, the castle is on the side of the island that faces us, although the spies tell me that the elevation on that side is higher, so you might not necessarily see it if you came from that direction."

Roland drew in several wiggly lines that went from the top of the map to the bottom. "These are elevation lines. Mind you, not any of this is very accurate, but some of us like to get an idea of where we're headed. See, all along these lines the height of the land is the same. So, if you ran along the line, the hill would slope from right to left, or left to right. Sometimes you can tell, sometimes you can't. In this case, the land slopes which way?"

"To the right," answered Robert. "Since you said the high side of the island is facing the shore."

"Correct. Now, if this was an accurate map, how would you go about attacking this castle?"

At that point, there was a knock on the door, saving Robert from thinking too hard about that question. Roland got up to open it.

It was an attendant with breakfast, served from the castle kitchens. The maps were soon replaced by a delicious-looking array of eggs and bacon.

Robert's learning didn't stop over breakfast. Roland

described the various types of siege equipment to him, explaining how they worked and should be used.

"My father once told me that it takes twice as many men to take a castle as it does to defend it. We don't necessarily have twice as many men as are in that castle. That means we need to plan more, and think of a better way to do things. That includes effective use of surprise, siege equipment, and politics."

"Kind of like the politics that got us this castle in the first place?" Robert asked with a wry grin.

"Right. Although..." Roland put down his fork and lowered his voice. "You'll find that not everyone is happy with Cogniard's ways of doing things. He likes to win. And he will win at any cost."

After breakfast Robert was allowed to explore the castle, and promptly did so in earnest. He stopped by the carpenter's shop, the cartwright's shop, the blacksmith's shop, and more. He was always interested in how things were made, and found himself enjoying the morning fully.

On his way back to the castle for lunch, he decided to stop by the stables and check on his horse. As Roland had told him, a scout's life depended on his horse and equipment and he should always be aware of the condition of his tack and horse.

Amaury was contentedly eating the hay he had just been served and he nickered quietly when Robert walked up.

Giving him a pat, Robert walked around his horse checking for cuts or bruises and inspecting his horse's feet and shoes. He noted that the shoes should be replaced soon, and figured that he had better get that done before they left for the island.

After satisfying himself that Amaury was in good shape, he left the stall and went to the tack room, where all the saddles and bridles were stored. Several young boys were in there, cleaning and polishing the castle's set of harnesses. They glanced up when he walked in, but ignored him once they realized they didn't know him.

Except one. "Hey, Robert! I haven't seen you in forever!" It was Glen, a boy several years younger than Robert, who had lived near the monastery where Robert had grown up.

"Hey, Glen. I didn't know you worked in Tynemouth Castle!"

"Well, I didn't know you were a scout! Actually, Mother and I moved to the castle grounds after our house burnt down." Robert remembered the days that they had spent at Glen's house. They were among the few days that Mark and Robert were let outside of the monastery grounds, and it was only because Robert's father somehow knew Glen's family.

Robert proceeded to tell Glen just what had happened since he saw him last, and all the stable boys were awed with the story. He soon found that they all wanted to be scouts, and looked up to him as a role model for their future escapades.

"Well, I was going to check on my tack while I was here," he mentioned, not wanting to distract them from getting their work done.

"It's right over here," one of the boys quickly said, and ran over to bring it to him. "I put your horse away when you came in."

"Good, you did a fine job," said Robert, taking the almost new saddle and bridle set. He sat down and started to go over the leather pieces, testing each joint for strength.

"Hey, you got a problem over here," said Glen, pointing to Robert's saddle. Sure enough, there were several stitches pulling out of the tough material that attached the stirrup to the saddle.

"Hmm. Whereabouts would that have happened?" Robert thought back a few days, then found himself telling the story of the ride through the woods on his first scouting trip with Roy, Ted, and the spies. Except, of course, he didn't mention the true purpose of the mission.

The boys were enthralled by the story, and Robert soon found himself retelling bits and pieces of his entire life, urged on by the eager looks and questions. Right in the middle of another story, he heard a trumpet sound.

Instantly, all the boys were on their feet.

"Army's here!"

"We've gotta help with the horses, Robert," explained Glen. "But if you want that saddle fixed, I know someone who's with the army that can fix it. Want me to show you?"

"Sure," said Robert. "But only if you're not needed with the horses first."

"Oh, that's all right. Our job is to take care of the horses, but we also take care of the people, so nobody will mind, as long as I'm not lazing around." He grabbed the saddle and led Robert out the stable door and toward the barbican.

When they reached the gate, the first contingents of the army were already streaming through the small opening. Colorful banners and brightly dressed knights contrasted with the plainly dressed scouts and the motley collection of peasants-turned-soldiers as they all pressed to get through the gate.

Forced to wait for the traffic to subside, Robert and Glen watched the army come in. Robert waved to Fulke, and beside him he could see Glen puff out his chest in pride.

After the main section of the army had filtered through the gates, the assortment of tradespeople and merchants tried to as well. They were turned back by the gate guards, however, who were well aware that the army alone would fill the entire castle to overflowing.

"Come on, Robert. They'll hafta set up shop outside the walls. We can get your saddle fixed out there." Robert followed Glen through the large gates and out onto the path that curved down the steep hill into the town.

He was stopped by Roland, who had been in conference with Cogniard just outside the gate. Robert explained what he was doing, and Roland nodded his approval, commenting, "You have a page now, I see."

Glen grinned and blushed at the same time, and Robert laughed. "Yes, I knew him from South Shields, when I lived at the monastery." Roland smiled and let him go, returning to his conference with Cogniard and the castellan, although Robert was positive there was a funny look in his eyes.

"I know who that was!" Glen almost shouted. "That was Roland! My dad knew him, when he fought for the Earl. The first one, that is."

"The first one? Oh, you mean the Earl before Cogniard."

"Yeah, he was a great earl, but apparently he plotted against the king, or something. Anyway, my dad knew him too." Robert was very aware that Glen had never known his dad.

Everything Glen knew about him his mother had told

him. Glen's father had died in this very castle, where he had been killed foiling a plot to kill the former Earl of Newcastle. Robert had heard this from his own father while staying at the monastery. He wasn't sure how his father had learned all the details, but he had been a good friend of Glen's father.

The two boys wandered among the tradesmen who were setting up their stalls outside the castle in the early afternoon sun. Soon Glen saw a stall he recognized, and pointed toward it for Robert's benefit.

"See? There's the best saddle maker in England. After all, he's my uncle." Robert grinned when he saw the place. It was the same booth that he and his friends had left so hurriedly and in such embarrassment at the last encampment.

It was too late to go back now. Glen was leading him into the stall. The old man was unpacking boxes of supplies and he looked up as they entered.

"Hello, son. How's your mother doing?"

"Fine, Uncle Bryce. I brought a customer for you."

"So I see. I think I recognize him, even."

Robert grinned. "Pleased to meet you, sir," he said. "My friends aren't with me, so whatever ruckus they would have caused --"

"Oh, don't worry about your friends. My Kate seems to

have taken a disliking to them, but they're good boys. And Kate's not here right now, so it's alright. What can I do for you?"

Robert showed him the saddle, and the old man frowned. "Under a bit of strain, was it?" he asked.

"Yes, and I had just gotten it, too."

"I can tell. It's a good saddle, though. The strain was just too much for it at the time. I can have this fixed pretty quickly. I think I could even make it stronger."

"That would be great!" Robert watched as the man set aside his unpacking and set right to work. Glen, having seen all this before, was immediately bored.

"Where's Kate, Uncle Bryce?" he asked.

"Well, I expect she's out finding her friends in the castle, as usual. They usually go down to the river... oh wait. I'm sorry, she actually headed up to your mother's house with our money. She left just before you boys came."

"Oh, let's go find her, Robert. We should be able to catch up with her." Robert followed the eager stable boy back out into the sunshine and up toward the castle again, none too sure he wanted to meet this girl his friends had such an aversion for.

Instead of leading Robert back through the main gates, Glen cut through the stream of travelers on the main road and started following the wall.

"So where are we off to now?" asked Robert.

"We always go this way. There's a small gate toward the back, and it's right by our house."

"Really. It's also right near the worst section of town, according to Roland," Robert rejoined. His words were soon proved to be true, as they started passing dilapidated shacks and thrown-together shelters. The people all stared at them hungrily. Nervous, Robert shifted the dagger on his belt closer to his hand.

"You say Kate always went this way? With money?"

"Oh yes, all the time," said Glen, oblivious to the looks they were receiving from the population of that little hut village.

"Her and what army? She'd be cleaned out immediately if she walked in here with anything halfway valuable."

"I suppose," said Glen, eyeing the poor inhabitants for the first time. "But I'm sure she hides it well."

His confidence proved to be misplaced, for as they were passing a rocky crag that stuck out into the "street," they heard Kate's unmistakable voice.

"And why do you suppose you can do that? You think you can just walk up to me and take my money?" By this time Kate had come into view, haggling with a skinny, one-toothed vagabond who eyed the sack at her waist with greed.

Robert was immediately aware of the danger. His instincts told him to run in and start pummeling the serf, but his brain stopped him. If the man was intent on the money, he wouldn't be afraid to fight for it. Also, if he started fighting, there would surely be more to help him. Furthermore, if Robert and Glen were the only ones helping Kate, the outcome of the fight wouldn't be too certain. He decided to play it safe.

Glen was looking at him, his eyes asking what to do. Robert just whispered "Stay with me," and continued walking.

It was only a few steps to the arguing duo, and the man was getting more and more demanding. Kate, on the other hand, was getting angrier by the second.

Robert walked up and stopped, standing just beside Kate. The man stopped talking, and stared at him, expecting him to say something. He didn't say a word, but just looked at the man, challenging him to continue the argument. He made sure his hand stayed far away from the dagger at his belt, attempting to portray the idea that his authority alone was enough to make anyone obey.

Finally, he made his move. "We were just passing through, I believe." He moved forward, and behind him Glen pushed Kate, still fuming, into a slow walk,. Robert could hear the man's ragged breath, but he didn't look back. Then Glen whispered, "He left!"

Robert turned and grinned at the boy. "Worked, didn't it?"

"Well, wouldn't it have been easier if you had just given him a good punch?" asked Glen, somewhat disappointed. Robert could see he hadn't been up to a fight either.

"Scouts try to think before they do, Glen. How many friends do you think that man had?"

"I don't care how many friends he had, he would have let me by without anyone's help," stormed Kate. "I don't need every random 'gentleman' in the county trailing me to make sure I'm-"

"You were wondering how many friends he had, Robert? That would be about two. And they have knives." Glen sounded worried. Kate stopped talking, her point obviously lost. Just ahead of them stood the same man. Two others stood next to him, greedy eyes glistening.

Robert started to think quickly. They were on a fairly steep hillside, and he could get an advantage by trying to knock some of his opponents down the hill to their right. They might be able to come back up, but it would take time. He calculated the amount of time they had, then slipped his dagger out of its sheath and passed it to Glen, who had come up to his side.

"Stay calm, and walk right behind me. Keep the guy on the left occupied, if you can." They walked in a line, directly for the gap between the man on the left, who was their original challenger, and the other two; one of them was heavyset and balding, the other a grinning, snaggle-toothed farmer.

Without slowing, Robert walked right up to them, as though he would go through. They were somewhat surprised, but Robert could see that they weren't planning to be fooled this time.

The instant he thought they would attack, he turned to the right and gave the fat man a shove, knocking him into the farmer. The farmer lost his balance and rolled down the hill, as Robert had hoped, but the larger man grabbed Robert's arm and gave him a yank that sprawled him unceremoniously into the dust.

Lights danced in Robert's eyes, and he rolled onto his back, kicking out with both feet blindly at the shadow that was hovering over him. He felt his feet contact the man's stomach, and heard a deep groan.

Just as he was beginning to get his sight back, he saw a knife flashing down toward him. His hand was up in an instant, deflecting the blow. Unfortunately, the knife was redirected right toward him.

Robert felt the pain ripping through his face as the knife cut cleanly across his temple. Rolling, he shook the blood out of his eyes and put his hand up to block against a second blow. None came.

When he got back on his feet, he saw Kate grappling with

the man who had the knife. In his seconds of planning, Robert hadn't even considered her help, although he was glad to have it now.

Her aid had come at the perfect moment, but there was no way she could overpower the fat man with the knife, who was already wrenching his hand away and maneuvering for a stab.

Robert was there in an instant, grabbing the man's free arm and pinning it behind his back. Then he rotated, tripping the man and slamming him against the ground. With him safely pinned, he looked up to check on the other men.

Glen was gamely fighting the one-toothed predator, although his knife was now gone and he was half of his opponent's size. He was desperately hanging on to the man's right hand, which held the knife.

Kate was already on her way over, and Robert turned his glance to the hill, where he could see the farmer was just making it back onto the road way, crouching and not looking too healthy.

Knowing he couldn't fight one man while pinning another, Robert brought his hand down on the base of the farmer's neck, hoping Brother Arnold had showed him the right spot.

He must have remembered something, at least. The man sighed, then fainted, and Robert turned to see a heavy hand swinging his direction. He sprang up just in time to block his new opponent's blow. Then he backed off, trying to get an opportunity to trip him. As he did, he heard shouts on the wall, and saw a watchman leaning over.

"The guard is on the way!" he shouted.

Robert had other things to worry about. His opponent was charging, so he sidestepped, then stuck out his foot and gave the man a shove. He toppled down the hill once again. Robert didn't give him a second glance.

Glen had seen how Robert had brought the fat man down, and he repeated the move, still hanging onto his opponent's knife arm. Just as the sound of running feet reached their ears, Glen had knocked his opponent off balance and managed to pull the knife from his grasp. He now used it to keep the man still, with Kate's help.

The guard immediately took over. With a glance at Robert, the leader ordered his men to truss up the three would-be thieves. The farmer tried to run, but was soon outpaced by the more athletic guards and hauled back.

"If you please, sir, could you accompany me to the guardhouse to explain the situation, and lodge a complaint?" the officer of the guard asked politely, and Robert assented. Then Robert turned toward Glen, who was whispering to Kate.

"I suggest you accompany this lady to her destination,

Glen. She might need someone to protect the robbers from her."

Uncharacteristically, Kate turned and said, "Thank you, Robert."

Robert grinned. "Anytime, for a cousin of Glen's."

CHAPTER 16

After morning topics the next day, the boys reported to the smithy as usual. When they walked through the door into the brightly lit shop, Mark looked at the latch and couldn't believe it was the same room that had been so tense last night.

It wasn't. Drydon was missing. In his place was Allen, his back to the furnace, arms crossed on his chest, and a scowl on his face. After the boys had all entered, he began to speak.

"Drydon is not here today. You will commence making the various fittings that Ruskin needs for his work. He will show you how." Allen motioned to a slight man in the shadow of the flue, and walked briskly out.

John Ruskin was the tailor, but he also made harnesses and bridles, as well as anything else a man could devise from a combination of leather and metal. He was skilled in his trade, and he soon had the boys producing what he needed.

Saddles, bridles, and other pieces of tack in all shapes and sizes were cut from freshly cured leather and sewn up. For every four horseshoes, Mark reminded himself, there was a horse that needed a saddle and a bridle, and these could break as fast as a shoe could be thrown, especially in a battle. Thankfully, there was plenty of tack on the island already.

The new activities made the time fly, and soon the work period was over. Mark went to the armory and sat down with his back against the wall next to Ijn. He had already told Ijn about the secret conversation the night before. He was about to mention that Drydon was gone when Ijn stood up. Motioning Mark to follow him, he walked into one of the siege weapon mounts.

"I saw one of your two friends," Ijn said in a low voice. "I was measuring land for the pasture, and I found a boat. It was camouflaged well, and sitting upside down, close to the shore."

Ijn paused, then continued. "I kept going and when I was a good distance away, I turned and saw somebody near the boat. He put something down, and left. I waited a bit, and then went back to the boat. He had put a box of papers underneath it, and there were several more boxes as well."

"They're leaving soon," commented Mark. "Just like the one guy wanted."

"It can't be any later than tomorrow, and it will probably be tonight, when it's dark," said Ijn. "We should go tell Allen."

Then Mark remembered Drydon, and mentioned that he hadn't been in the shop. "Let's see where he is, and get him to come with us. It'll lend some more credibility to our story."

The boys left the observation area and entered the armory. They decided to take a few of the boys with them, just in case they ran into the upperclassmen. The situation was still tense, even if the younger boys did have their freedom.

The group walked down the hall to the spiral stairs and entered the lower floors, where everyone else lived. Drydon's room was near the end, and there were several vacant rooms adjacent to and across from it which had belonged to sailors who had accompanied the Earl on his overdue voyage. When they reached the smith's room the door was slightly ajar. Mark pushed it open, then stepped back in shock.

The room was a mess. Clothes were strewn across the floor, dresser drawers were hanging askew, and the bed was unmade. Random objects were lying all around the room, and several pieces of parchment were ripped up on the floor. But that wasn't what shocked him.

Drydon wasn't in his room, but Lord Cornuel was, as well as Ijn's father and several other high-ranking officers. There were officers everywhere. It was a full-fledged meeting, and Mark had just barged right into it.

Lord Cornuel spoke. "If you're looking for Drydon, he isn't available right now. Please close the door when you leave." The boys quickly backed out, and walked up the stairs.

"Yikes! What was that?" asked Mark

"Drydon was never that messy. I can almost guarantee there was a fight in there," said Ijn.

"And Drydon's gone," said one of the other boys.

"It has to be those two. They must know, or must have guessed that Drydon heard them," said Ijn. "And you know what that means."

"I'm next," said Mark. "If they know I was there."

"Either way, we're going to Allen now," said Ijn. "I'm not taking any chances on having you abducted."

They knocked on Allen's door and were told to enter. Mark and Ijn went in, and the others waited in the hall. Mark told Allen what he and Drydon had heard, then Ijn told him what he had found near the beach.

Thomas Allen frowned, squinting his eyes, and rubbed his chin with his hand. "All right, boys," he said. "Don't say anything about this to anyone else. We'll take care of any problems." The two boys nodded and left, returning to the armory with the group.

As they entered the armory, they heard Allen's door open and close, and the sound of running feet echoed down the hall. He wasn't wasting any time. The boys noticed that it was already getting dark outside, and before several minutes had passed they heard a column of men passing by quickly, weapons clanking.

After conversing for a while, the boys started to drift off to their beds. Mark and Ijn left with their groups and were soon preparing for bed.

The upperclassmen began to make trouble almost immediately. One wanted his clothes brought to the laundry. Several of his friends were ready to help enforce his demand. They were on the other side of the dormitory, and when Mark reached the spot he saw that one of them was Harold. He and his friends were standing by a pile of their clothes, demanding that Sven take care of them. Mark wondered why the upperclassmen insisted on continuing this fight. They had been humiliated the last several times.

Then he noticed something. There were more than a

couple upperclassmen in the room, and they were all waiting for trouble. They had staged this so they could have a numerical advantage. Harold had placed several people on each side of the room acting rather nonchalant. Not only that, but Mark remembered seeing several older boys out in the hall. He figured the boys in the hall could do one of two things: they could join the fight from behind, or prevent the boys left in the armory from helping.

He approached Ijn. "We're rather out-manned right now," he said.

"You're right," Ijn replied in a low voice. "The upperclassmen in the hall won't let the other two groups out if they try to help."

"We're going to get pounded if we make a fuss," Edward commented. "A tactical withdrawal might be in order."

"You mean chicken out?" snorted Mark.

"I'm going to go with Ed and call it 'foxing out,'" said Ijn. "We have the brains on our side. Let's use 'em."

As the boys discussed their options, the upperclassmen became more and more insistent, and Sven was getting nervous. The boys were standing around, unsure of what to do, watching the discussion. They had all expected a dirty fight, and not many had missed the large number of older boys.

"Let's just have Sven do what they say, and pick our fights better in the future," said Ijn.

"I don't like the idea of giving up either," said Edward, "but I can't see that we have victory as an option."

They were leaning up against the stone wall of the boys' barracks, and Mark was frowning deeply. The argument across the room had stopped, and it was quiet. Mark looked up to see Harold standing in front of their little group. He had a triumphant smile on his face and he said, "You're right. Your only options are give in or get it bad." He sat there, the smug look on his face, watching the group. Mark pushed himself away from the wall and Harold tensed, ready to fight.

"I'll take your clothes. You don't need Sven to do it." Mark looked Harold in the eye as he spoke. The older boy grinned and motioned to the clothes scornfully. Mark walked over to Sven and nodded to him, then picked up the clothes and walked out the door.

The group of boys sat stunned, and then one of the older boys commented, "Well. The castaway loses again." Younger boys scowled, confused, but Ijn suddenly caught on.

"The laundry isn't the only place he can bring your clothes, Harold," he said calmly. In an instant, the older boys, led by Harold, dashed out of the room in pursuit of Mark. He was just walking into the armory past a group of confused upperclassmen who had expected to keep the boys in, not out. Strolling past the oblivious younger boys still in the armory, he headed for the observation posts.

When the older boys stormed in, he broke into a run, dodging shelves and people on his way outside. Harold had just come out of the armory when Mark threw the pile of clothes into the bay.

Pandemonium broke loose. Harold and his group attacked Mark. The younger boys instantly attacked from the armory. The odds were easily in favor of the younger boys now, but Mark was isolated in the observation post, his back to the stone, fending off several people at once. Almost instantly, he realized he couldn't last long alone. He put his head down and charged into the group of upperclassmen toward the rest of his friends.

Hands grabbed at him from all sides, and he quickly lost his footing in the mess of moving feet. Harold had him in a headlock, so he grabbed the older boy and pulled him down as well. He rolled to the right and left, knocking people over on top of them. When he had broken Harold's hold, he struggled to his feet and jumped through the mess of tangled limbs to his friends.

As soon as Mark had gotten out, Ijn pulled all the boys back into the armory, where they stood a better chance of winning, because they outnumbered the upperclassmen and could surround them easily.

When the older boys walked out of the observation area, the fight had gone out of them. They knew they were only going to get pummeled if they started the fight again. Harold was still as mad as a hornet, but Mark noticed two others conspicuously standing next to him, ready to hold him back. Mark had heard the comment as he left the barracks, and he couldn't resist throwing it back at them.

"Well. The castaway wins again, eh?" The boys laughed as they saw the necks of several upperclassmen turn a brilliant shade of red.

"We still have to go back to the barracks, Mark," Ijn said. "Remember, they sleep in the same room."

"I wonder if we could do something about that?" Mark said. "Allen might put us all in one room."

"Allen is way too busy to worry about us," said Ijn. "Besides, we don't want to bug him too often."

"I don't think they'll want to fight after this," said Edward, walking over from the other side of the room. The others were arranged in the semi-circle that Ijn had placed them into to counter the possible attack from the observation posts.

The group all filed out of the arsenal and into the two rooms. The upperclassmen were already in bed, and the younger boys, getting ready for bed themselves, did nothing to antagonize them.

Just before they got in, Mark went to Ijn and said, "I still wonder what's happening with Drydon. If he's gone because he heard what I heard, then I don't feel really comfortable. These people aren't as dull as the upperclassmen. You can't just fool them."

"You're just gonna have to stay with your group all the time, and--"

"Listen..."

The boys quieted as they heard the clank of armor. The men were returning from Allen's expedition. Both Mark and Ijn got up and went to the open door. The group filed past, their armor muddy, and two of them turned in at Allen's room.

"Doesn't look like they got him," commented Ijn. "If they had, they would have brought him to Allen."

"Or Cornuel and the other officers," said Mark.

"I doubt it," said Ijn. "Allen generally takes care of everything and then reports it all to the officers."

They were still standing there when Allen's door opened and the two men came out. After them came Allen, who started down the hall in the boys' direction, but stopped when he saw them and motioned them into his room.

They sat in the chairs in front of his desk, and he took his seat behind it. The old chair groaned with his weight as he leaned back and rubbed his chin, frowning as usual.

"Tell me again exactly what you saw and heard," he commanded. The boys related their story again, and this time Allen took notes, not missing anything, and asking questions in his gruff way.

"You realize that one of these men could still be here, right?" he asked.

"I figured that," Mark answered.

"Would you be able to recognize his voice if you heard him talking?" asked Allen.

"I don't know. He was in the next room. I could try if you wanted, but I can't guarantee anything."

Allen sat there, thinking, then said, "I'm going to choose to trust you, for reasons beyond what you know. I need your help. You may have noticed that there is somewhat of a dissension among several of the hired men. What you saw was almost definitely a spy from Cogniard. When you put infiltrators with dissatisfied people, you get big trouble. This isn't even the beginning of what could happen. I need you and your groups to keep an eye out for anything suspicious, like you have done. I need you to let me know anything you see, and quickly.

"Your problems with the upperclassmen are your fault, and they need to disappear. We can't have that kind of thing going on right now. If Cogniard's man is smart, he could use it to pull both sides of the fight to him."

"If you don't mind..." Mark ventured.

"Go ahead."

"It would help a lot if we were in separate rooms. They wouldn't dare come in ours, and we wouldn't want to go in theirs, and--"

"I'll have it done in a day. Keep it quiet until then."

Chapter 17

After reporting to the guard house, where his face was quickly and professionally bandaged, Robert headed out to see Glen and Kate again. However, as soon as he walked out of the door of the guard house he realized that he still didn't know where Glen lived.

So instead of visiting them, he headed to the keep to see if he could track down Roland and be of some help. After all, he thought guiltily, that was what he was supposed to be doing here.

Roland was in the main hall, arguing with several of the overly-dressed courtiers who always accompanied Cogniard. Cogniard was also watching, but not taking part. Benedict stood to the side, and motioned Robert over when he saw him enter.

"They can never agree, whether it be on soup for supper or weapons for war. Roland is just a completely different character than these imported geniuses," Benedict said, a sarcastic lilt on the last words.

"So what is it?" asked Robert, smiling. "Soup or weapons?"

"Soup. It's the supply system for the men once we get them on the island. Roland wants to get all the men on the island first, then ship in the food, but these boys would rather send each group with its own supplies. Roland's right, but really, I mean, it's not that big of a deal."

Robert grinned. He could see that Cogniard agreed with Benedict. Just then, Roland saw him and took the moment to excuse himself.

"Hello, Robert. What have you been up to? Fought with a tree?" he asked.

"Yeah, the new leaves were really getting to me and I had to do something about it. Actually, it was three men who were trying to steal some money from a friend of mine."

"I take it they only tried, then. They didn't actually get it?"

"No, but they have a better bed to sleep in now that they're in the guard house." Robert went on to tell the story, not forgetting to compliment Glen and Kate. And he recommended that Roland keep an eye on Glen, as a potential future recruit.

"Well, with all the fighting over, I've got to show you how to handle some of the less interesting, but often more important, parts of leadership. We've been moved, too. We're now billeted with the scouts just inside the castle's postern gate, where we can leave on short notice if needed. I suppose we could have stayed in the keep, but I figured you would want to be with the men."

Robert read between the lines and interpreted his last statement as a suggestion of what he should want, if he ever became a scout leader.

Roland nodded to Benedict, and then led Robert out to the scout's camp, where tents were set up in random order, leaving a clear passage to the small postern gate.

The tent they entered was the largest one, and it had a portable desk and several chairs which were intended to seat Roland's officers. Robert took one and pulled it up to the desk where Roland had just sat.

"So, we've got this many scouts, and they eat this much food a day," Roland started, pointing out numbers on a piece of paper. "We need to figure out how much food we need for our stay at the castle, and how much food we should have brought to the island for each day that we stay there. And, we need to find out how much that costs."

This was something Robert was good at, although he

could just imagine Mark groaning at the thought of it, and couldn't help grinning.

"Think it's funny, eh?" asked Roland. "I could give you loads of this stuff all day, and you'd think it was better than a show."

Robert laughed, and told him what he had been thinking. Roland nodded.

"We never really forget about the people we've lost. Believe me. I've lost quite a few."

Robert agreed. He had thought of his brother, as well as his father, more and more often as time went on. But he couldn't let that hold him back. He picked up the pen and went to work.

It was several hours later when Roland leaned back and stretched. "That's it!" he said. "I've enough ink on my fingers. Let's go get a breath of fresh air."

Outside in the street, a lively group of scouts was playing "gameball," where a pigskin stuffed with dried peas was kicked, hit, or thrown in order to get it from one goal to the other. Robert immediately joined in, and found himself opposed not only by other scouts, but by quite a few of the castle dwellers themselves.

It was a long, lively game, and the sides were evenly matched. After an hour of trying to get the pigskin into the opposing team's goal, which was the postern gate, he dropped out. Returning to Roland's tent, he ducked back into the semi-darkness.

"Robert, right?" a voice said from one of the corners. "Roland said you were free until after supper. He'll meet you at the archery butts as soon as the meal is over."

Robert thanked the man, who was one of Roland's officers, and left the tent. He decided to go down to see if his saddle was done.

It was late afternoon when he ducked into the saddle-maker's shop, and he found the old man stitching away on what appeared to be a brand-new saddle.

"Hello, son. Your saddle is right over there in that corner. She's as good as new."

"Thank you, uh, Uncle Bryce?"

The man laughed.

"The name's Bryce Fendrel, but you can call me Bryce, that's fine."

Robert inspected his saddle and found it to be repaired quite well.

"How much do I owe you for this, Bryce?" he asked.

"Nothing at all, seeing that bandage on your face. Kate and Glen stopped in here earlier, and told me what happened. Thank you very much, and if there is anything else I can do for you, I'd be glad to do it."

"Oh, it wasn't a problem, really. It was interesting, though. I've never really fought in earnest with anyone before."

"Oh, you will, though. You're in the scouts, right? Don't be lazy. You'll need every bit of training you're ever going to have. Even if it's for one moment, once in your life, it can make the difference between life and death." Robert thought of Roy's shot in the woods, and agreed.

Bryce continued. "I wasn't a scout, but I did fight. I was a man-at-arms for the old Earl of Newcastle, and I would be still today if I could lift a sword that size again. Now I'm stuck with a needle. A little smaller, but just as sharp."

Robert took a seat on a nearby saddle rack. "So your brother was a soldier too, I hear," he said. "And a bodyguard to the Earl himself. So, what do you think about supporting the army that's going to attack him?"

"Well, I could refuse to support it, but that would be akin to being exiled, since nobody gets far here without Cogniard's permission. Most people are fine with that. As they say, rulers come, and rulers go."

"You don't sound like you're fine with that."

"I'm not. But, as I said, I don't have much of a choice. I just try to forget that I have anything to do with the army in this business. If my brother were here, he probably wouldn't agree.

"Cogniard isn't such a good man. He's a brave leader and a friendly man, but at the same time he's cruel and underhanded. Not like the last earl, who was always fair, at least."

"So if Cogniard is bad, and the last Earl was good, why does everyone here sit down and just take it?" Robert asked.

"Well, first of all, quite a few people moved in when Cogniard came. That was his way of trying to influence public opinion. Second, most people really didn't care. Those people are starting to wake up now, but most still don't think there is enough reason to worry. And they're right. Cogniard hasn't gone out of his way to offend anyone, and if he's unfair, at least he's unfair to everyone."

Robert snorted. "Well, I'm not in a position to say anything, seeing as though I eat his food. But you've given me a bit to think about. I'm going to go down into town and talk to Brother Arnold."

Slipping back out into the street, he grimaced at the thought of carrying his saddle all the way back into South Shields. Better to wait until the next day, when he didn't have a saddle to carry around.

After the meal, this time in the scouts' camp, he headed outside the castle to the archery butts, where Roland was waiting for him.

"How are your archery skills?" he asked when Robert walked up. Robert hesitated.

"Well, I was decent at one time, but I haven't practiced in a while, so..."

"Well, let's see, then. Take your bow and give it a try. Every scout needs to know more than one weapon, and the bow is the most important. By law, you should be practicing with it fairly frequently. Also by law, you shouldn't be playing gameball either."

"By law? Why?"

"Well, because it takes away from the time you should have to practice with your bow. England depends on its archers, and the past several kings have ordered mandatory longbow practice and outlawed gameball because it keeps people away from their bows. Not that anyone cares."

Robert accepted the bow from Roland and pulled an arrow from the multitude supplied by the castle's pages. Taking aim at the furthest target, he let the arrow fly.

Both watched as the arrow flew in a graceful arc, burying itself into the ground ten feet from the target.

"I can tell somebody isn't in practice," Robert said, grinning. "I think I'll be a lawful citizen for the next few days."

"I don't know who told you what was good or bad, but that was the farthest butt, and you came pretty close for not being in practice. But I agree. You will be a lawful citizen every day from breakfast to lunch."

Robert didn't reply, but picked up another arrow, and let it fly. This time he overshot the target by about the same distance.

"Well, I'm going to start now," he said. And he did, practicing with the bow until the sun dipped below the hills, and the pages began to pick up the used arrows and stow them away in a small outbuilding.

On the way back from the butts, Robert realized he was happy having something scheduled to do. He decided that from then on, every day he had free he would practice archery in the morning, and see if he couldn't find a spot to practice his horsemanship on Amaury sometime as well.

CHAPTER 18

The next few days in Mark's life were relatively uneventful. Work continued on the castle, and it was now showing serious signs of improvement. The outer walls, kept for last, were just being repaired. They could be seen from miles away by even the most dull lookout, who might report any repairs to his lord.

The stables, a group of low buildings to the north of the castle, were progressing nicely. The smithy still churned out useful parts and pieces for every workman on the island. But no one knew how to make weapons except Drydon, and he hadn't been seen for days.

It was a warm day near the end of the week when Cornuel announced a break in the work. The castle boys could have the day off to relax and enjoy the weather.

Mark and his friends trooped out of the barracks. They had no particular plans for the day, but they were in deep discussion as they walked along. The fate of the castle and the whereabouts of Cogniard were foremost among the topics, and the boys debated them vigorously.

"There's no way Cogniard could know where we are. This island looks as deserted as it did when we came here," stated Rich.

"You can't forget the boat that got away," reminded Jan.

"It would have to be a good-sized boat to make it to land, and it wasn't that big, was it, Ijn?" asked Rich.

"It wouldn't be really comfortable or safe, but it could've made it from here to shore on a calm day," replied Ijn. "And it was calm that night."

"So what happens when Cogniard gets the message that we're here?" asked Pieter. "Does he have an army on hand, waiting to attack us? If he does, it must've cost a pretty penny to keep it all these months."

"Speaking of which, he must be pretty discouraged, not having seen hide nor hair of us since last year," commented Louis, the only one who had been with the Earl on the mainland.

"Or just happy, because he doesn't have to worry about us," said Jan.

The discussion continued as the boys made their way

along the seashore, their feet compacting the wet sand. The water was still too cold to swim in, but the weather was just right for a walk along the shore. As they neared the stables, they could see a number of people crowded there, and soon one broke off and ran toward them.

It was Alfred, the boy Mark had helped in sword practice, and he seemed excited. "The sergeant set up the lists for tilting, and we're all going to have a try at it," he said breathlessly. The boys quickened their pace toward the stable, always ready for a bit of horseback riding. When they reached the tilting grounds, there was already a line of eager participants, waiting for a turn at the game.

It was a simple process in which a post, with a ring attached to it, was set into the ground. The aim was for the rider to put the end of the lance through the ring and take it off. This was a surprisingly hard thing to do, because the heavy lance required substantial strength in the arm. On top of that, the horse would be shifting sideways to keep its balance at top speed. This made a tricky combination for any level of rider.

The first riders were mocked with much vigor as they all failed to come anywhere close to the target. The number of mocking voices, however, gradually disappeared as one by one they each failed to meet their own standard.

By this time most of the boys had already had a try, except for Mark, his friends, and several of the older boys, who were content to watch for the time being.

Seeing that Mark hadn't tried his hand yet, Harold swaggered over. "So, Mark, I bet you think you can do this too," he said. He turned to his friends. "You think the monks taught Mark how to ride a horse?" They all laughed dutifully. He turned back to Mark. "I highly doubt you can."

Mark just smiled. "You just want me to challenge you," he said.

"You're right. I bet I can get it faster than you can," Harold replied.

"I've never tried it before," said Mark, "but I wouldn't mind starting now."

Harold smiled triumphantly, and raised his voice. "Clear the lists. Mark says he can do this in fewer tries than me."

Mark knew it was useless to protest; excited voices were already spreading the rumor that Mark had challenged Harold.

The current occupants of the arena moved out of the way as Harold herded Mark over to a group of horses. "Pick a good one, because you're going to need it," he remarked, leering. Mark walked around the group, finally picking a small roan with a white stripe. It was easily the smallest horse there, but to Mark it looked more nimble than the others, and what he had already seen of it was good.

A young boy led the horse over to a large stump and

threw a saddle on him. Mark jumped onto the broad back and grabbed the reins. He hadn't ridden a horse in months, but he still felt fairly confident.

Harold rode over on a large destrier, or warhorse, dwarfing Mark's small mount. Harold looked slightly uncomfortable as well, and Mark figured that the horses hadn't had much use in the past year.

Harold began. "Right," he said. "This is how we're going to do it. We'll ride toward the post, and take a try at the ring. If we don't get it, we go around again, and repeat until we do. If we both get it on the same turn, it's a tie, so we go around until one person gets it and the other doesn't."

"Sounds fine to me," Mark replied.

The two boys rode their mounts over to the small pyramid of stones that marked the starting point, and turned them around. With a kick of his heels, Harold sent his horse dashing toward the post, and Mark quickly urged his mount to follow.

The hooves of Harold's horse kicked up clouds of dust, and Mark could just see the post approaching at a rapid pace. Though the haze, he could just make out Harold's lance missing the ring by inches, and then the post was only a few feet ahead. He steadied the heavy wooden lance, and aimed it directly at the center of the ring.

The post flew by, and Mark had to look back to see if he

had caught the ring. It was still hanging there, swinging slightly from the passing of his horse. He cantered his horse back around behind Harold, who was already headed full tilt at the ring.

The second and third tries ended the same as the first: neither contestant came anywhere close to the ring. On the fourth try, however, Harold struck the ring with his lance, and the jar caused it to fall off.

Mark pulled his mount to an abrupt stop, and waited for Harold to come around. The horse was breathing hard but still reasonably energetic, pawing at the dusty ground. As Harold trotted up on his horse, he was in an exceptionally foul mood. Neither contestant had expected it to take this long, and the question now was whether or not Harold had won.

Harold, of course, was adamant that knocking the ring off was as good as spearing it on his lance, but the large group of younger boys were equally sure that it was not. The matter was settled when even Harold's friends sided with Mark, and both boys pulled their horses around for another try.

This time, Harold pierced the ring on his first try, and as Mark rode by the post, Harold was replacing the ring. Mark came around again and headed straight for the post.

This was it: the last try he had to show that he was Harold's equal, if not his better. He felt the muscles of the horse's back rippling under the blanket, and the coarse mane whipped up in his face as he leaned forward in concentration. The dust swirled, and he squinted his eyes as a gust of wind pushed it toward him. Then the post swept by.

He could have blamed it on the horse's mane, the wind, or the dust, but as he rode back to his friends, he had no excuse. They helped him off as Harold jeered and mocked; then they headed back to the stables together. The rest of the boys stayed at the tilting yard, unsure of how to react to this unsettling defeat.

On the way to the castle, they passed the well, and Mark stopped there to clean himself. "I'll catch up in a bit," he said, lowering the bucket.

The fresh, cool water felt good on his hot, dusty face as he poured it over his head. It soaked half of his shirt, but he didn't care. He sat down next to the well and let the warm sun soak into his skin.

As he sat there with his eyes closed, somebody came up and sat down next to him.

"You realize that Harold has been doing this all his life? He's out of practice, but there isn't anybody here that can beat him when it comes to the tiltyard."

The voice sounded vaguely familiar to Mark, and when he opened his eyes, his suspicions were confirmed. It was Lukas sitting next to him.

"I really didn't challenge him, but I guess he wanted to be proud of himself for something. I should've known not to even answer him," Mark said.

"You know, he's not that bad of a guy anyway," Lukas said. Mark snorted.

"No, seriously, he wasn't that bad when you weren't here. It's just that when you came, you challenged his little monarchy, and he's been in a bad mood ever since."

"And it serves him right," asserted Mark. "He has no right to do what he does."

"No, he doesn't, but it's not like he's viciously trying to make life bad for anyone younger than him," replied Lukas.

"Well, you believe what you want, but I think he is."

"Actually," continued Lukas, "he's interested in metalwork, same as you."

Mark was reluctant to accept that Harold could be a normal human being, but after a good half-hour, he grudgingly agreed to at least be civil to him. After all, Allen had also told him that it was in the best interests of the castle. With this decision made, Mark stood up and headed back into the keep.

As he headed down the spiral stairs to the boys' barracks, he decided to keep away from Harold and at least to act normal toward him. He didn't really want to make trouble, but he still didn't like the idea of serving the upperclassmen.

As soon as he walked into the armory his good intentions flew out the window. Harold and his friends were standing in a group around Mark's friends, and they were in a shouting match that would have hurt anybody's ears.

The instant Harold saw Mark, he redirected his wrath toward him.

"Who do you think you are? Do you think you can touch my stuff and get away with it?" he shouted, his voice shaking with anger.

"I already told you, Harold. *Mark hasn't been down here yet,*" shouted Rich. "There's no way--"

"Shut up! I'm not talking to you anymore. I'm talking to this fleabag here." He pointed at Mark.

"What do you want?" asked Mark, annoyed and confused, and well on the way to becoming angry.

"My bed is trashed, my gear is ruined, and you're the culprit!" Harold fairly screamed.

"I didn't touch your moldy st-- uh!"

Harold's fist connected solidly into Mark's stomach, spinning him backwards and into the wall. Mark pushed himself off the wall and hurtled back at Harold, but Pieter had already shoved him into his group of friends.

As Mark headed his way, one of the upperclassmen extended his foot and tripped him. He fell forward and into Pieter, who tripped, spinning to the ground. Mark could see Harold's foot heading their way, but it was stopped by Ijn as he jumped over Mark and Pieter.

The fight was well-balanced, the lower number of upperclassmen holding their own. The very fact that it was such a close fight ensured that it continued unabated.

As Mark was fighting with one of the upperclassmen, he shoved him backwards, knocking him into the rack of swords. The upperclassman, whose name was Anthony, turned to the rack and grabbed one of the light swords, lifting it off its pegs and bringing it to bear on Mark. He was about to say something when Mark slammed into him, ripping the sword out of his hand. He broke away and swung the sword in a wide arc, slamming the flat of the blade on Anthony's shoulder.

A second later, Harold grabbed a sword and singled out Mark. They began to hack away at each other ceaselessly. The others soon dropped out of the fight from fatigue, pain, or both, but Mark and Harold never stopped. Their dueling swords cut through the air, only biting into flesh on rare occasions. Both were skilled swordsmen.

As the fight continued, Mark began to get tired, and it showed. As he and Harold moved around, circling each other and watching for an opening, his movements became slower and slower. The point of his sword began to drop, and it took more and more effort to effectively block Harold's thrusts. A key parry, however, left him with a chance at a strike, and he took it. The point of his blade ripped across Harold's sword-arm. The wound was not large, but it soon became apparent that Mark was gaining despite his weariness.

It was at this point that Mark remembered what Lukas had been telling him about Harold. He began thinking about how this fight had started, and he realized that all this must have been a misunderstanding. He had no idea what Harold was accusing him of, and he hadn't done anything to offend him.

Mark stopped pressing Harold, took a step back, and dropped his sword. It clattered to the floor in the sudden silence.

Harold looked scornfully at him, as though he were an idiot. His knuckles were white as he gripped the hand-and-a-half sword he had taken off the rack.

Then Mark spoke. "Look, Harold, let's stop this right now. We can work this out later. I don't want to hurt--" He jumped aside as Harold took a broad swipe at him.

He wasn't fast enough. The sword cut into his unprotected side, and bowled him over into the hard-packed dirt. Harold had the sword back in play instantly and stood over Mark, but he was tackled by his friends. Mark was left on the ground, unconscious.

CHAPTER 19

Robert was out at the butts early the next morning. The cool spring air felt good on his skin, and he liked the "twang" of the bow as it sent the arrow flying across the sky.

He was getting his instinct back, he thought. Each arrow got closer and closer to its target. He didn't only practice on one target, but on every target, switching positions and styles as well as the hand he used.

Robert quickly found that, while seemingly easy to do, four hours of archery practice was dull and tiring. This convinced him even more to vary his shooting style, and by the time lunch came, he had improved his skill with his left hand as well as his right. He also tried standing, sitting, kneeling, and even lying on the ground, although with varying degrees of accuracy.

After grabbing lunch from the castle kitchens, he walked down to the stables with bread in one hand and water in the other. His bow was strapped across his back, the string coiled in a pouch in his pocket, and a feather in his cap, just like every other scout in the castle.

When he got to the stable he let Amaury eat what was left of the bread. Politely declining the eager stable boys' help, he saddled up and rode out of the castle.

He was heading for a plot of land that he had spotted from the castle walls. It was a series of rolling hills with clumps of timber and numerous fallen trees. There was also a large field nearby, and Robert hoped it was relatively smooth. He wanted to try his bow from Amaury's back.

The ground proved to be quite to his liking, and he started off by testing his horse on several fallen limbs. The young sorrel eagerly jumped the obstacles, and Robert was satisfied enough to try some larger tree trunks. Soon he was pointing Amaury at logs that were several feet above the ground.

Having proved his horse's ability, he rode over to the large field and pulled Amaury to a stop. His eyes scanned the edges, looking for a suitable target. A large stump stood out and, gauging the distance carefully, he took a practice shot.

Happy with his initial try, he nudged Amaury into a walk, then slowly brought him up to a gallop, taking shots along the way. When he passed the stump, he reigned in and rode over to inspect his success.

The first arrow, fired from a standstill, had hit the stump, but it was the only one. All the others were spread out from five feet all the way up to thirty feet from the stump. Shaking his head in frustration, he picked up the arrows and placed them back in the quiver, determined to do better the next time.

He tried again, and then again, each time learning that it wasn't as easy as it looked to hit a target from the back of a moving horse. He was getting better, but not nearly as quickly as when he had re-learned normal archery.

Finally becoming tired, he dismounted and led his equally tired mount at a walk toward the stump. He tied Amaury's reins to a low hanging branch in the nearby forest, and then sat down on the stump and put his head in his arms, resting.

After a few minutes he heard a voice in front of him.

"Good evening to you, sir."

"And to you," he replied, lifting his head from his arms. The man in front of him was in his late twenties, athletic, and looked quite alert. His eyes were constantly scanning the area around him, even as he smiled back at Robert.

"Out for a little archery practice, eh? I always was fond of the bow. But the sword comes in handy as well, don't forget. Even to a scout."

"You look like you could be a scout, the way you watch everything. I didn't even hear you come up." Robert was surprised this man wasn't a scout, given Roland's eye for talent.

"Well, there are more that want me to be a scout. But I have other loyalties in life as well." He left it at that, and continued to discuss seemingly unimportant things.

Robert wasn't completely untrained in the art of getting people to talk, and he saw very well what this man was doing. The conversation went from his position as scout, to his duties, and all the way back to his life at the monastery. But Robert trusted the man. He didn't know why, but the voice sounded clear and honest.

When the man asked his opinion of the former earl, Robert knew instantly why he was probing. He gave an evasive answer.

"I grew up in the monastery, as you know. The monks weren't real keen on having the main topic of the day be politics." Robert noticed the young man's eye sharpen.

"So. What is your opinion now, then?"

"Well, I have this feeling that you want me to say I'm all for him and he's much better than Cogniard, but unfortunately for you I'm not going to say that. I do work for Cogniard after all, and owe him, as well as Roland, a great deal for the position I'm in now. I've got a future, which I wouldn't have if I hadn't met either one of them."

The man nodded. "You'll come around, yet. I'm Tim, by the way. Pleased to meet you." He shook hands with Robert. "Either way you think on the topic, I'd like you to go to 87 Low Friar's. Tell the Brother I sent you." He turned and walked away. Robert gaped after him.

87 Low Friar's... Low Friar – that was the road the monastery was on! He knew the monastery was 70 Low Friar's. That would make Brother Arnold's house very close to 87! And the man had said "tell the Brother!"

He shook his head and watched the man's receding back. Was Brother Arnold part of a conspiracy to overthrow Cogniard? If he was, then the conspiracy must have some validity. His father had trusted Brother Arnold, so Robert was ready to as well.

On the other hand, he knew that Roland was also a very honorable and trustworthy man, and Roland served Cogniard. He determined to visit 87 Low Friar's the next day, and see if that was Brother Arnold's house or not. Until then, he would put the matter out of his head. Treason wasn't the type of thinking that got people promotions.

Rising from the stump, he untied Amaury, restringing his bow for another few tries at shooting on horseback. It was tough to put Brother Arnold out of his mind, but when he did, he noticed that his shooting was improving, even if it was only slightly, and he headed back up to the castle.

Roland was coming out of the gate as he was going in, and the older man immediately did an about-face to join Robert.

"We've got things to do," he informed Robert. "How did archery practice go?"

"Oh, not bad, considering. I went down to some field, too, and practiced shooting on horseback. It's not as easy as it looks."

Roland laughed. "Those skills rarely are. You're right, for sure. It took me a while to get used to it too."

He led Robert to the keep, where they entered Cogniard's study and took a seat next to several other important-looking men.

"We have a meeting here in a couple of minutes. I was just heading out to see if you were at Bryce's, when I met you coming in at the gate."

"How did you know I knew Bryce?" asked Robert in surprise.

"Word gets around in a scout troop. You were talking

about a young lady yesterday, I believe? Bryce's daughter?"

"Oh, that. I can see how you might start jumping to conclusions. I'd be careful about one of those conclusions, though. It might prove inaccurate, you know."

Roland laughed merrily, then looked up and nodded at a heavily-built man who was towering over them.

"Who's this young fellow?" the man asked in a deep voice. "And why is he in our conference?" he added with an undercurrent of distrust.

"This is Robert, my newest scout. I'm teaching him the skills he needs to make a good scout leader." Roland's attitude had changed instantly to an impeccably polite, careful way of speaking. "Robert, this is Sir Whittington, Cogniard's top liaison with the king."

"Pleased to meet you, sir," Robert dutifully said.

"And you, I'm sure," the man replied.

At that moment, Cogniard walked in and took a seat. Apparently this was the signal for the meeting to begin.

Cogniard began by giving everyone a brief overview of the current situation, which Robert was quite familiar with. After he had gone through this, he was about to continue, when one of the knights present asked, "How do we know for certain that this island is, in fact, the hideout of the former earl?"

"Spies," Cogniard replied. "Roland, I'll defer this to you to introduce."

"And," said Roland, "I'm going to defer this to Robert, who knows just as much as me on this particular topic."

Robert felt his stomach give a violent heave, and he was certain his face had turned completely white. But he leaned forward and began to explain, in as official terms as possible, what was happening with the spies.

"A few days ago, in fact, the day the army left for Tynemouth, we sent a forward party, myself included, with several spies to find an island that we assumed was there, but couldn't be sure. The spies were launched in a boat in the middle of the night, and directed by two beacons, which led them in the general direction of the island."

Robert continued talking, telling the story of the spies, the pigeons, and the notes received. It was odd explaining things to his superiors, especially to men of the highest rank he would probably ever meet. His own voice sounded far away and funny, but he could see that most of the men were interested in what he was saying, and that gave him the courage to go on.

When he closed with the last message from the spies, which Roland had handed to him so he could read it word for word, he fielded a few questions, then turned back to Cogniard.

The Earl nodded his acceptance with a quick smile, and continued.

"We have the unexpected opportunity of speaking to Donald and Fred ourselves, as they have arrived back safely from the island. They were suspected, but not before taking a prisoner and leaving their work in the hands of others better placed than they."

He rang a bell, and a page came in. The boy was sent for the two spies, and the room was silent until they arrived.

"Greetings, milord," said Donald, echoed by Fred, as they came in.

"Hello Roland, Robert," said Fred, as he took a seat next to them.

"Donald, could you give us a report? Just tell us everything, from the beginning."

"Of course, milord." Donald started his story exactly where Robert had started his, and Robert was proud to see that every fact lined up. Once Donald got to the point where they left in the boat, Robert was all ears.

"So we pushed off, and kept our eyes on the beacons. It was hard, no question about it, and I never would have made it myself, especially after we lost the beacons in the rain. But Fred has good eyes, and even better, a sense of direction, and he managed to row the boat right up to the island."

"With the help of a sail," Fred put in modestly. "I couldn't have rowed that far."

"So anyway, we almost passed it, but Fred saw it off to the side, and once we saw the island we were home free. We pulled the boat on shore and hid it as best we could, then crept up close to the castle.

"On first view, the castle was vacant. There was nobody to be seen. If we had passed the island in daylight, we would have passed it off as deserted."

"As most captains did, I'm sure," commented Roland.

"So we waited until morning and watched the castle while we hid in a grove of trees. Even before the sun came up, people began appearing from nowhere, working on restoring the castle. It had obviously been in bad repair. From the amount of work that had already been done, it appears that they've been at this for quite a while."

He went on to describe in minute detail the castle's defenses, the number of men, and the morale. Anything that a commander could have wanted to know was included in the long description of the castle, and when he was done, there were no questions.

"Absolutely amazing," offered Sir Whittington. "I believe that leaves us with no doubt where to go next."

"And I did forget, but both Fred and I would like to

thank Roland and our escort for their excellent work," Donald added. There were nods all around. Robert was certain he had only added that for his benefit. Spies did tricky things like that, after all.

"So now that we've gathered our intelligence, we can move on to our planning."

"I do have an objection, lord. I think we should keep this only to the ears that need to know." The injection was from Sir Whittington. All eyes swiveled to Robert, who sat stock-still in his chair.

"I think Robert has proved to all of us his ability," commented Cogniard easily. "I'll leave that call up to you, Roland."

"I have not a single reason to distrust Robert, but if Sir Whittington would be more comfortable without him, that's fine with me. He has already served my purpose, and that very well, in this meeting."

Robert took that as his suggestion to go, and he stood up. "Thank you, my lord," he said, turning to Cogniard. Then he nodded to Roland, and left the little chamber.

On the way out of the keep, he told himself it was obviously not a slight that he had been forced out, since it wasn't common to trust boys his age. But if everyone else trusted him, why couldn't Sir Whittington?

He continued to the stables, saddled Amaury, and set off

at an easy walk toward 87 Low Friar's. Now was a good time to check if that address was really Brother Arnold's house or not.

CHAPTER 20

The room was silent as the small group of people watched Charles O'Neill. He was examining the still form in the bed at the front of the infirmary. Mark had been carried there after Harold had finally been pulled off him, and his attacker was now lying in the next bed, suffering from relatively minor wounds. He watched closely as O'Neill finished his inspection of Mark.

"Hold on, this might hurt a bit," grunted Charles O'Neill as he pulled a bandage tight around Mark's side. Harold's first cut had broken one rib and damaged several others. O'Neill had set the bones, and now he was going to wrap them up tight and hope for the best.

"One more bandage and we should have you done up fairly well," he said as he completed wrapping Mark's wounds. There were several major wounds as well as a few small bruises and scratches. According to O'Neill, the soonest he would be out of the infirmary would be several weeks. That would give time for the bones to heal if they were broken. By that time he would be in fairly good condition.

Several minutes later Mark opened his eyes and looked around. It took him a while to come back to his senses completely, but after a bit he was well enough to talk.

As it was, he didn't feel too bad - as long as he kept still. The deep gash in his leg hurt him every time he moved, and his ribs hurt when he breathed deeply, but otherwise he was managing fine.

After O'Neill had finished putting the final touches on Mark's minor wounds, he helped a few other boys, then left. The only other occupant of the infirmary was Harold, who would leave in a day or two. He hadn't said much to Mark, but it was easy to see he wasn't the same person anymore. He had watched O'Neill take care of Mark and seen exactly how much he had hurt him. His somber attitude told Robert he was sorry. He thought back to what Lukas had told him, and knew that Lukas had been right. It was only little things that had gotten blown out of proportion that caused all this. And most of it was his own fault.

Harold had evidently been thinking the same thing, for, after O'Neill had left, he began to speak. "I'm sorry,

Mark. I must have been out of my mind. I can't believe I got that mad over what happened... I didn't even stop to question if you actually did it. Did you?"

"I'm still not positive what you're talking about. After you beat me in the yard...Wow! That seems like a long time ago!"

"You're right, it does. It seems like several days ago, instead of this morning."

"But anyway, after you beat me, we headed back inside, and I stopped at the well to clean up a bit. While I was there, I talked to Lukas for a while, and then I came to the armory. When I walked in, you were all arguing, and we pretty much fought over nothing."

"I'm sorry. That was my fault. When I came back from the yard to put my gear back, I found all my stuff ransacked. There wasn't anything that hadn't been touched."

"Who would do that? Do you have any enemies besides us? I don't think anybody I know would have done that."

"I really don't know who would have done it if it wasn't you or your friends."

"You know, it almost sounds like what happened to Drydon's room."

"Why? What happened to his room?"

"Somebody tore it apart, and nobody's seen him since, that I know of. I think it was, well, the spies, but I guess you don't know about that." Mark proceeded to tell Harold about the events preceding Drydon's disappearance, how he and Drydon had heard the spies, how Ijn had found the boat, and how the boys had seen the mess in Drydon's room.

"So," Mark continued, "after he disappeared, I was scared myself, because I had heard the same things he had, and I figured they might come after me next."

"Actually, you shouldn't have been scared at all," mused Harold, "because before you came, I was always the one in Drydon's shop, helping him out. If they were going to go after anybody, it would have been me."

"And it looks like they did," said Mark. "If what you say is true, they almost definitely were the ones who messed with your stuff."

"So I basically started a big fight over nothing," Harold said regretfully.

"Maybe that one," Mark assented, "but the others were my fault. I was too ready to pick a fight. I think the spies saw that, and used it to their advantage."

"We could argue about that for days, but what we have to do now is find who those people are, and give them a bit of their own medicine," proposed Harold.

"Allen mentioned earlier that we should stop fighting, and he said that Cogniard's men could use it to separate us, but I think what his men just did was a big mistake," said Mark.

"Exactly. We'll bring everyone together now, not fighting each other."

As they were talking, Allen came in, with a troop of boys behind him, both old and young.

"I see you've reconciled yourselves," he said. "That's good, because half my job is done. I came in here to ensure that all you boys will now treat each other like normal human beings, and since you two have already started, I'm sure the rest will not hesitate to follow." He glanced at the rest of the boys and then walked out of the room.

"So what's happening here?" asked Ijn.

"Harold and I have pretty much figured out that it was Cogniard's spies that got into Harold's gear, and together, we're going to find out who they are," Mark replied.

"What spies?" asked one of the upperclassmen.

"Can you explain, Ijn?" Mark said. "I just went through this with Harold."

So Ijn repeated the news, and when he finished it was nearly time for supper in the main hall. When the gong rang, the boys filed out, and Mark was left with Harold in the infirmary.

"You know, when I came into the armory after Lukas had talked to me, I was ready to quit fighting," said Mark. "He completely turned my attitude around."

"He's always been that way," mentioned Harold. "Always ready to make peace. He has a lot of influence."

"I can tell. I bet he's done this more than once," Mark commented.

"Yes. You probably won't believe this, but Drydon and Allen used to get in shouting matches fairly frequently. Just before we left for this island Lukas spent quite a bit of time patching things up."

"How long have you been with the earl?" asked Mark.

"I was with the men he and Cornuel recruited on the continent, back after Cogniard had just taken his land, compliments of the king," said Harold.

"Whoa, I didn't ever hear about this!" Mark interjected.

"That's right, you wouldn't know any of that, either, would you?" mentioned Harold.

"How about you just start from the beginning, however long ago it was, and tell me everything. We've got all the time in the world."

"Okay. Here goes. About twenty years ago, I think it was

1410, the Earl inherited his earldom when an uncle died. Now our Earl became the Earl of Newcastle, and he moved there from Edinburgh, where he had been living. When he came, he found that his uncle's castle was in disrepair, and not strategically situated. He moved to another castle, or, more accurately, a fortress, on a peninsula that jutted out above the sea. I remember seeing it once from a distance away, when we passed it on the way to the island. There's a several-hundred-foot drop from the castle to the sea, and it's only approachable by a series of twisting paths. They called it the Eagle's Nest. It's said to be an attacker's nightmare and a defender's dream, and it took a considerable amount of time to build.

"It turned out that the earl's closest neighbor was Cogniard, and he wasn't very friendly. The earl's uncle was a peace-loving man, and had bribed Cogniard to keep the peace, which was why he had no need for a good castle. The earl, of course, refused to pay any tribute. Then Cogniard started an argument over some lands that were obviously the earl's. When it looked like Cogniard was ready to fight it out, the Earl sent his wife, Catherine, and his children to different places in Britain to keep them safe. To this day, only he knows where they are. Rumor has it that Catherine went to her family in Norwich, but they wouldn't take the children. However it worked out, the Earl keeps in touch with them regularly.

"Cogniard never fulfilled his threats, but there was always

tension between him and the earl, and when the Earl found that Cogniard's lands weren't really his, he jumped at the opportunity to rid himself of this unruly neighbor. That's how he came to know Lord Cornuel, who really owned the land. The Earl plotted with Cornuel to take back Cogniard's lands, but the plans were discovered, and Cogniard acted quickly. About five years earlier, King Henry VI had come to power, and Cogniard had gotten on his good side. He convinced Henry, with a little blackmail, to take the earl's lands from him as punishment. The Earl was left without land or title. Cogniard was sent to capture him, but he escaped with Cornuel.

"He and Cornuel traveled across Britain, gathering a group of loyal supporters. They later found this island, which they've used as a base to consolidate their forces. Cornuel inherited a fortune from his father, and used it to hire about half of the people here, expecting Cogniard to find them soon. Some of the hired men show true loyalty to Cornuel and the earl, but most, as you can see yourself, are influenced quite easily. I'm sure the spies were planted in the group of hired men by Cogniard, although we have no idea who they are. I also think that the vast majority of the hired men would be decent subjects if only several of their leaders were taken care of. So, that's where we are today, and it looks as though we will have a showdown soon, if those spies made it back to Cogniard."

"Well, that should satisfy my curiosity for a while. So the

Eagle's Nest was the castle he built?" asked Mark.

"Right," Harold responded. "That name came when people began calling him the Eagle. When he had an eagle emblazoned on his shields in silver against a blue background, it made it official. Most people around here call him the earl, although you might find several men who came from Newcastle that call him the Eagle. We still have the eagle as our symbol, too."

"I do remember that. I saw that when Cogniard's men almost got me. I still remember how surprised I was that soldiers would appear out of nowhere."

"Allen picked the best bowmen in the castle and put them in the tower, where you had lit the fire. Of course, they put the fire out, too. Then he took the best swordsmen and gave them the official dress of the house of Newcastle and sent them out. It was probably the most organized front we've shown Cogniard yet. I'm sure he did it to impress both Cogniard's men and ours, and it worked. Even though Cogniard never heard of it."

"So if the old castle was the Eagle's Nest, that makes this place Eagle's Island, I guess."

Harold laughed. "I haven't heard that one yet, but it sounds good. Maybe it'll catch on. Certainly a little more interesting than Moore's Island."

The boys began to pick over all the occurrences of the past few weeks, using up the time that they now had so much of. Mark began to get to know Harold better, and realized that he really did have an interest in metallurgy. Harold told stories about working in the blacksmith's shop that Mark could relate to, and soon they were talking about Drydon's alloys.

"He really knows how to make swords well," said Harold. "The only thing he doesn't know how to do is reproduce the sword that the Earl has. He inherited it from the original Earl of Newcastle, who was his grandfather. The sword should have gone to his uncle, the one who he inherited the earldom from, but his grandfather detested him because he was gutless, so he gave it to the Eagle instead. The Earl knows that the men recognize that sword as the symbol of the knowledge of his house, and he doesn't want to lose it. The men know that a sword like that would be the ultimate gesture of partnership, and they won't accept that Cornuel has any authority without that sword.

"Really, though, it's not the sword that is the symbol, but the knowledge that it takes to make a sword like that one. The true retainers trust the original house of Newcastle, and all other lords are inferior if they can't match the sword. The original Earl wrote down how his smiths made it, but it was lost and Drydon can't imitate it. If he could, it would lend credence to Cornuel's authority."

"Was there a dagger like it as well?" asked Mark, recalling the dagger he had found on the ship. He knew the sword he and Drydon had made couldn't be anything but the one Harold had just mentioned.

"I hadn't heard of one. Why?" asked Harold.

"I found a dagger in the shipwreck. The sergeant treated it like a sacred thing when he found it," Mark said. "It shone like nothing I have ever seen before, and it was perfectly balanced. The sheath and grip were mostly blue leather, the hilt was silver, and the pommel was silver. There was silver on the sheath as well."

"That's exactly like it!" exclaimed Harold. "I've seen the earl's sword, and it shines so brightly you can't look at it sometimes. I bet the dagger was meant to go with it!"

"You said Drydon couldn't make it? And Cornuel wanted a copy?"

"Well, Cornuel wasn't as concerned about it as the Earl himself, but yes, he did want a copy. The sword could really inspire men. You could see it from far away."

"If I'm correct," said Mark, slowly, "that's exactly what Drydon and I made the night we heard the spies. I didn't realize it was that important. He said Cornuel wanted it made, but he had no idea how. I showed him what I had learned from the monks in South Shields, and he said it was exactly what he wanted."

"You mean another sword like that exists?"

"Yes, it's lying on a shelf, wrapped in cloth, right now."

"If it really is the same, Cornuel will want to know right away," said Harold.

"It still has to be finished," said Mark. "It only has an iron crossbar and handle."

"We have to finish it and give it to Cornuel," Harold determined. "He'd be able to rally all his men."

"We can't just do it from memory. We'll have to copy the dagger."

"And Allen has the dagger."

"We can tell Allen. We need to reproduce it, and I'm sure he'll agree. Together we can handle it, right?"

The boys determined to notify Allen the next time they could, and their conversation soon drifted off to other topics relating to the castle and its lord. By this time the infirmary was sliding into darkness and the conversation faded. Soon the two, so recently archenemies, were asleep, as O'Neill saw when he looked in later after returning from a talk with his friend John Ruskin.

CHAPTER 21

Robert looked up as Roland walked into the tent. Even though the head scout tried not to show it, he was tired and perturbed.

"I take it you enjoyed yourself at the meeting," commented Robert, fishing for information.

"You'll make a spy yet, Robert," said Roland as he dropped into a chair with a wry grin. "But you can't fool me. Yes, the rest of the meeting was a bit stressful, to say the least."

"More arguments about food?"

"Not food this time; it was, I'd say, more about personnel."

"Was it that a big of a deal when I left that you had to argue about it?"

"No, it wasn't that. You're fine, but we're having a bit of trouble with a minor resistance movement here in town. They want the other Earl back. Not that I can blame them. Cogniard isn't as easygoing as he could be, even if he's much better than most. The others want him to come down hard on the movement. And crush it. But I say that if he does that, he'll help them more than he hurts them. In my opinion, he should give them a reason to like him before he expects them to fall at his feet in blind allegiance."

"I can see how that would get interesting. I take it your relations with Sir Whittington haven't improved?" Robert remembered well Roland's stiff politeness when the man had spoken to them.

"Let's just say that that man is fit for court, not reality. He doesn't know a peasant from a pitchfork." Roland rose from his chair. "But I've got another mission for you, set for tomorrow morning. It's more Cogniard's mission than mine. Report to me when you wake up."

He left the tent, and his footsteps faded softly into the night. Robert thought about what had happened that day, ending with his visit to Brother Arnold.

The Brother had been waiting for him, it seemed, and didn't let Robert just sneak by as he'd had intended. His hopes were to find out if 87 Low Friar's was Brother Arnold's, but when he came to that address, Brother Arnold was standing in the street.

With a friendly yet firm grip on Robert's shoulder, the Brother had led him into the house labeled "87." Once inside, he had inquired about Robert's position as scout. His voice had been strained, yet proud at the same time when he heard about the benefits Robert was enjoying.

In the end, it had seemed more like an interrogation than a meeting, but Robert had remembered at the last what he said about Cogniard.

"Tread lightly with Cogniard," Brother Arnold had said. "Tread lightly. Don't get too involved with his schemes and plans. You may learn to regret it."

The words echoed in his head even now, as he sought to get some sleep. He knew he had a mission to go on tomorrow, but he couldn't forget those words. "You may learn to regret it."

The next morning Robert rose early, presenting himself to Roland, who was already at work and just as tired as the night before. Even as Robert approached him, he was dismissing yet another messenger, and the sun was only just peaking over the tops of the hills.

There was a new look in his eyes as he gave Robert his orders. It was full-blown worry, causing wrinkles Robert had never seen before in his face. With a visible effort the man pulled himself together and continued with his orders.

"At that point, you need to make a decision. If you think you can trust Cogniard and Whittington, and you want to live by their laws, return. If not, I want you to take a sharp left and literally disappear into the woods and fly. Fly like an eagle, away from this place. Go, my young friend. Go now."

Robert could tell Roland was more than worried. The man held himself together, but after Robert left the tent he could hear him snapping orders to his pages in a manner he had never heard before.

It wasn't long before Roland's mood quickly became the last thing on Robert's mind. Two warnings within two days! He had no doubts that Roland was warning him, the same way Brother Arnold had just last evening.

"Scar's looking handsome there, Robert," teased Fulke as he walked out of the camp. Robert flashed him a quick grin. Fulke had heard all about the fight from Glen, whose house was actually right near the scout's camp, next to the postern gate. Glen and his friends were now convinced that scouting was the ultimate adventure.

Glen had the horse ready when he reached the stable. "Here's Amaury for you, Robert," he said.

"How did you know I was leaving?" asked Robert.

"Roland told me. He also said to say goodbye. Are you leaving for good, Robert?" Now Glen was worried too. Robert quickly saw that Roland was giving him yet another nudge in the right direction.

"It might be a while, Glen. Long mission, you know."

"Well, I'll see you in a little bit then." Glen waved as Robert mounted Amaury and rode away from the stable.

As he passed through the main gate, he heard Brother Arnold's voice from the shadows.

"Have a good flight, eagle!" His heart thumping, Robert kept riding. He saluted to the gate guards, then pushed Amaury into a trot as he left the castle behind him.

As he started to post to the staccato rhythm of Amaury's gait, he felt his leg bump against an unfamiliar object. He was surprised to see a sword attached to his saddle, mounted in a scabbard positioned for a quick draw. He felt the hilt, and noted that it was like new, with leather grip and a simple, functional design.

His curiosity now aroused, he checked the saddle bags next. Inside was enough food to last him for several days, as well as a small knife, some fishing line, hooks, and a carefully drawn map. Roland hadn't been taking any chances.

The ride to Ashington was uneventful, and he arrived in the center of the town without incident. He remembered that the original purpose of his mission was to check with Mayor Denton about any volunteers for the army, so he headed down the road to the mayor's house. It would give confirmation that he was completing his mission, he thought. If he deserted the army they would assume the act had occurred on his way back to the castle, if he at least started back in that direction.

But Roland had said, "When you hit Ashington..." Robert changed his mind. Roland's words seemed to suggest that he leave Ashington without seeing the mayor. He turned his horse around and rode out of Ashington at a walk. When he spurred Amaury into a trot, he heard galloping hooves behind him, and turned to see five horsemen close behind.

Robert instantly recognized Cogniard's men and instinctively knew that Cogniard had somehow heard of his plan to escape. He set Amaury into a gallop and headed straight for the woods, leaning forward on his mount's neck.

An arrow landed in the ground far ahead and to his right. So they had brought bows. But they certainly hadn't practiced with them. He pulled his own bow from his back and re-strung it as Amaury galloped over the rough ground. Turning in the saddle, he let a shot fly back at his pursuers.

The arrow missed, but it certainly did its job of scaring the men. They broke out of the close formation they had been riding in and spread out into a line.

Turning forward again, Robert saw that he was coming to a stream. A stream much too big to jump. His heart sank. Pulling Amaury into a sharp turn, he pointed him to the right. There was a narrower section of stream several hundred feet down.

He could almost feel his pursuers' glee. They were now able to cut him off. He knew they would reach the stream at almost exactly the same moment as he did. Leaning over Amary's neck, he urged him faster. It wasn't enough.

When they reached the stream, Robert pivoted Amaury to the left to make the jump. At the same time he felt an arrow, fired at close range, pierce his horse's back just below the saddle.

The stallion half jumped, half reared, as he tried to obey Robert's command. Even before he left the ground, Robert knew the game was up.

Amaury crashed into the opposite bank with a sickening thud and a "snap." Robert already had his feet out of the stirrups, and he grabbed the sword and leaped onto dry ground. Seconds later, he was spinning into the ground. The first pursuer's horse had managed to clear the stream and had bowled him over.

Picking himself up from the ground and retrieving his sword, Robert saw that he hadn't been the only one to fall. The horse that had hit him had been knocked off balance and had fallen as well, momentarily pinning its rider to the ground.

The sound of another horse landing brought his attention back to the stream. He brought his sword up and blocked the sweeping blow of a spear shaft as the rider attempted to catch him by surprise.

When he looked downstream he saw a small ford and two more riders crossing it. That made four horses on his side of the stream, one of which was struggling on the ground, its rider trapped underneath. Where was the fifth?

A horse's scream told him. The last rider had attempted to jump the stream just after Robert, and had similarly crashed into the bank. Two horses were now struggling in the muddy water, with one man trapped between.

He should have been watching the others. A heavy hand grabbed his neck, almost choking him. Quickly he spun and lashed out with the sword. It was a failed blow, catching the horse in the neck and further enraging the rider.

Robert's sword was ripped from his grasp and he felt his arms pinned behind his back. His little flight was over.

He was placed face-down on the ground and quickly trussed up. Behind him, he could hear the soldiers' efforts as they tried to help the fallen horses, efforts that were thwarted by their thrashings. It was soon apparent that they had managed to rescue the pinned man, and then he heard one man say, "What about the boy's horse?"

"The sorrel? You'll have to kill it. Its leg is broken."

"Shame. That's a nice horse."

Robert had to agree with their decision. He knew that a horse could only be useful with the best of care after a broken leg. But he still felt awful as he heard the soldier draw his sword.

After they had taken care of his horse they put him on one of their own. A soldier mounted behind him, grabbing the reins around him. Out of the corner of his eye, Robert could see the lifeless form of Amaury in the ditch.

The ride back was a long one. Two horses were injured, one limping and the other with a large bruise on its shoulder. The rider of the limping horse had a broken leg and had to be helped along by one of his comrades.

"You did too much damage for a little pest," said the man behind him. "Don't even try to escape now."

Robert had dropped that thought the instant it came up. His head was throbbing, and the cut on his face had split open again.

He didn't reply to the soldier, but kept a grim silence, wondering what Roland, Benedict, Kate, and even Glen would think. He'd been warned to leave Cogniard, but he still didn't know why. And now, even though he had failed in his attempt and would probably be kept a prisoner, he still didn't know why he had been urged to escape.

He told himself it was on good recommendation, and that was the truth. He would have to trust Roland and Brother Arnold that it had been worth the effort. Obviously there had been eyes on him before the plan or these soldiers would not have been ordered to capture him.

They entered Tynemouth Castle in a slow procession. Robert hoped nobody could tell he was a prisoner. They might guess by the look on his face, but for all they knew he was just getting a ride back into the castle. Bound. Robert dropped that hope.

It didn't turn out to be as embarrassing as Robert would have predicted. Villagers merely glanced his way, then looked at the ground. It seemed that this type of scene was all too common. Robert thought he saw Tim in the crowds, but just before he caught his eye the horse sidestepped, and Robert had to catch his balance.

As they passed through the inner gate he knew at least one of the stable boys saw him. And when there was one, there were more. Glen would know by the end of the day.

Then he saw Roland. Robert nearly missed him. The scout leader was leaning against an old box elder, almost hidden by shade from an old smithy nearby. Out of sight of everyone but Robert's group, he slowly raised his hand in a Roman salute.

Robert could almost have cried right then. He didn't care that he was going in the dungeon, he didn't care that he was bruised and cut, or that Amaury was dead. All he knew was that he had failed the best friends he had ever had. Roland above all, Brother Arnold, Glen, Kate, and the rest of the scouts to a lesser degree. The old scout leader was still on his mind as his guard led him into one of the many dungeon cells.

When Roland and Benedict had given him a tour of the castle they had shown him the dungeon as a place to store any captives he would bring in. It had looked bleak then; now it looked worse. The door slammed shut behind him, and he was left in the semi-darkness of the cell.

He didn't know how long he lay there, thinking. It was hard to tell time without the aid of the sun, but he thought it must have been way past supper when he smelled food coming up the aisle.

The prison-keeper was a gruff, cruel-looking man named Gault. Robert had met him his first time in the dungeon, but luckily the man didn't recognize him. He was certain there would have been more than one snide comment.

Supper wasn't the only thing the man brought. With him was a little page who all but held his nose at the sight of the prisoner occupying the cell. Although disgusted at the boy's attitude, Robert was still thankful for the bandages, cream, and bowl of water he brought.

It should have taken only a few minutes to clean the old wound and apply the bandages, but Robert made it stretch into an hour. He meticulously cleaned every corner of the cut, and artfully arranged the bandages to provide the best cover without running out.

The rest of the day dragged on. Robert felt perfectly awful. He had plenty of time to rehash his mistakes.

First of all, he told himself, he should have obeyed Roland's instructions to the letter and not ridden down the road toward the mayor's house. He was certain that he had let his pursuers catch up with him.

Second, he should have paid much more attention. It was all a game until he saw the riders behind him. By then, the game was up.

Third, he should have used his bow more quickly; and fourth, he should not have led his horse toward a stream. After some consideration, he decided that the last two could never have been done at the same time anyway, and gave up blaming himself.

Having come to that conclusion, he picked up a stone and started scratching pictures into the wall. And hoping nobody he knew would come to see him in the dungeon.

CHAPTER 22

The next day Harold was released from the infirmary, and O'Neill told Mark that he might have to spend less time there than he had originally thought. Harold was still aching a bit, but he was ready to leave, the infirmary being somewhat of a boring place to be for hours on end.

Before he left, Harold promised Mark that he would start work on the sword that day.

"But how are you going to do it?" asked Mark. "The shop is used all day, and you have things to do at night. Besides, the spies might be watching for you."

"I have time in the evening. I'll make time, anyway. I don't have to be worried about being waylaid by a bunch of boys!"

Harold laughed, and Mark smiled. He was still unsure of how safe the shop was.

"The armory might be their meeting place," he said. "If they meet there again, you could be in trouble."

"They won't dare, after having been heard the first time."

"Still, there's always the chance..."

"How about this: I actually will be busy the next few nights, but as soon as I have some time I'll tell you, and you can send as many of your army as you would like. They can make up some good excuse for being in the shop, and we can work on the sword."

"Actually, since you have to go to Allen to get the dagger anyway," said Mark, "why don't we just talk to him. He could post a guard outside. That would keep it more of a secret."

"Of course. That sounds great. I'll ask Allen to meet us in the shop at sundown in several days. If O'Neill won't let you out of the infirmary, well, we'll just sneak you out anyway."

The next few days passed quickly. Mark was mostly alone in his sickbed, but he received several visits, including one from Aronii. He had come without any reason whatsoever. At least, that's what he would have Mark believe. Mark was fairly certain there was something behind his visit, but he couldn't figure it out. At any rate, the samurai was easy to talk to and he stayed for a while, talking to Mark about himself and Ijn, also asking Mark about his past and what he hoped to do in the future.

To the latter question Mark answered laughingly that he wouldn't mind being a general, but that being an Earl would be good fun as well.

"That way, you have your hand in everything, and you look at the big picture," he said.

"But you also have a lot more to worry about," Aronii said.

"It would be more of a challenge than a problem," Mark answered, "and the better you rule, the less you have to worry about."

The commander smiled, and Mark thought he could detect a glint in his eye that went beyond the humor Aronii found in the statement. Soon after he left the room, telling Mark to get well soon and warning him that fighting was very un-Earl-like.

In a few days, Mark was feeling much better. And, although O'Neill was set against it, he finally gave his permission to let Mark visit the shop one evening, as long as he came right back to the infirmary afterwards.

When it was time, Harold appeared at the door. After greeting him, Mark grabbed a pair of crutches. His legs weren't that bad, but O'Neill had warned him that it wouldn't take much to injure the partially healed wounds again.

When they reached the shop, Allen was already there, inspecting several harness pieces that had been made by Mark's group in his absence.

"Pleased to have your presence here, Mr. Mark. I wasn't expecting you to be out of bed yet," the tough old sergeant said.

"He's here to do the honors," said Harold. "So far, all the credit for this is his."

"And what, pray tell, is the 'this' that we are talking about?" asked Allen, his heavy brow furrowed as he leaned on the anvil.

"Mark? Why don't you show the sergeant what you've done."

Mark hobbled over to the shelf where the sword had been placed several days earlier. He pulled the sword down from the shelf, turning toward the sergeant. As he was pulling the oiled cloth off, the door swung open. In a flash, he covered the sword and put it behind his back.

Several men entered the smithy and began to cross toward the hearth. Allen's gruff voice stopped them in their tracks.

"What do you need?"

"We were scheduled to use the shop this evening," a distinctly French voice replied coolly. Mark's heart jumped into his throat. He knew that voice. It was the voice of the spy, the voice he had heard only several days earlier! He studied the man intently as the sergeant made his very diplomatic reply.

"Not anymore."

"Excuse me?"

"The shop is officially full."

"Allen, I've just about had enough of your games. If you think you can kick me out of the shop, you can think again. I know you're Cornuel's favorite, but Cornuel doesn't own the castle."

Mark could tell by the tone of his voice that the man was not used to being disobeyed. He appeared to be a very important person around the castle, and Mark was surprised that Allen was being as aggressive as he was.

"I don't have all night to wait," Allen growled as he stalked toward the three men, his face scowling.

"Cornuel will hear about this. The Earl, too," the Frenchman shot over his shoulder as he walked out.

"Who is that?" asked Mark as the door closed. Allen locked it.

"Mr. Pierre Lytton the Third," he said. The note of

disdain in Allen's voice made Harold's eyebrows rise. Allen usually didn't divulge his opinions to his students.

"It's him, the voice I heard," Mark blurted out. Allen's eyes narrowed and he looked sharply at Mark.

"We'll talk in my room when we are finished here," was all he said. Walking back over to the door, he latched it. "You may proceed."

Mark slid the cloth off the sword for the second time and placed it on the anvil. The light of the fire reflected off it onto the ceiling. Allen's eyes narrowed to slits.

"You made it?" he asked. There was no question he recognized the significance.

"Drydon and I," Mark answered. "We began it the night before he disappeared, and we never finished it."

"We wanted to borrow the dagger Mark found so we could finish it," Harold put in.

Allen looked at Mark. "Just for future reference, I'd prefer if you didn't tell anyone else about the dagger."

Mark blushed and nodded his assent.

"However," Allen continued, "this is very important. We have to keep this as quiet as possible. What I'm going to do is lend you the dagger every night. I'm also going to get you in touch with Stephen Greville. He's an old soldier friend of the earl, and nobody can work silver like he can."

"We were also worried about the spies..." Mark started.

"That, too. I'm going to send three of my men along with the dagger. They go where it goes. The sword is in their hands as well."

Mark and Harold nodded, and then Allen dismissed Harold and walked with Mark to his office. As Mark sat in the chair in front of the desk, he thought about the first time he had sat there. Although only a couple of weeks ago, it seemed much longer. The memory of arriving here prompted thoughts of his old home, and he wondered once again what had happened to his father, and how his mother was doing. He had been so busy with his new life in the castle that thoughts of this type had started to become fairly scarce.

Allen broke into Mark's thoughts.

"Are you absolutely sure that was the voice you heard?"

"Positive. It was a very French voice, and it had the same edge to it, like he wasn't telling all he knew. It's as though he's constantly plotting..."

"I think that's more your introduced imaginations, but I'll trust you that it's the same voice." He paused, then continued, as though to himself, "You know, it's going to be very tough to crack this nut. He came on board just before the Earl found the island. Without some very convincing proof, the Earl will never believe he's a traitor. I wouldn't be easily convinced either if someone told me that a friend who saved my life wanted to kill me."

"Lytton saved the earl's life?"

"In a manner of speaking, yes, back in '27, when he lost his lands to Cogniard. The king intended to kill the Earl as well, but Lytton talked him out of it. Even then, the king was going to imprison him, but some messages went missing and it gave him time to escape."

The sergeant put his hands behind his head, and appeared in deep thought. After a while he frowned, then looked at Mark and rapped out his order.

"I need your help, it seems. I want your boys to keep an eye on Lytton. Don't have one person follow him, but have people everywhere."

Allen paused, then continued. "You don't need to be afraid of the upperclassmen, so split up. Assign people as messenger boys. Never mind, I'll do that."

He grabbed a scrap of old parchment and jotted himself a note. "Give me a list of people who could be messengers and I'll try to get a few into positions that might have potential. Just try to have somebody in every corner of the castle. If you get in a scrape, make up an excuse that has to do with me and I'll back you up. Get any information on Lytton you can, and if at all possible, get somebody who is not one of your boys to observe any evidence."

"Here," he said, grabbing another piece of paper. "I'll give you a list of people you can trust. If anything looks suspicious, send someone to them. Memorize this and burn it." Allen scribbled out a few names on the sheet of paper and almost threw it at Mark. "Now leave my office before someone gets suspicious and please try to act like I don't favor you."

Mark hid a smile and scooted out of the room, leaving Allen to his paperwork on food supply and training. He returned to the infirmary and placed himself back in bed, noting that he didn't feel infirm at all.

The next morning, Harold came to the infirmary and told Mark he was going to be picked up by one of the men-at-arms that were guarding the sword, and that they would begin work on the hilt that evening.

The rest of the morning and afternoon, Mark kept thinking about the sword. He was visited by all his friends as they had time, and he learned that the castle was nearing completion due to the hard work of everyone who had pitched in after their normal duties.

Thomas was working on the masonry with his group, who were finishing off the crenellations on the massive outer walls. Mark made sure he passed along Allen's request to watch Pierre Lytton, as well as to Ijn, who came in later. The stables were done, Ijn said, and he was helping to disassemble the scaffolding on the completed walls with Greg, who had been helping the carpenters.

Greg came in as well, reporting that their work had actually been done a few days earlier. After that they had helped fill the ammunition stockpiles located around the castle.

As Harold had promised, a knock came on the door immediately after supper, and a young member of the guard stepped in to escort Mark to the smithy. When Mark saw him, he knew instantly that it was the same person who had escorted him back to the castle after his encounter with Cogniard's men.

His name was William Braithewaite, and he had been in the class just above Harold, finishing his training just before the Earl had left on his now overdue trip. Harold's class, he said, would graduate soon after the Earl returned, and they would then be incorporated into the body of squires that assisted the men-at-arms.

When they came to the smithy, William stayed at the door with one of his fellow squires. Mark entered. Harold and Stephen Greville were waiting for him, as well as Robert MacCrae, who was Allen's assistant, and two men-at-arms.

"So this is the famous sword-maker," commented Greville, a wiry, white-haired man in his seventies. "After looking at that blade of yours, I'm not sure we can produce a hilt fine enough to complement it!" His twinkling eyes told Mark he was joking, and Mark laughed.

"To tell the truth, the sword was mostly made by Drydon. I just helped a bit," he replied.

"Well then, we'll get on with it. What we have to do is finish the blade, then we'll move to the hilt. The blade, as I'm sure you know, needs to be scraped and ground. After you get it cleaned up with the shop stones, I've got some of my own that you can use on it." He pulled several small grinding stones of different finenesses out of his bag and placed them on the table. "By the end of this week we'll have this sword done."

"Only working nights? How are we going to do that?" asked Mark incredulously.

"We won't be working just nights," said Harold. "Allen moved the whole shop up to the new building in the courtyard this afternoon. If you had looked around when you came in, you would have noticed that the shop is a little bare." Mark looked, and it was, in fact, quite bare. The only shop tools left were the tools that they would be using.

"Why did he do that?" he asked. "It couldn't have been just so we could work on the sword."

"Well, actually the plan had always been to get the shop out of the underground section. They'll have more air up top, which means better fires and less work," said Greville. "But that wasn't supposed to happen for a while yet. Allen knew we needed the time to make the sword, and when he wants something done, he'll move mountains to get it done."

"I guess," said Mark, wonderingly.

"And, therefore, we probably shouldn't be putting those mountains back in place by sitting here and gabbing," put in Harold. "Grab the tools and let's go."

Mark and Harold set to work honing down the blade. They scraped off the excess steel, and then set up the grinding wheel, working the blade to a smooth, flat surface.

Meanwhile, Greville laid out his smaller grinding stones, and after the boys were done with the comparatively rough work on the sword they started on the fine stones.

"These are pretty smooth," commented Mark. "I've never seen any sword smoother than we have this one now."

"Well, this sword is a special one, obviously. I want you to smooth that sword until a block of wood slides around on it like it's ice." The old silversmith showed them how to get the perfect angle on the blade, and then went back to working on the design for the hilt, which he was copying from the dagger.

Mark was bone-weary when he left the smithy that night.

As he entered the infirmary, O'Neill looked up from his workbench where he was mixing several herbs.

"Hope you're good and tired. Swedenborg has some new poultices for you in the next room." Christopher Swedenborg was O'Neill's assistant, who studied with him in his spare time.

Mark nodded, and entered the sickbay. Swedenborg was attending to a new arrival, a boy from Ijn's group who had fallen off the scaffolding. He turned and walked over to Mark, keeping his voice low.

"I know O'Neill might disagree with me, but you can probably go back to the barracks now."

"Are you sure? I don't want to disobey him."

"I'm sure. Go sleep in the barracks. Just be careful with your wounds." This curt reply was accompanied by a significant look.

Mark grinned and thanked him, turning around to head for his room, the room he now considered his home, filled with his friends.

CHAPTER 23

Robert's scratched-in-stone drawing had grown into a masterpiece. It was the only thing he could do to occupy himself. The drawing had spread from a single stone to several stones, all in the lower corner of the wall. It was a detailed drawing, as detailed as a scratched drawing could be, and it depicted an island castle.

With the recently violent turn of events, Robert had convinced himself that Cogniard was not all he seemed to be. Roland, he still trusted. And Brother Arnold, of course. But his capture and imprisonment was proof that something was wrong, and he no longer felt he owed anything to Cogniard.

That led him to consider the resistance movement. He was certain that either his visit with Brother Arnold or his talk with Tim in the field had prompted this action. If Cogniard was so afraid of him that he was clapped up the instant he even talked to the "enemy," then the enemy must certainly be more organized than Robert had first assumed.

The island castle drawn on the wall was evidence of his hope that the people who lived there were better than those who now imprisoned him.

The prison keeper, Gault, came by to give him his breakfast of leftover stew and some water. He hardly felt like eating the moldy-looking food, but he did anyway. He reasoned that if he ever got a chance to escape again, he wouldn't fail like the first time. And that required eating as much as he could, to stay healthy.

He was just finishing his breakfast when Gault returned. This time, Kate was with him; Robert noticed she treated the prison keeper like he was some sort of filthy rat. Gault unlocked the door and let Kate in, then strode away, smirking.

Robert was unsure whether he should be embarrassed to be sitting in a dungeon or happy to have a chance to explain what had happened. He chose to be happy.

"What's going on, Robert?" asked Kate, as soon as the sound of Gault's footsteps had disappeared.

"I really don't know, except that a couple of days ago I started receiving warnings to leave. They weren't from just anybody, either, so I followed their advice, at least up to the point where I got caught." Robert had gone over this reasoning many times in his head already.

"So you'll just be tried like a deserter? They can't do too much to you then, can they?" Robert could see Kate was picking at things to encourage him.

"Nobody sends five men-at-arms to recapture one deserter," he returned. "And I think there's a lot more going on here than just that." He told her about the resistance movement in Newcastle, and about his talks with Tim and Brother Arnold. He made sure not to mention any names, knowing that it was quite likely that Gault could be listening.

"So you were thought to be part of a resistance, then? How come nobody else got caught?"

"That's a good point, I suppose," Robert said, thoughtfully. "It would be unusual to arrest one person and let the others have time to escape."

"Maybe they did escape."

"It's possible, but not likely, especially if they all had as many men assigned to catch them as I did."

They continued to discuss the possibilities, but didn't come to a conclusion. Robert was quite happy to have somone to talk to, so he was disappointed to hear Gault returning.

"You've got to go now, lassie," he said. "No more time to talk to the criminals."

"Then I think you'd better keep your mouth shut," she fired back as she walked out the door. With a wave to Robert she disappeared out the door and down the hall.

Five minutes later she was back, peering through the bars at the front of his cell.

"I've got to be quick," she said. "Because I told him I left my scarf here."

"When it's so warm out?" Robert asked, grinning.

"Whatever. He's stupid enough anyway. Listen. When I walked out, there was an important-looking man standing there, waiting to talk to him. So I told Gault I needed to return to your cell for my scarf. Then I waited just out of sight, and listened to what they were saying."

"Interesting," said Robert. "Did they actually talk about me?"

"Well, I heard Gault say, 'He thinks he's in there for that worthless resistance movement' and then the other man laughed and said, 'Let him think that. He'll never know until he swings.'"

"Well, there goes that idea. I don't like the thought of being hanged, though. I'd rather have stayed with being a traitor."

"Found your scarf yet, girl?" Gault had returned and was jangling his keys impatiently.

"I must have dropped it on the way here," said Kate, acting like she meant it.

"Well, you won't find it by talking. Time to go, for the second time."

Robert watched them go down the corridor, then returned to scratching his drawing on the wall. His mind wandered everywhere, trying to find the reasons for his imprisonment and his already decided sentence. And he thought about hanging.

"It doesn't look like that."

The words were so sudden Robert almost screamed.

"Easy now," the voice said. "You'll have to start over if you want it accurate."

"How do you know?" Robert asked as soon as he found his voice. "And where are you? And how do you even know what I'm drawing?"

"Next cell over. You're not the only one who's fallen into Cogniard's bad graces. And I overheard your conversation." When Robert looked toward the voice he could make out a dim shadow in the next cell.

"So have you been to the island? What's all this about? I don't even know who these people are," he said, moving to the grating that separated the two cells.

"Well, before Cogniard comes and moves me, which he will, I'll tell you what you want to know even more." The shadow laughed a little as Robert frowned in confusion.

"This is what I have to tell you. You have a brother, and he's on the island."

"What?! What are you, some kind of fortune teller? I don't believe a word of it." Robert started thinking this was just some old man losing his mind. The man had guessed that Robert had a brother, but that didn't prove anything.

"Well, let's see. Do you remember Brother Arnold? Yes? And the books he had... one with a description of how to make a sword in it. You and Mark memorized that description. And you probably remember how mad the cook was, too."

Robert tried to keep his face from showing his astonishment.

"Are you saying Mark is alive?" he asked with eagerness. "Only Mark could have told you that story."

"Yes, that's what I'm saying. He's alive and kicking. Literally, too." At this moment Gault walked up and snarled at them.

"Shut up. No talking in the dungeon. I'm gonna move you, old man." Just as the prison-keeper pulled his neighbor out of the cell, Robert called out, "What's your name?"

"Drydon."

After that it was a long day. The sun peeped into the cell for about five minutes, shining through a small, grated window in the upper corner of the cell. He basked in its glow for the time that it stayed, then turned his attention to the window.

He hadn't noticed it before, because it was up in the corner and the grate was the same color as the stone. His cot was just below, and if he stood on it he could see outside. Well, if one could call the public sewer "outside." Now he knew where the smell was coming from. Surprisingly, it didn't smell as bad as he thought a sewer would, and he wondered if the castle architect had channeled fresh water from the river Tyne into it to dilute the nasty mess.

After exhausting his interest in the beautiful view of the public sewer, he took a look at how the grate was fastened to the stone. He wasn't going to get his hopes up yet, but it would be wise to consider every option.

The grate was made of wrought iron, with a frame of the same material around it, all of one piece. This design meant that if he were to try to escape through the window, he would need to remove the entire grate at once.

The grate itself was fastened to the stone by means of four large bolts. Curious, Robert took a better look. The bolts looked like they entered right into the stone. With closer examination, he saw that the bolts actually entered between two stones, one on the inside of the wall, the other on the outside.

He stopped looking at the bolts and sat back down on his cot, staring at his drawing on the wall. There was no possible way that to remove those bolts without a hammer and chisel, and even that might not do the job.

For a moment he thought about removing the entire stone that covered the bolts from the inside. But after scratching at the cement that bound the stones together, he gave up that idea as well. It was just as hard as the rock.

He spent the next hour staring at his drawing, wondering what the island castle really looked like. Every once in a while he would scratch a few lines in, clarifying a feature. The boredom was awful.

It ended abruptly. Sounds of footsteps coming down the corridor broke him out of his reverie. It wasn't just Gault, either. He could hear the clink and clank of metal on metal, as well as the scuff of more than one pair of leather boots on the ground.

It was an armed guard, with Gault in the lead, holding the keys to his cell. As Gault opened the cell door, the guards arranged themselves around it. They left no opportunity to escape.

With rough hands, two of them ushered Robert to the door and out into the corridor. After Gault closed the door they headed down to the dungeon's entryway. There, the officer of the guard thanked Gault with a curt nod. Robert noticed the disgusted look on his face and wondered if anybody, anywhere, liked the rude prison-keeper.

"Out of the frying pan, into the fire, eh?" One of the soldiers elbowed him jovially. "Or rather, into the boiling water, since it's a ship. Hmm, that would make--"

"Shut up, man. We don't make a habit of telling our prisoners more than they need to know."

Robert had heard enough. He was being transferred somewhere. On a ship. A distant prison? Or… the island. Maybe he was going with the invasion force. "He'll never know until he swings…" How did that all fit in?

He left those thoughts behind, and thankfully breathed the fresh air as the guard led him out into the road. As they marched quickly out the postern gate, which was closer to the water, he saw the officer of the guard that led him look back inquisitively. And then he dropped back and began to talk to Robert.

"Are you…possibly… the young man who we came to help right here?" he asked, as they passed the scene of

Robert's earlier encounter with the would-be thieves.

"Yes, that would be me," Robert said, slightly embarrassed.

"Ahh, I see. I recognized that cut on your face." They walked along in silence for a while, heading to the mouth of the River Tyne.

"Have you ever seen an eagle?" The sudden question caught Robert off guard.

"Uhh, no, actually, I haven't," he replied. All of a sudden, an inspiration flashed into his mind. "I did try to fly like one once, however."

The officer's disappointed look after his first answer broke into a sharp, interested one. "And how did that flight go, may I ask?" He watched Robert's face closely.

"I was hoping too high, I suppose. I tripped over five stones as I was launching myself and landed in a pigsty."

"I am very sorry to hear that. I do wish I could help you, but I doubt my wings are strong enough to carry us both." He gave Robert a hint of a smile, then returned to the front of the group, where he began to converse with the soldiers in raucous tones.

Robert's heart was beating fast. In sending him off, Roland had said "Fly like an eagle." On a chance, he had continued the theme with the officer of the guard; and now he had found, or so he thought, what the watchword of the resistance was.

He was almost certain that this man knew what he was trying to convey: that he had "flown" from the castle, and that he had been caught by "five rocks" and put in a "pigsty." If he had, it proved that he was a member of the resistance to Cogniard, and that he was a friend.

Robert recalled the last words he had said. "I doubt my wings are strong enough to pull you out." That meant, almost certainly, that he wouldn't be getting any help from the resistance. At least he knew he had friends.

He was jerked back to reality by the sight of the ship before him as the group walked up the gang plank. It was resting low in the water. Full, he was certain, of supplies for the army that would soon be heading to the island.

But that wasn't what he was thinking about. He was thinking about the last time he had sailed on a ship of this size. With his father and his brother.

He ignored the soldiers as they locked him up in the ship's brig and left him alone. He was thinking about everything that had happened over the last few weeks: from the first journey, so promising, to this one, so devastating.

CHAPTER 24

The next morning, Mark nodded to William Braithwaite as he opened the door to the shop. When he entered, the first thing he noticed was the grim look on the faces of the unusually numerous guards.

"Well," said Greville, the twinkle still in his eye, "how do you like your new bedroom? I know it has a little larger fire than you were counting on, but it should do nicely…"

"What's happened?" asked Mark, confused.

Sergeant Allen turned away from Aronii, whom Mark hadn't noticed before, and responded, "Mark, we just about lost you and Harold last night. That exchange with Lytton may have been a little too heated for our own good. Harold's bed was poisoned. We put a chicken in it to test the poison, and it was dead in five minutes. Your infirmary bed had the powder as well."

A cold sweat broke out on Mark's forehead. Had Swedenborg known? That look...

"In light of that, the guard here has been doubled and you are not to leave this room. I had the appropriate supplies transferred here from the barracks and the pantry. We aren't taking any chances."

In slightly different moods than the day before, Harold and Mark set to work on the sword. The work progressed; by the end of the day the blade had a mirror finish, and Greville's block of wood did slide around like it was on ice.

The next few days blurred into one continuous collage of smithy, sword, and dagger. Mark and Harold worked late and got up early, the uncomfortable cots not giving them any reason to sleep in.

The sword took shape quickly, and on Friday morning Mark and Harold knew it would be finished that day.

They had just completed their relatively plain breakfast when Harold pulled the sword from the sheath that Ruskin had made for it.

"She's almost ready, Mark. We've just about completed the biggest advancement in sword-making since the discovery of iron."

"Yeah, right, and I'm the new earl. It is a pretty nice-looking sword, though."

Just then, William opened the door and leaned in. "The sergeant wants the sword the instant you finish it. He said he would be in Cornuel's chambers."

True to their estimate, the sword was finished just after their noonday meal. Mark passed the oiled cloth over it one more time, and slipped it into its sheath.

"Alright, boys, let's head out," ordered MacCrae. The guards formed around Harold and Mark as the group exited the smithy.

They were just approaching the stairs in the dimly lit hall when two men jumped out of the shadows with drawn swords, threatening. Obviously surprised at the number of guards, they hesitated for a fraction of a second. It was a crucial second.

"What..." MacCrae's face flushed as he pinned one man to the floor. Another guard had the second man against the wall at swordpoint.

"Lock those men in the prison. The rest of you, watch your backs. Let's MOVE!"

The group trotted down the corridor, swords drawn. As they came up the stairs and out into the light, the courtyard was in turmoil. It seemed the entire population of the castle was gathered there. They were shouting Cornuel's name and shaking their fists. It was obvious something momentous had taken place in the time they had been busy.

The armed group pushed through the crowd to the keep, where Cornuel had his apartments. As Mark studied the crowd, he noticed several very active men weaving in and out of the masses, shouting louder than all the others, and inciting them to riot. He mentioned this to Harold, who gritted his teeth, muttering, "Those spies..."

They reached Cornuel's rooms quickly, and were instantly admitted. The sergeant was there, and he nodded curtly to MacCrae, then called to the next room, "Lord Cornuel, you ready?"

Mark saw Cornuel enter from the door to his left, and drew in his breath sharply. The lord was looking almost royal in a full suit of armor, polished to a brilliant shine. Light from the open balcony made the plates glow. A royal blue surcoat trimmed in silver covered his breastplate and thighs. In his hands was a pair of blue leather gloves, lined inside with silver silk. His helm, held under his arm, was topped with a solid silver depiction of an eagle diving like a lightning bolt.

Mark knelt on one knee and held out the sword in its sheath, with the blue and silver leather belt. Cornuel took it from him almost gently, and Mark saw that his movements were cool and determined.

He belted the sword to his side, then pulled it slowly from the sheath. The light from the mid-afternoon sun flashed into the room, reflecting off the brilliant blade.

"Thank you, Harold, Mark," he stated calmly; then, replacing the sword, stepped out onto the balcony above the rioting crowd.

Instantly, the people were silent. With characteristic grace, Cornuel began to speak.

"Two years ago. Two years ago, we stood together on this spot… and pledged to raise up a castle like no other. This castle was to be known, not for its wealth, not for its might, though it might have those, but for the grit, determination, and unity of its people. Where are we today? What has changed since that spring day?

"Yes, we have gone through troubles. Starvation, sickness, and death. Alarms, threats, and tense days. We carried through with the grit that was to make us great… and we survived. We continued on to finish the greatest castle ever built, whose might and wealth were measured in brotherhood and unity. What has changed since that spring day?

"Today, we face a challenge from our enemy, the entire purpose of our endeavor. The goal to which all of our trials and troubles have pointed is here. We have destroyed those troubles with our grit, and challenged those trials with our unity. And I ask you now, before the

Earl and *before his sword*, has *anything changed since that day?"*

Lord Cornuel stood on the balcony, holding the sword high, as waves of cheers rolled past him and into the room beyond, where his private audience sat astonished. Mark's heart raced, and he felt dazed as he heard Cornuel reminding the people of their duties in the face of the now-encountered Cogniard.

"Masterful, just masterful. I don't know how he does it," exclaimed MacCrae. "The people were ready to draw and quarter him when we came through."

"The people were incited by the spies," said Mark.

"Doubtless some of them were incited by the spies, but I'm willing to bet that it wasn't the work of a moment," Allen commented.

"Everything changed in an instant, though, like we had a different crowd out there," Harold said.

"There was only one thing, Harold. One thing." They turned to face Lord Cornuel, who had returned from the balcony. "You and Mark changed their minds, with this sword." He slid the weapon back into its sheath and took a seat. "Allen, whip these people into shape. Let's turn the heat up on our friend Cogniard."

In that moment, the orderly daily life that had persisted ever since the castle was built was shattered. As Mark had surmised, Cogniard had sailed in and was sitting off shore with three large ships. He was waiting patiently, as though stalking the island.

Guards patrolled the walls until sunset, and then their number was doubled; every man was watching the sea. Cogniard had to be kept offshore. If they could intercept his landing, he would be vulnerable.

No torches were given to the wall guards, as they would only serve to blind them in the darkness. Men below the wall, on the exterior, patrolled far and wide with the torches to cast light into the inky darkness.

Cogniard had chosen his time well. No moon aided the defenders; and when, in the early hours of morning, a patrol ran into Cogniard's landing site, it was far too late to stop it. The enemy's camp had been made on the beach, directly in front of the main gate.

As that same patrol sped back to the castle, it was met by an enemy patrol. After a short skirmish they managed to break contact. When they arrived back at the castle, they reported to Allen that Cogniard had arrived and was there to stay.

The next morning as the sun began peeping over the far horizon, Mark was leaning on the cold battlements, his joints stiff from the long hours of guard duty. The leather padding of his armor chaffed at his skin, and the heavy helmet had produced a sore neck and a slight headache.

As he watched the activity in the enemy camp, Ijn came

up the wall stairs to relieve him. Since Ijn had been on the patrol that had discovered the camp during the night, he was just as tired as Mark.

"How's it going up here? You don't look quite as cheery as you did four hours ago," Ijn said, not looking so cheery himself.

"The same goes for you. It looks as if Cogniard's in for the long haul."

"It's certainly possible. The spies would have told him that we were low on food, and not expecting another supply ship."

"That's true, but that's not why I say it. I've been watching these chaps since they got out of their tents, and they're building something down there."

"Where's that?"

"Right at the front, just out of arrow range, of course. It looks like a shelter of some sort."

"If that's a shelter, Cogniard must be a short man, Mark." Aronii's laughing voice came from behind the boys. They turned and greeted Ijn's father, who continued. "It looks more like a platform. If I didn't know Cogniard better, I'd say he was ready to give a speech."

The three watched the structure grow. It was made of rough boards that must have been brought from the ships. The men were working calmly, and not consulting plans, as far as the small group could see.

"It can't be any form of siege equipment. Even the simplest catapult has to be made well if you're going to get any range out of it," commented Louis, who had joined them.

As noon approached, the platform neared completion. Returning from the barracks, Mark saw a noticeable difference. Planking had been applied to the top, but he could just make out a square hole in the center. When he pointed it out to Aronii, the samurai's brow lowered.

"I don't like it. I don't like it at all. They're fixing to hang someone, and I happen to know someone very important to this castle who is currently missing..." He let his thought drop in the warming forenoon air. As the boys stared glumly at the growing gallows, Lord Cornuel and Sergeant Allen approached Aronii.

"What do you make of it?" asked Cornuel. Aronii repeated his assumption, and the three men strolled off down the wall, preparing themselves for the worst.

When it came, it was both a relief and a puzzle to the inhabitants of the castle. The rumor had spread that someone was going to be hanged if the castle did not surrender, and the common interpretation was that the Earl had been captured by Cogniard. This was not to be.

As Mark stood watching the increased activity around the platform, a boy was led to the dangling rope. Mark took one look and turned away, his face as white as the clouds. He sat down on the ramparts, his head in his hands. How had his brother gotten into this?

Crazy thoughts went spinning through his head. Obviously, Robert was in serious danger. Was there any way he could rescue him? He almost considered running straight down to the platform. There were few guards...

He slowly brought his mind under more rational control, and began to think logically. He could sneak out to the platform, and rescue Robert, but the chances for failure would be too high. And, if he were caught, there would be no reason for anyone in the castle to help Robert. They had no idea who he was.

Could he get Ijn to help? Harold? The whole group of boys? He liked that thought the best, but he knew they didn't stand much of a chance. The platform was close enough to the enemy camp that no decent-sized rescue force could get there without being noticed, and one that could sneak in would be too small to help.

He saw Cornuel striding across the dusty courtyard. From the wall a messenger came running, no doubt to tell him the news. As the man approached him, the lord turned to a hailing from the other direction. Another page was sprinting across the courtyard. The two met the lord by the stairs to the wall walk, and after a few seconds of discussion, both were sent off at a run.

"What's up, Mark?" A hand fell on his shoulder, and Jan sat next to him on the wall. Pieter appeared on his other side, and he could hear Richard behind him. They had just come off guard duty and had seen the planned victim.

Mark didn't know why his brother was on the platform, or how he had gotten there, but he knew that his life was going to be offered for the surrender of the castle. Without hesitation, he decided not to reveal his relationship to Robert. He would never forgive himself if the castle was surrendered because of him. He got up and walked to the stairs.

"I'm fine. Just a little tired." Then he looked back at his brother on the scaffolding and almost threw up over the wall.

As he crossed the courtyard where Cornuel had been ten minutes earlier, William ran up to him.

"The sergeant wants you to report to Aronii's rooms immediately," he told Mark. Mark just nodded and changed course, heading for the keep. William looked at him again, then headed off to the walls.

Aronii's apartments, which were lavishly decorated in the Eastern style, were on the opposite side of the keep from Cornuel's. Mark didn't even notice the furnishings as he sat down on a couch. Ijn came in a moment later, followed by Aronii. Then Lord Cornuel entered with Allen, and Mark saw that they were deep in discussion.

"All right." Aronii's voice began. "Mark, Ijn, you were called here for a reason. You were chosen for a mission that will be dangerous, but, if you succeed, it will give us a little help. If you will take a look out that window, you will see two ships. They arrived about an hour ago and are busy ferrying supplies to their camp. Cogniard has detected them, and based a small force on the creek to deter them. He knows he must, because they carry the Earl and his men." Mark looked up sharply, and saw Ijn do the same. Sure enough, two ships were anchored at the far end of the island.

"The Earl has to be informed of the situation here. You boys know as much as we do about this, and maybe more, thanks to your being involved in the issue of the spies. We need you to go to the Earl and tell him everything you know, especially about the hostage situation. He will be very interested in the boy they have out there now. If he sends you back to the castle, I need you to come back immediately, regardless of the situation." Mark and Ijn nodded, not planning on doing anything less.

"Now, you may have noticed that the castle is surrounded by Cogniard's men. You would normally not be able to leave, but we still have a few tricks up our sleeve. If you recall the cave in which we usually store our ships, you will know that an underground stream runs from there to the creek where Cogniard has based his deterrent force."

Aronii handed a map over to Mark and Ijn, then

continued, "The underground stream can be blocked in such a way that the water can be pumped out and men can go through. Unfortunately, we are not in a position to do this, because Cogniard's men are at the other end. However, at this time of year, the stream does have a low level, and there is just enough air that you might be able to go through. We need you to travel underneath those hills to the earl."

Mark didn't hesitate a second. "When do we leave?" he asked. He was ready to do anything that would help his brother.

"I need to tell you a few more details, and then you can go." Aronii proceeded to give them the critical information to tell the earl, and then said, "Go quickly. The life of that boy depends on you." He gave Mark a searching look, and left the room.

Mark's heart gave a jolt. Did Aronii know that the boy was his brother? Or had he seen Mark's reaction, and guessed there was a connection?

He looked at Ijn, and they stood up and left the room to go to the armory for supplies. There was no turning back. He and Ijn were leaving on a mission that could determine the fate of the castle – and of his brother.

CHAPTER 25

The stone walls were wet to the touch, the stairs almost slippery as Mark and Ijn descended to the large grotto. They were dressed in black clothes and armed with small dirks. Aronii expected that they would exit the underground stream at dusk; the black clothes would keep them from being seen by Cogniard's men.

The large cave yawned overhead as they stepped out of the stairwell. The mid-afternoon sun only reached the very front, and the back of the cave was shrouded in shadows that danced to the flickering of the torches in the wall sconces. Allen had provided a small, dense piece of wood soaked in tar that he said would burn as long as they needed, and Ijn now lit it with one of the wall torches.

"All right. Here we go. Time to swim," commented Mark as they approached the back of the cave. "And... it looks like Aronii was wrong."

The underground stream had already been blocked up and pumped out. It gave enough room for both boys to easily walk without even getting their feet wet.

"Any ideas what this means?" Mark asked as they began to jog down the empty tunnel.

"Probably..." started Ijn, as he halted at the edge of the small stream that remained and doused the torch, "that we aren't the only ones here. Keep your voice down and hug the wall. If Father didn't know about it, then anyone here is not our friend."

The inky darkness was like a cloak around them as they moved quickly, feeling the wall of the tunnel with their left hands. Five minutes after they had entered the cave, they heard voices behind them.

"They can't be far ahead," whispered a low voice. "We entered just after they did... [splash] ... stupid stream."

"If you hadn't fallen in aforementioned stupid stream," retorted a second, sharper voice, "we would have caught them by now."

The flickering of torches was now quite visible, and the boys were in danger of being spotted.

"Get in that little depression there," Ijn whispered. "I

think we can both fit." Mark nodded and the boys squished into the small hiding place.

Footsteps intermingled with slashes came closer every minute. Then the two men came into view around the corner. Mark and Ijn held their breath as the torchlight slowly illuminated them, hoping the men wouldn't look up.

A few seconds later the light passed, and Mark felt Ijn let his breath out. Mark relaxed as well. The two men had just passed them, and were headed away.

A heartbeat later, the second man slipped. His torch hand rose to give him balance as he twisted sideways... and stared right at Mark.

"Vaught! Right here! I've got --" His voice was cut short as he dodged Mark's dirk thrust. He grabbed for his own sword, but was a second too late. Ijn's dagger caught him under the ribs, and he rolled into the stream with a splash.

The first man turned around. When he saw them, he took off running, shouting at the top of his lungs. Mark sprinted after him with Ijn close behind.

The older man's feet couldn't last long on the rock-strewn floor of the tunnel, and as the nimbler Mark closed in the man turned like an animal at bay and drew his sword. The first swing didn't have room to gain any power, but it caught Mark in the upper arm and knocked him sideways into the shallow stream.

As Mark rolled over and spat out the brackish water, he saw sparks fly. Ijn had just blocked a sweeping cut by the swordsman. Mark stood and came at the man from behind. The man's powerful swing turned him sideways, right into the short thrust of Mark's dagger. He crumpled, and Ijn grabbed his torch and tossed it into the stream.

Mark could almost see Ijn wiping his forehead in the inky darkness and let out his breath. "Whew, I thought our mission was finished there, if you don't mind me saying so."

"Not at all," Ijn answered. "I thought *we* were finished there." They continued in silence, each wondering what was going to happen next. Several minutes later, Ijn spoke.

"How's your arm? I saw him get you."

"Not bad. Thankfully, his sword was dull and he didn't swing hard. It's just a long cut, not very deep." Once again, silence, this time broken only by sounds of the outside world as they approached the stream's hillside exit.

They could see that the stream had been blocked off by a large wooden barricade. It appeared to be operated by ropes and pulleys from the small building next to it. According to Aronii, this device should have been open, and the water level should have been at their necks. The ingenious mechanism, however, was not what caught their attention.

Two columns of men were filing into the tunnel, armed to the teeth. Mark and Ijn looked quickly around. This time there was a large enough cutout in the wall to safely hide them both.

The boys crouched against the wall as the men filed past. The lines seemed to go on for hours, but it was only five minutes later when the last man passed.

"Three hundred. Three hundred men going in through the back door to the castle, and we can't do a thing about it." Ijn was furious.

"Now hold on just a moment. Watch this." Mark crawled to the opening of the cave. Ijn was right behind him. The stream's banks were vacated, and far down the stream they could see the enemy's hastily erected guard camp that was intended to block the earl.

"They've left," Ijn whispered. "They're gone. All the troops just went into the tunnel."

"Wait…" Mark walked forward to the wooden barricade and drew his dirk. Wedging it in between the planks, he tore out a large section of the structure. Water began to splash into the pool below.

"Does that suffice for 'doing something', Ijn?" asked Mark. "They'll still be able to make it, just like we were going to - very slowly, and one breath at a time."

"That'll work, that'll work. Now let's get this thing done."
They could hear the water pouring slowly through the
tunnel as they scrambled out of the small valley that the
stream had dug and set off for the earl's camp.

Ijn led Mark, who was unfamiliar with this part of the
island, along the edge of the fields. The forest on their left
would have impeded their movement, and they couldn't
very well travel in the open for fear of being spotted by
Cogniard's men.

As it turned out, they could have spared the trouble. A
guard at the camp they thought was deserted saw them in
the distance and raised the alarm.

The boys were first aware of the pursuit when they heard
hooves pounding in the soft turf not very far away.
Casting a glance over his shoulder, Mark saw three men
on horseback galloping toward them.

Shouting at Ijn, he broke for the woods. His friend
followed quickly. When they were safely in the woods,
Mark saw the horsemen rein their mounts in at the edge
of the forest and tie them there. Ijn noticed as well.

"If we get to the beach we can outrun them," he shouted.
The boys cut across the forest and the pursuit continued.
Dodging bushes and branches, they tore through the little
forest. Their pursuers were gaining on them.

When they reached the beach they fared no better. The
spongy sand was tiring, and they were slowed immensely.

The men behind them had been joined by several more, and soon they were almost surrounded. There were runners at their flanks and several more at their rear, gaining quickly.

Knowing that their best chance for safety was getting to the earl's camp, they pressed on. The men drew closer and closer, until Mark and Ijn could hear their pursuers breathing quickly as they slogged through the sand behind them.

Then Ijn tripped. In an instant, Mark stopped in his tracks and ripped out his dirk, stabbing at the nearest unprepared pursuer. The others hesitated for a moment, which gave Ijn time to get up. But now the flank runners had closed in, and they were surrounded.

Standing back to back, they faced their enemy, dirks ready. The men, eager to get revenge for their wounded comrade, closed in with their swords drawn.

The fight was lost at the first swing. Their dirks couldn't match the length of the swords, and Mark and Ijn were separated instantly. Mark felt himself overwhelmed by multiple blows and brought to the ground. He squirmed and desperately dodged the blows raining down.

Then it stopped. Mark lay there, his right eye swollen and cuts covering his body. He could see the sky, starting to turn a shade of pink as the sun began to set, and he wondered how Ijn was.

Then a face appeared in front of the pink sky, and he heard a voice sneer, "Just as I thought. I couldn't mistake him."

Then, addressing Mark, "How are you doing, Mark Sheffield? Your brother is ready to be hanged, and he might want some company. In fact, you'll be right with him, maybe as soon as tonight." Mark heard Ijn's sharp intake of breath from a few feet away, and he winced.

The speaker ordered both boys to be bound, and Mark was manhandled to a standing position as they tied his hands. Ijn looked at him, but didn't say anything until they had begun walking back to Cogniard's camp.

"I didn't know that boy was your brother," Ijn cried. "No wonder you looked a little dazed!"

Mark just nodded, and then Ijn continued excitedly, "But that boy was… that means you're --"

"Shut up! Keep quiet there, or we'll make you quiet real quick!" One of the guards prodded Ijn with his sword, but Ijn was still grinning. Mark didn't know why; and, he told himself, he really didn't care at that point.

Just as they reached the edge of the woods they heard the thundering of hooves behind them. Instantly, Mark could tell it wasn't the same sound as the light horses that Cogniard's men had been riding. These were warhorses! He twisted his head in time to see a group of horsemen galloping toward them, clad in silver and blue, with the diving eagle on their helms and blue plumes waving in the wind. A second later he was shoved roughly forward, and chaos ensued.

Each one of Cogniard's men had a different idea about which way to go, and Mark was grabbed on every side. The net change was exactly zero, and the horsemen hit the group like a lightning bolt. Men were knocked to every side as the horsemen encircled Ijn and Mark. Within a minute, every member of the would-be kidnapping party had been disabled or captured. Mark found himself standing inside a ring of horses, their sweating haunches in his face.

A knight on a huge bay warhorse wheeled his mount and raised his helm.

"Did you come from the castle?"

"Yes, sir," Mark replied.

"As I thought. I assume you need to get to the earl?"

Once again, Mark replied in the affirmative, and the officer whispered to one of his aides. The soldier rode off at a gallop. Then, after two men offered to carry Mark and Ijn double, the rest of the group followed at a leisurely trot.

In a few moments they could see the beach where the Earl was unloading his ships. A larger contingent of horsemen was guarding the area, and more supplies were constantly being ferried across the gap between ship and shore.

When they were almost to the camp, a small group of horsemen rode to meet them at high speed. In the lead was a gray charger carrying a tall man who was fully armored and magnificently outfitted. Behind him the familiar flag snapped in the wind, carried by a squire. In an instant, Mark knew this was the earl.

As their group stopped, Mark and Ijn slid off their horses and walked toward the oncoming party. The Earl reigned in his horse sharply, the gray almost rearing as he stopped on his haunches. Ijn knelt to bow, but Mark stood in a daze as the horse snorted, his mane and tail whipping in the wind… He had seen that horse before! The Earl reached to calm the horse, and in that slight action, in that split second, Mark knew he had seen the Earl before!

CHAPTER 26

There was pure joy on the weather-beaten face of the old campaigner when he raised his helm and smiled at his son.

"Father!"

The knight swung down from his horse and enveloped Mark in an iron-clad hug, then grabbed him by his shoulders and held him at arm's length.

"A little rougher, a little tougher... I never thought I'd see you again!" He laughed, then his face turned serious. "Have you seen Robert?"

Mark's dream came to an abrupt halt, shattering into a million pieces. His face turned white, and he put his hand on his father's horse to steady himself.

"What is it, Mark?" His father was worried now.

"Robert's on the beach… with Cogniard. They built a gallows this morning, and we expect it'll be his life for the castle…" He buried his face in the gray mane. "It was the first time I saw him since the wreck…"

His father was affected as well, but kept his composure. Then Ijn took over.

"If I may, your Highness," he began. The Earl nodded, his face hard. "The Lord Cornuel sent us to inform you of the situation so you could help in any way to rescue your son."

"Hold on, Ijn." The Earl was familiar with Aronii's son. "Bertrand!"

"Yes, sir!" The officer on the bay warhorse snapped to attention.

"Get every man mounted for a raid immediately." The soldier saluted and set spurs to his horse, his two aides following close behind. Then the Earl nodded to Ijn, who related the recent events at the castle and explained their position.

By the time he had finished, Bertrand had summoned the mounted contingent and brought them to the earl. A total of forty heavily armed knights sat at attention, awaiting their commander's bidding. Bertrand rode up to the earl, his two aides each following with an extra horse.

"Sir. I brought two horses for the boys, if you please."
The Earl nodded, and Mark and Ijn mounted the two
riderless warhorses. Without armor, the two boys looked
small on the backs of the two large horses whose size was
only increased by the plate armor. Bertrand smiled. Then
the earl's raised hand brought the world into a frozen
silence. The mailed hand hung in the air, then snapped
down.

Shattering the peaceful twilight, forty-four heavy horses
went from a stand to a full gallop in the blink of an eye.
Thunder rolled through the fields as iron-shod hooves
thudded into the sod. Leaving in their trail churned
messes of spring soil, the iron spearhead was headed for
Cogniard's host.

...

The rough rope chafed at Robert's neck. His forehead
was grimy from a constant slow trickle of perspiration
that had plagued him from the moment Gault had
summoned him. He could hear Kate's unsteady breathing
behind him as he had all day. Out of the corner of his eye,
he could see her hand on the lever that held his life in the
balance. Literally. Gault had gotten Cogniard to arrest her
as well, using her conversation with Robert as the
incriminating evidence. Robert was convinced he'd just
done it out of spite, and bringing Kate here now was
nothing more than pure cruelty.

Gault's dagger was pricking into the back of Kate's hand, ready to force the lever down at any moment. And that moment was not so far away.

Robert had heard Lord Cogniard's interchange with the castle's occupants. It was then that he had realized who he was, and why he had been chosen for this. As an heir of the "Earl of Newcastle" – why had he never heard that name? – he would be a prize worth having. And bartering.

The sun was setting slowly. He could see the clouds coloring behind the castle, and he felt the tinge of cool air beneath his rough clothes as the wind took to another one of its tempestuous bursts. The same wind had been blowing sand into every crevice of his body, even collecting on his eyebrows at times.

He could tell Gault wasn't in a good mood either. His heavyset body was sweating profusely, and he kept shifting, making Kate eye the dagger nervously.

The waiting game had become unbearable long ago. Cogniard had returned to the castle gates several times, demanding that the castle be vacated, and Robert could see he wasn't happy with the results he was getting. Truth to tell, that made Robert pretty nervous. If the castle didn't give in before nightfall… he couldn't bear to think of Kate's hand being forced down on that lever…

He had heard Lord Cogniard tell Master Smith how to set

the height of the gallows. It wasn't very encouraging. "Just about six inches of slack… and a springy board. We can't have him losing consciousness too quickly." He glanced up now at the "springy board." It didn't look too flexible to him.

Just then he caught the sound of Lord Cogniard's voice coming from the camp behind him. It had a hard quality to it that Robert didn't like.

"Get their attention. We'll give them one more chance. Then he gets a taste of the rope."

…

Mark could feel the rippling cadence of his mount's thickly muscled back underneath him. To their side, the sun was setting, and its last rays cast eerily long shadows next to the rumbling cavalcade.

They hit the stream at a full gallop. On the other side was the enemy blocking camp, looking eerie in the twilight. Leaving behind them a froth of foaming water, the horsemen tore through the camp.

There were about ten men there, and Mark saw more than one knight put hand to sword as several attempted to stop them. The rest of Cogniard's guards merely stood gaping at the solid flow of horseflesh and iron.

The rhythmic beating of hooves and the clink of armor continued unabated, the entire column changing direction as one body coming out of the camp. The knights were well trained and skilled in what they did. Mark could see it hadn't taken a single day to recruit these men.

Then his thoughts turned to his brother, on the hastily erected wooden platform, awaiting his death. He didn't even know if Robert was still alive, but, if he was, he knew his father would challenge odds of ten to one to get to him. The heavy horse would be right behind. And by the looks of it, that's exactly what they were about to do.

. . .

Robert felt like he was listening to Lord Cogniard's voice from miles away. He could hear the angered tone, and the insinuating threats of torture and violence, both well backed up by the all too real rope around his own neck.

"And, if you do not give your answer immediately, I will give a countdown from ten, whereupon your earl's only remaining son will be hung from the neck like a common criminal."

Cogniard turned and nodded to the assembled host behind him. They drew to attention, unsheathing their swords, and Gault's knife put more pressure to Kate's hand. She instinctively moved her hand away, and the trapdoor under Robert shifted.

"You dirty monster!" she hissed at Gault, jerking her hand up.

326

"And your answer is?" Lord Cogniard turned with triumph to the castle. There was a tangible silence, and then the scribe at his side raised his voice.

"Ten… nine…" Robert held his breath. Kate shifted. Gault sniggered. "Eight… seven…" From far away, Robert could hear a rumble, and a slight shaking of the platform he was standing on. "Six… five…" There was an unmistakable shaking of the ground, and every eye turned to the north. Robert thought the sound was coming from behind a slight bulge in the terrain. "Four… thr-?"

"For *Newcastle!*" With a brilliant flash of light, the earl's horsemen came around a small outcropping. As the late evening sun reflected directly off bright shields and raised swords, their war cry shattered the tension in the still evening air.

"*Newcastle!*" Instant pandemonium broke out among Cogniard's men. Robert saw Gault freeze and Kate jump back. Tearing his eyes off the oncoming horses, Gault reached for the lever… and yanked.

…

Mark saw Robert drop. He shouted louder, and urged his mount on, leaning into the wind. Robert disappeared from his field of view, and then the horsemen hit the wall of infantry.

The crash was tremendous. Screams of horses and shouts

of men were heard as the unstoppable flow of flesh churned into the packed infantry. Iron-shod hooves hit helmet, breastplate, and shield in the ranks, clearing a path towards the gallows. Mark pushed his mount forward, forward, toward his brother.

...

As the trapdoor opened under Robert, he felt the noose tighten. Hanging by the neck, choking for breath, he clawed at the rope. In front of him, Kate's eyes were huge. She gasped, turned away, and saw Gault climbing down into the mass of soldiers. His right hand, holding the knife, was grasping the edge of the platform as he found footing on the rough beach.

Grabbing the knife, Kate slammed her foot down on the exposed fingers. With a very unmanly shriek, Gault released the knife and fell to the ground.

Without hesitation, Kate spun around and buried the knife into the rope where it wrapped around the beam. Robert dropped below the platform.

Kate took one look around, noting that the underside of the platform was exposed, and jumped down after him. Very few of the men had seen what had happened, and those who did had other things to worry about. Except one.

Gault, with his right fingers hanging helpless, ducked under the platform and threw a punch at Kate. She ducked, then threw a handful of sand into his eyes. Doubled over in pain, he backed away as two more men approached, brandishing swords threateningly at Kate, who stood between them and Robert.

One began to circle around, and Kate backed up, holding the dagger ready. Then the second leapt forward and took a powerful swing at Robert's only hope of survival.

With the blade halfway through its powerful arc, there was a crash and a rending screech as several thousand pounds of horseflesh hit the platform and divided around it.

. . .

Mark found himself squeezed against the gallows as the charge came to a sudden stop, forming into a rough circle around the wooden platform. Looking back at Ijn, he saw him clambering onto the wooden deck. Immediately, he followed his friend onto the platform and down through the trapdoor.

The first thing Mark saw when he landed on the ground was a girl with her dagger sunk to the hilt between the plates of a swordsman's armor. The soldier's sword was stuck several inches into a wooden support column, and his face showed shock at the instantaneous change of fortune.

"Mark!" Ijn was closely engaged with another swordsman. Although he was parrying his opponent's thrusts with the short dirk he still carried, he was being pushed back quickly. Mark came up behind him and brought the man's attention to himself, letting the girl's dagger do the rest.

There was a brief moment of silence, as the four youths recovered from the adrenaline rush. The sounds of battle still continued outside, but they had won their fight.

"Mark, meet Kate, my would-be executioner." Robert spoke up from the ground, a little raw around the throat, but still quite alive. "Kate, meet Mark, my twin brother."

"I didn't need that introduction really," laughed Kate. "He looks just like you."

"Robert and Kate, meet Ijn, the next ruler of the Far East!" They all laughed, then Ijn spoke up.

"We aren't done. I think they might need some help out there yet." The truth of his words was immediately apparent when they pulled themselves onto the platform. The cavalry was hard-pressed, backed up to the platform and fighting for their lives. Masses of infantry were beginning to regroup, and with the element of surprise and the weight of the charge gone, the knights were readying for a long fight.

"I see they need help, but I'm not sure how we can do that… I have one dirk to throw, but that's about it." Mark knew he couldn't very well fight mounted with a dirk.

Just then there was a shout from the direction of the castle. Turning to look, the four saw the castle gates wide open, with streams of blue and silver pouring out. Column after column of heavily armed infantry moved out of the castle at a slow jog. At their head was a small contingent of cavalry, with the flag of Newcastle snapping in the brisk breeze. Blue plumes waved, and silver shields flashed in the brilliant orange glow of the setting sun.

The effect of the infantry charge was not nearly what that of the cavalry had been. Cogniard's men closed ranks and met the charge head on, not succumbing to its weight despite the colorful pageantry.

The action did, however, seriously relieve the cavalry at their station. They pushed their advantage, thereby gaining a little breathing room around the platform.

It was at that point that Robert looked over his shoulder to see Ijn snatching a sword out the air. With a bow, the boy turned and presented it to Robert, flourishing one of his own.

"Compliments of my father," he said. Aronii was at the head of the castle column, and had contrived to throw two of the light samurai swords across the heads of the enemy, directly to the little group on the platform.

"Not bad!" Mark exclaimed. "Now let's join this fight!"

"You can, but I don't have a horse!" Robert shouted over the din of battle.

"Neither do I," Kate said.

It didn't turn out to be as much of a problem as they thought it would be. There were more than a few riderless horses around the platform – a boon for them but a sign that told all too well how the battle was going.

Robert, Mark, and Ijn pushed their horses into the thin line of defenders, all agreeing to keep Kate back. Frustrated though she was, Kate didn't object for once. The fighting was brutal.

The small group of defenders fought valiantly, waiting for the column of men streaming from the castle to rescue them. Looking over the heads of the massed infantry, Robert could see the castle's troops making more and more progress, slowly but surely. He was confident that if they held out long enough they would be rescued.

However, even as he watched, a large mass of infantry began to move their way. Unlike the ferocious but uncoordinated attacks of the common infantry, this group posed a serious threat. Robert recognized them as Cogniard's personal bodyguard, and he knew they were tough.

Mark was right next to Robert, and he saw them too.

"Where's Father?" he shouted to Robert, blocking a sword cut from a large, wild-eyed mercenary.

"Right here," his father replied, riding his horse up next

to them. He swung his large sword in a great arc, ending with a loud crash on the breastplate of a foot-soldier. "We need to get some momentum or we're lost here," he shouted to his men.

With that, he was urging his horse forward into the crowded pack of soldiers in front of his. Robert and the rest of the cavalry followed, glad to be moving again. Standing still, the large warhorses did no good, but a moving destrier would put terror in the eyes of any foot-soldier.

Except Cogniard's guard. As the small cavalry contingent gained momentum, cutting through the fleeing mercenaries, the band of pikemen formed into a solid line. The rows of battle-hardened men raised their shields. Every pike faced forward. To the charging cavalry, it looked like a wall of spears.

But they didn't hesitate. Following the lead of their earl, the entire contingent of heavy horse threw themselves onto the seemingly invincible wall.

With a rending crash, the two veteran forces met. Amidst a large field of common fighting, this was where the real warriors fought.

Mark leaned into his swing, sending the light samurai sword crashing into the gap between helmet and breastplate on a nearby pikeman, who stumbled backwards. With the man went Mark's sword, caught in the narrow opening, the handle smooth and hard to grip.

Without a sword, Mark thought himself useless. He ducked quickly to the side to dodge a pike aimed his way. Then an idea came, and he urged his horse forward. The steed's heavy hooves might be able to do more damage than the sword itself.

Robert saw Mark breaking from the ranks and quickly followed, cutting his way through a mess of pikes. Next to him, Ijn's horse reared, and then collapsed onto the crowded beach. It rolled over, pinning Ijn to the ground.

But Robert was already far ahead, intent on supporting his brother. Another knight moved forward to defend the fallen boy, but a skillful pike-thrust found its way though his heavy plate armor, and he fell to the ground next to Ijn.

The Earl himself was in a tight spot, fending off three pikemen and trying to keep his little band together at the same time. His sword quickly dispatched one of the pikemen, but a counter-thrust by another veteran warrior knocked the legendary blade out of his hand.

With gritted teeth, the Earl grabbed for his mace, but it was gone, knocked from its usual spot on the saddle sometime during the fight. Instead, he leaned forward and grabbed one of the pikes that was waving around him, trying to find an opening. He wrenched it out of the pikeman's grasp and reversed it, bringing it to bear on his other opponent.

Meanwhile, Mark and Robert were deep into the masses of enemy pikemen. Far from their friends, they were fighting desperately for their lives. Turning to look back, Robert saw that the little band of cavalry was being cut to pieces. Looking forward, he saw an endless sea of hostile faces.

The next instant, something hooked him from behind, and he felt himself pulled backward.

"Mark!" he shouted. His brother turned to help, but the pikeman who had hooked Robert was too quick. With a heave, he pulled Robert backwards over the right side of his horse.

Caught in the stirrups, Robert dangled there, defenseless. Distracted for a moment, his brother succumbed to a pike-thrust in the shoulder and crumpled in his saddle. The veteran pikemen were about to make short work of the two when Cogniard's commanding voice was heard.

"Save those two alive!" he shouted. "Anyone who touches them answers to me!"

Back in the main body of cavalry, the Earl saw Robert pulled down, and turned to command his forces to the rescue. All his astonished eyes saw were five lonely knights fighting courageously at his back.

...

From the castle walls, Alfred watched the desperate battle. He was disappointed to be left behind, but he wasn't alone. The youngest of the boys in training were held back, told they were valuable to the castle, and then left to watch the walls.

Having been personally trained, once, by Mark, Alfred had initially felt he should have gone along. But now, he shuddered at the thought. He had seen the ill-fated charge of the cavalry brigade, seen it fall apart, and seen the Earl captured.

It was bad news for the cavalry, but the long column from the castle had stuck together like glue. They were slowly but surely pushing Cogniard's men back to their ships. By the time the sun had set, every enemy soldier had been chased back to the ships or left lying in the sand.

The last rays of the sun caught the dirty white sails of the invasion fleet, slowly creeping back to the mainland, bearing the Earl and his two sons.

CHAPTER 27

Below the deck of Cogniard's flagship, Robert lay against a heavy oak beam. His mind was spinning. Blood trickled slowly from a cut across his arm, and his wrist felt like water after the long fight.

But he considered himself lucky. Next to him, Mark lay unconscious, the loss of blood finally bringing him down. The wound in his shoulder was still bleeding, despite Robert's best attempts to stop it.

The Earl himself was housed in the second of three cabins on the ship, being the principal prisoner. His lodgings were equal to those of Cogniard himself, for this short trip at least.

It was early morning, and still dark, when the small flotilla of ships cast anchor at Tynemouth. Deciding to leave the unloading until morning, the weary remnants of an army fell asleep onboard the ships.

. . .

Dark shapes filtered out from under the priory cliffs. Creeping to the shore, they became seaborne ghosts, and floated silently closer to the fleet. Small lights danced in their midst, carefully sheltered.

Onward they drifted, their prey heedless of the danger. Once they were close enough, the small lights began to multiply, bursting into larger tongues of flame. And still the fleet slept.

With the flames casting their uncertain light, it could be seen that this group was a band of determined men in several small boats. A score of bows were pointed toward the sky, their arrows furnished with oil-soaked rags, now alight.

One fiery arc slipped through the night air, and in a moment a multitude more followed. Hissing like serpents, the tongues of fire embedded themselves into the sides of the ships. It didn't take long for the old wood of the ships to take fire. Flames licked upward, curling around the rigging and masts.

Aboard the smaller boats the plotters watched, hard-eyed, as the fleet went up in flames. It only took a minute for the stillness of the morning to be broken by the shouts of the surprised sailors, then of the weary army, as they scrambled to quench the flames. Several of the occupants deserted the ships immediately, and more followed, but the rest couldn't swim, and battled the flames in desperation.

The attackers drew their bows once more. As the first of the swimmers approached them on their way to the shore, they stood watching.

"Get ready," a tall, gray-haired man said. "But do not shoot. We will identify them as they come by. Then we can start a ferry to shore with prisoners."

"I'm ready, Roland," a low voice growled. "I've got friends on that island, and if anyone hurts them, they'll answer to me." James Drydon stood in the little boat, his arms crossed, daring anyone to defy him. Next to him, Tim lowered his bow.

"You'll pay the price if Cogniard gets away, my friend," he replied.

"And you'll pay the price if an innocent person gets killed, Tim," Roland replied from a second boat further down the line.

. . .

Inside the ship, Robert's head was filled with the shouts of the crew and crackling ferocity of the fire. The smoke wasn't too bad yet, but he could see the flames licking at the ship's timbers overhead.

The boys' guard had disappeared at the first cry of "fire!" and hadn't returned. Robert turned to Mark and shook him. The boy opened his eyes and looked at Robert blankly.

"The ship's on fire, Mark! We need to get out!" Robert's shouts didn't register quickly, but once they did, Mark tried to get up.

Still weak, he collapsed. A flaming piece of decking crashed down next to him. With a start, Mark realized the situation they were in, and the adrenaline started to flow.

Despite his weakened state, he managed to stand, and Robert helped him to the stairs. From above, a hand reached down and helped them up to the deck. Robert didn't even have to look up to know that it was his father.

In the confused, fiery night, the three of them managed to make it to the ship's rail. A rope net was draped over the side, and Robert and his father helped Mark down it and into the water.

All three collectively gasped as they entered the water. It was bone-numbingly cold, and the salt stung their wounds.

Without any hesitation, the Earl began to swim to shore. He was supporting one side of Mark, and Robert followed along, keeping at Mark's left shoulder. They swam that way for what seemed like hours, until the Earl let go of Mark and swam quickly off to the right.

Robert struggled to hold Mark's head above the water. He was almost ready to go under when a large chuck of wood floated in front of his face. He grabbed on, hauling Mark's arms across it as well.

On the other side of the deck beam was the earl, smiling slightly.

"We've a much better chance now," he said. "I'm sorry I left you like that, but I had to grab this thing."

Robert just nodded, too weary to speak. The two of them pointed the beam toward shore, and began to propel themselves forward.

Robert had his head down and couldn't see anything when he heard the shout.

"Over here, Tim, I've got three of them."

"Let's see your faces, scum!" another voice shouted. Robert wearily raised his head, and saw the Earl do the same.

"I don't recognize them."

"Neither do I!"

"Hold it!" a familiar voice shouted. "It's the Eagle!"

The rest of the night was a confused blur to Robert.

Roland and the resistance brought them straight to shore. From there they were transferred by a cart to a back-alley inn, where a kind landlady dressed their wounds and gave them food to eat.

The night wasn't over then, however. The resistance had planned an attack on the castle if the firing of the boats went well, and the Earl now led this attack. Robert recalled snatches of the fight, scenes here and there that stuck in his memory.

The castle's defense had been left to a meager crew. The gate-keepers were surprised and overcome, and there was almost no resistance from the sleepy guards. Once the alarm got out, however, there was a pitched battle in the castle courtyard.

Robert would never forget the fierce look on Benedict's face as he led Cogniard's men in a last desperate attempt to hold the castle grounds. Over a cup of wine, the castellan had been jovial, intelligent, and conversational, but he was a true fighter. His few troops rallied around him, loyal to the end of the losing cause. Even when Robert's father offered him mercy, the man scowled and cried "Never!" He hadn't surrendered.

The stable-master that had looked at him strangely was well-known to the earl. Robert had seen him come around the corner of the gate in the early morning light and stop in his tracks. His eyes had become huge when he saw their little force, and it was the work of a moment for the Earl to command his seizure.

"Even I don't have the heart to kill a traitor in cold blood," the Earl had said. Robert remembered thinking how different this was from the attitude that had him swinging from the end of a rope.

The small resistance force had then secured the castle. Mark was sent for, and he and Robert took refreshment with their father in the keep. Among the guests were Roland and Brother Arnold, both of whom welcomed Robert and his brother with open arms.

Roland had been unaware of Robert's identity when he signed him on, but the subsequent contact with Cogniard and Sir Whittington had excited his suspicion. He had risked his position in the attempt to keep Robert safe, and when that failed he had looked up the resistance group.

Brother Arnold had known Robert and Matt all along, as a former man-at-arms who had become a monk for the express purpose of guarding them. Needless to say, he was heavily involved in the resistance. He made sure to tell Robert that his fishing partner, Ulric, had once been a courageous man-at-arms before retiring to his current position.

Many stories were told, and many fine points were cleared up. Weary though they were, the men made sure to set the guard in order before retiring to bed at nearly ten o'clock that morning.

CHAPTER 28

High in a stone tower, a young man looked out over the sea. He was watching for sails. The sails of a scouting ship that had been sent out just that morning, searching for clues to the whereabouts of the captured earl.

The young man was deep in thought. He had fought in a battle for the first time last night. It was because his cousin was in danger. Both of his cousins, he realized, and his uncle. Even though every extra man had marched to the rescue, his relatives had been captured and sent to the mainland with Cogniard's retreating ships. It had all ended in failure.

Over the horizon the sails of a small ship could be seen. The earl's nephew narrowed his eyes, watching. It wasn't the same ship. His heart sank again.

A hand grasped his shoulder. "How are you doing?" Cornuel asked him.

"Not very well. I see a lot of trouble ahead, if the earl, as well as Mark and Robert, are in captivity. We don't have the power to take them back."

"You realize that you'll be Earl in his place, if… he doesn't come back?" Cornuel wasn't ready to give up either, but he wanted to face the facts.

"I realize. I have no interest in it." Both had been intently watching the sail. It wasn't the same ship, but it plied its course directly toward the island.

"It's one of Cogniard's ships," said Cornuel. He disappeared back down the tower stairs, and the young man could hear him rapping out orders to prepare the defenses yet again.

. . .

From the bow of the ship, Robert and Mark watched the castle eagerly. They couldn't wait to be back. Robert was in good health and excited to see inside the island castle that his father had been telling him all about. Mark was much better than the previous night, but was still easily tired. Despite this, he was in high spirits and ready to see his friends again.

"Look, someone's in the tower!" he said, pointing. A tall figure could be seen watching the ship as it approached.

"And on the walls," commented Robert.

"Allen will have the men in defensive positions for sure," their father said, standing behind them. "He won't take any chances with Cogniard's old ship pulling into his bay."

As he spoke, the ship pulled closer to the cavern where it was to dock. On the island, the tall figure could be seen disappearing from the tower. Several minutes later, the earl's standard was run up on the pole over the keep.

"If we had a flag, I'd run it up right now," the Earl said. "As it is, Allen will have to sit on the edge of his seat until he recognizes us."

That moment came soon, and a hoarse cheer went up from the soldiers on the wall as they recognized their lord in the ship.

The news must have spread quickly. When the ship reached the dock, there were crowds of men awaiting it. Every man was cheering, and it brought a lump to Robert's throat.

A moment later, the crowd parted. The young man who had been in the tower walked through, and bounded up the gangplank to the ship, clasping the earl's hand.

"It's good to see you again, Uncle," he said.

"And to see you, Lukas," the Earl said heartily.

"Lukas is our cousin?" Mark exclaimed. "Lukas, I had no idea!"

"Neither did I," the young man replied, "Until I saw Robert with a rope around his neck. One look was enough to tell me then, but I couldn't say anything."

"Why not?" Mark asked.

"Cornuel and Allen knew almost from the beginning, but wanted you to find out for yourself. That's why they sent you to your father."

"What? Cornuel and Allen knew I was the son of the earl, and they didn't say a word the entire time I was here?"

Lukas laughed. "I remember them thinking it through," he replied. "They wanted to make sure you weren't a spoiled brat before they conferred any honor to you. Besides, you made enough trouble as it was!"

"Speaking of Cornuel and Allen," the Earl broke in, "where are they? And Aronii, too."

"Cornuel was going to stop by his room before coming down here. He had to pick something up," Lukas replied.

"And Aronii?"

"He's… with Ijn."

"Ijn? Was he hurt?" Mark looked sharply at Lukas.

"Yes, I'm afraid he was," the young man replied. "His

horse fell on his leg and broke it up pretty bad. Swedenborg says he might lose it."

"Swedenborg! What does O'Neill say?"

"O'Neill is dead."

"I'm sorry to hear that. I'll always be grateful to him for fixing me up."

"O'Neill was a traitor, Mark."

Mark's head began to spin. "Is everyone a traitor? What happened to the dunce of a Frenchman, Lytton?" The Earl cast a disapproving glance at Mark.

"Pierre was my right-hand ma –"

"I'm sorry, milord, but Pierre was a traitor as well."

Now it was the earl's turn to be surprised. "So… where is he then? Dead, too?"

"No, he's in the dungeon, awaiting your decision," Lukas replied.

The Earl frowned. "Where did you say Allen was?" he asked.

"I'm sorry, sir, I didn't say. Allen is dead."

"Allen? Dead?" asked Drydon, standing behind them on the ship's deck.

"Yes. He was killed in a last-minute attempt to recover what was left of the cavalry."

At that moment, Cornuel entered, followed by a girl in a long gown. Cornuel approached the earl, then knelt and presented him a sword. The earl's sword.

"A little worse for the wear, but yours nonetheless, brother. We recovered it after the battle."

The Earl took it in his hands and held it up. A cheer resounded from the crowds behind Cornuel. It only took a look from the Earl to quiet it.

"Cheer, my friends, but cheer quietly, for it was hard-won." Then he bowed his head and walked toward the stone stairway. The others fell in behind him.

Robert looked up to see Kate walking next to him. He hadn't even recognized her in the courtly gown.

"Uh, how are you?" he asked, a little embarrassed at finding himself speaking to such an important-looking woman.

"Are you mad?" she hissed. "They make me wear this thing like I'm a fine lady or something. It's hot and sticky!" Robert stifled a laugh.

"How did you get out?" he asked, his face serious all of a sudden. "We entirely deserted you."

"You were captured, by the way, you didn't desert me. I

just hid under the platform like a coward until your troops made it to me. They didn't know me, but thankfully they treated me well. Ijn was able to vouch for me, and that was when they forced me into this." She grimaced again. "I think I'll be happy to go back to the mainland."

Cornuel caught that, and smiled. Then he turned sharply to the earl.

"You never told us what happened! How did you escape?"

"All in good time, friend. I'd like to rest for a moment before I tell *that* story, too."

They came to the top of the stairway, and met Robert MacCrae about to go down.

"Are all those worthless soldiers just standing down there?" he asked Cornuel. "We've got a guard to keep!"

"I think it'll be alright, seeing the circumstances, MacCrae," said the Earl with a slight smile.

"My lord!" MacCrae took a step back and knelt. "I'm sorry, I didn't realize you were back!"

"MacCrae has been promoted to Allen's position," Cornuel stated to the earl. "Pending your approval, of course."

"Of course," the Earl replied. "Please rise, MacCrae.

You've got a big job to do, and even bigger shoes to fill."

"Yes, my lord," MacCrae said. "I'll do my best."

Several hours later, another ship floated into the bay, unnoticed. If Lukas had been watching this time, he would have recognized it as the scout ship they had sent out earlier. It stopped short of the dock, and lowered a boat to ferry its passengers to shore. A tall, stately lady rose to step from the boat onto the pier. Several attendants helped her. They were knights, dressed in the colors of Newcastle, spotlessly clean and polished.

The lady herself was older, her hair beginning to turn gray. She carried herself like a queen, and wore a long blue gown with a lining of scarlet, and trimmed with ermine. The knights treated her with utmost respect as they led her up to the earl's chambers and knocked.

. . .

Robert and Mark had just finished an excellent repast in the earl's private room when they heard the knock. William Braithewaite walked with a slight limp over to the door and opened it, ready to inquire who wanted to see the earl. As soon as he had opened it, however, he dropped to one knee.

"My lady," he said.

"Mother!" said Robert and Mark.

The Earl just smiled.

ALLAN BYRNE

ABOUT THE AUTHOR

Allan Byrne started writing early on in life. After many short stories in school, he started writing this book, and finally finished it over 12 years later. He currently resides in Michigan and works as a mechanical engineer.